New York Times bestselling author Tessa Bailey can solve all problems except for her own, so she focuses those efforts on stubborn, fictional blue collar men and loyal, lovable heroines. She lives on Long Island avoiding the sun and social interactions, then wonders why no one has called. Dubbed the "Michelangelo of dirty talk," by *Entertainment Weekly*, Tessa writes with spice, spirit, swoon and a guaranteed happily ever after. Catch her on TikTok at @authortessabailey or check out tessabailey.com for a complete list of books.

MY KILLER VACATION

TESSA BAILEY

PIATKUS

PIATKUS

First published in 2022 by Tessa Bailey
Published in Great Britain in 2022 by Piatkus

17 19 20 18 16

Copyright © 2022 by Tessa Bailey

Cover Art and Design by Okay Creations

A CIP catalogue record for this book
is available from the British Library.

ISBN 978-0-349-43528-2

Printed and bound in Great Britain by
Clays Ltd, Elcograf S.p.A.

Papers used by Piatkus are from well-managed forests
and other responsible sources.

Piatkus
An imprint of
Little, Brown Book Group
Carmelite House
50 Victoria Embankment
London EC4Y 0DZ

Hachette Ireland
8 Castlecourt Centre
Castleknock
Dublin 15

An Hachette UK Company
www.hachette.co.uk

www.littlebrown.co.uk

CHAPTER 1

Taylor

To all the people who've called me cheap in the past...

How do you like me *now*, jerks?

It is only through pinching pennies and rationing resources for years that I have been able to afford this truly luxurious beach house for six whole days—on a second grade teacher's salary. The bright white jewel with sparkling windows is right on the Cape Cod coast, boasts a wrap-around porch and walkway straight down to a semi-private beach. My toes are already wiggling in anticipation of digging into the sand while the New England sun bakes my skin north of translucent and most importantly *of all*, my baby brother gets a change of scenery to recover from his heartbreak.

Wheeling my suitcase in one hand, holding the house key poised for immediate lock insertion in the other, I look back over my shoulder to find life returning to Jude's boyishly handsome features. "Damn, Taylor. I guess ripping your napkins in half paid off."

"No one needs a whole napkin if they eat carefully enough," I sing back cheerfully.

"No arguments here. Not when you've scored us this view." Jude adjusts the surfboard under his arm. "So, someone owns this place and rents it out? I can't imagine anyone not wanting to live here year round."

"You would be surprised. Most of the homes on this street are rentals." I nod at a nearly identical home across the narrow lane with shingled siding and purple hydrangeas bursting in all directions in the front yard. "I looked into that one, too, but there was no clawfoot bathtub."

"Jesus." He draws out the sarcasm. "We'd practically be camping."

I stick my tongue out at him over my shoulder, stop in front of the entrance and slip the key into the lock, turning it with a heightening sense of excitement. "I just want everything to be perfect. You deserve a nice vacation, Jude."

"What about you, T?" asks my brother.

But I'm already pushing inside and oh. Oh yes. It's everything the owner promised online and more. Panoramic windows overlooking the turbulent Atlantic, a hillside of seagrass and wildflowers tumbling down to that sapphire ocean. High, beamed ceilings, a fireplace that turns on at the push of a button, big inviting couches and tasteful nautical-themed décor. There is even a hint of something in the air... a scent I can't quite put my finger on, but it's got a kick. And best of all, the ocean plays a gentle soundtrack that can be heard anywhere in the house.

"You didn't answer me," Jude drawls, leaning his board against the wall and poking me in the side. "Don't you think *you* deserve a nice vacation, too? A year of Zoom classes with children who were secretly playing Minecraft off camera? Then straight into another year of bringing a new class up to speed, basically covering two years' worth of material? You deserve a trip around the world at this point."

I suppose I do deserve this vacation. I *am* going to enjoy myself, but I'm much more comfortable focusing on Jude's good time. He's my baby brother, after all, and it's my job to take care of him. It's been that way since we were children. "I forgot to ask if you've heard from Mom or Dad at all recently?" It's a question I always hold my breath after asking. "They were in Bolivia the last time I spoke with them."

"Still there, I think. Potential riots on the horizon and they're clearing the national museum, just in case."

Our parents always had the weirdest job at career day. Officially, they are archeologists, but that title is a lot more boring than their actual duties, which include being contracted by foreign governments to protect and preserve art during times of civil unrest when priceless treasures could potentially be destroyed. Inevitably at career day, a child in the front row would say, "You're kind of like Indiana Jones," and my parents—who were prepared for this— would bellow, "Snakes! Why does it always have to be snakes?" Perfectly synchronized.

They are such fascinating people.

I just don't know them very well.

But they gave me the greatest treasure of my life and he's currently sprawling out on the closest piece of furniture, as he is wont to do, effortlessly belonging everywhere he goes in flannel and Birkenstocks. "You take the biggest room, all right?" he yawns, dragging suntanned fingers through scruffy dark blond hair. When I start to argue, he points at his mouth and makes a zipping motion, indicating that I should shut up. "It's not up for debate. I couldn't even afford to chip in on this place. You get the master."

"But after everything with Bartholomew..."

A shadow crosses his face. "I'm fine. You can't worry about me so much."

"Says who?" I sniff, wheeling my suitcase toward the kitchen. Seriously, what *is* that aroma? It's kind of like...a big meal was prepared in the kitchen very recently and the garlic and spices are still lingering in the air. "You take your nap—"

I laugh under my breath when his snore cuts me off. My brother could fall asleep on the wing of a 747 with a flight in progress. Meanwhile I have to perform a very specific night-time ritual of stretching and exfoliating and precise pillow placement to wrangle a measly four hours. Maybe the waves will lull me to sleep while I'm here, though. One can hope.

With a hopeful exhale and squaring of my shoulders, I stow the handle of my roller luggage and pick it up against my chest, my utilitarian teaching flats carrying me up the stairs. That clawfoot bathtub has been calling my name since I saw it online, buried in the background of one of the pictures. Not featured, as it should have been. There is only a shower stall in my apartment back in Hartford, Connecticut and I *dream* of baths. Several of the accounts I follow on Instagram are dedicated to luxurious bath time rituals, including people who eat full meals while submerged in hot water and bubbles. Spaghetti and meat-balls, right there among the suds. I'm not sure I'll ever take bath time quite so far, but I respect their enthusiasm.

The master suite is big and inviting, decorated once again in a nautical theme, the palette consisting of creams and whites and light blues. Though it was sunny when we arrived, clouds are currently passing over the sun, darkening the walls. Quiet. It's so quiet. The bed invites me to come take a nap, but nothing short of a hurricane warning is going to keep me from taking the bath I've been envisioning for weeks.

When I walk into the bathroom, I don't even bother trying to hold in my squeal when I spot the tub at the far end, silhouetted by a floor-to-ceiling picture window. Leaving my suitcase just outside the door, I kick off my shoes, my spine tingling with excitement...although, that pungent smell is upstairs, too? Isn't that odd? Maybe the previous renter was the type to eat *their* meals in the bathtub and they accidentally let it rot?

Hmm. The rest of the house is immaculate. That doesn't really track.

There must be a dead mouse or rat in the wall somewhere, but I am not going to let that stymie our good time. I'll simply call the owner and ask him to send over pest control. A minor blip on the overall radar of the vacation that will be taken care of in no time. Jude won't even have to wake up from his nap.

The clawfoot tub beckons me from the far side of the bathroom and I can already hear the white noise of the water running. Can already see the steam curling and fogging up the windowpane. Maybe I can get one tiny little bath in before I call the owner about the smell?

Experimentally, I close the bathroom door and the stink is significantly dulled.

Bath time it is.

I do a little shimmy on my way to the tub, flipping on the hot water faucet with a flourish and sighing, looking out over the sparsely populated beach. Most likely, everyone is home recovering from the fourth of July, which was only yesterday. The rental fees were significantly cheaper this side of the fourth, and my wildly popular brother had several barbeques to attend over the long weekend, anyway, so arriving on the fifth—a Tuesday—worked out for both of us.

With the tub halfway to full, I return to the bedroom briefly to take off my clothes and fold them neatly on the bed, to be placed in the travel hamper as soon as I officially unpack. Holding my breath against the smell, I start to return to the bathroom when something important occurs to me. I found this rental on StayInn.com and at the very top of their renter checklist was this: always make sure the fire and CO_2 alarms are working upon arrival.

"Better do it before I forget..." I murmur, glancing up at the ceiling, though the detectors are probably out in the hallway—

Two little holes.

There are two little holes drilled into the crown molding.

No. No, no way. I have to be imagining that.

Goosebumps prickle down my naked limbs and I fold my arms across my breasts. The pulse in my temples start to pound and I shiver. A conditioned response to being surprised, that's all. I'm sure it's just where the nails were hammered into the molding. Surely those aren't *peepholes*. Dammit, I knew I was getting in too deep with my true crime podcasts. Now everything is a life or death situation. The beginning of a grisly hack job that law enforcement will inevitably claim is the worst they've seen in their twenty-year career.

That's not what is happening here. This is not a new episode of *Etched in Bone*.

Dateline's Keith Morrison is not narrating this little panic attack.

This is just my simple, boring life. I'm just a girl on a quest for a bath.

Turning in a circle, I search the perimeter of the ceiling for any other holes of that size and come up empty. Dammit. Of course those two holes are on the side of the room that faces the center of the house. There could be an attic or a closet on the other side. Gross. *Please let your imagination be working overtime.*

Still, I'll never be able to relax now, so I quickly shut off the bath with no small sense of regret and wrap a towel around my naked body, returning to the space beneath the holes, regarding them warily, as if they're going to jump down and bite me. I've heard of this kind of thing, obviously. Voyeurism. Everyone has. But it's not the kind of problem one would expect to have at a beachfront property that cost a month's worth of paychecks. Those cannot be peepholes. No way. Just a defect in the wood. As soon as I confirm that, I'm neck deep in hot water and this perfect vacation is off to a flawless start.

Before I can allow myself to get scared, I venture into the hallway outside the bedroom and open the adjacent closet, releasing a pent-up breath when there is no peeper inside. Although...there are no holes either. Not in the immediate closet. But there is a removeable panel on the shared wall. A crawl space?

Speaking of crawling, that is what my skin is doing.

Was the house so quiet and dark when we arrived? I can't even hear Jude snoring anymore. Just the distant drip of the bathtub faucet. Drip. Drip. And the sound of my breathing now as it accelerates. "Jude?" I call, my voice sounding like a curtain ripping in the total silence. "Jude?" I call louder.

Several seconds pass. No sound.

And then footsteps are coming up the stairs. Why is my mouth dry? It's only my brother. But when my back hits the wall, I realize I'm cowering there, my fight-or-flight instinct preparing me to dash for the bedroom and lock the door. If what? If someone other than my brother is coming up the stairs? What kind of a horror movie do I think I'm living in? *Calm down.*

My parents infiltrate riots to save artwork in the name of preserving history. Obviously their bravery is not a hereditary trait. Two little holes in the crown molding have my heart jackhammering. Even more so than the first day of in-person classes with a mob of second graders who'd been cooped up for a year with limited physical activity.

Could you be any more pitiful, Taylor?

If I needed proof that—at twenty-six—my life is too safe and predictable, here it is. One wrench in the engine and my routine-oriented self is ready to self-destruct.

I slump against the wall when Jude's yawning face comes into view. "What's up?"

Swallowing my nerves, I gesture vaguely at the closet. "So this is probably me being crazy, but there are two holes near the ceiling in the bedroom. And I think they correspond to that crawl space up there?"

Jude is awake now. "Like peepholes?"

"Yeah?" I wince. "Or I could just be imagining things?"

"Better to be safe," he murmurs, passing me into the bedroom. Hands on hips, he observes the holes for a long moment, before meeting my eyes. And that's when cold licks down my spine. His expression is suspicious. Not teasing, like I was hoping for. "What the fuck?"

"Okay." I let out a slightly unsteady breath. "You're not laughing and pointing out some flaw in the construction, like I was hoping you would."

"No, but let's take stock, T. If those are peepholes, there's no one peeping now." He returns to the hallway to stand beside me. Both of us stare up at the crawl space. "But neither one of us is going to relax until we're positive, right?"

I groan, visions of my bath dissipating like wisps of smoke. "Should we call the police?"

He considers my totally irrational question. Really considers it, stroking the scruff on his chin. This is one of the reasons I love Jude so much. We're siblings, so naturally we've had our share of bickering fights and outright shouting matches over the years, but he's on my team. It's a given. He doesn't accuse me of being crazy. He takes me seriously. The things that are important to me are of equal importance to him and I will always, always do everything I can to make his life easier, the way he's done for me in the near-constant absence of our parents.

"I think I'll just pop off that panel and have a look," Jude says, finally.

"I don't like it." Jude might be well over six feet tall now, a grown twenty-three-year-old man, but he'll always be my little brother—and the thought of him confronting a possible peeping Tom on my watch makes me nauseous. "At the very least, we should have a weapon handy."

"Need I remind you that I took jujitsu for six months?"

"Need I remind *you* that you only hung in there that long because you were waiting for the instructor to break up with his boyfriend?"

"They were clearly on the rocks."

"I'm sure your dimples helped speed things along."

"You're right." He gives me an intentionally creepy smile. "They are the true weapon."

I shake my head at him, but thankfully the shivers are subsiding.

"All right." He claps his hands together. "Let's take a quick look and pray we don't find a jar of fingernails or some shit."

"Or a GoPro," I mutter, bracing myself against the wall, hands covering my face. I watch through the cracks of my fingers as Jude slides into the closet, reaches up and eases aside the panel to reveal a small space. Very small. Immediately, however, daylight streams in through the two holes and it is impossible to ignore the fact that they are the exact width of an average set of eyes and they go straight through to the bedroom. Peepholes. One hundred percent. "Oh God. Yuck. Is there anything...or anyone up there?"

Jude grasps the edge of the crawl space and does a quick pull up. "Nope. Nothing." He drops down. "A person would have to be tiny to fit up there. Or really flexible. So unless my powers of deduction fail me, the peeper is a gymnast."

"Or a small woman?" We trade a skeptical look. "Yeah, that doesn't really fit the peeper profile, does it?" I pull my towel up tighter beneath my armpits. "So what do we do?"

"Send me the contact info for the owner. I'll give him a call."

"Oh. No, I'll do it. I don't want this to disrupt your vacation time. Go take your nap."

He's already on his way back to the stairs. "Send me the info, T."

For some reason, I still don't want to be alone with the peepholes, so I scurry along after my brother in my towel. "Fine." I chew my lip. "I think I'll check the laundry room for a stepping stool and some tape to cover up the holes."

He tosses a wink back at me. "In case the peeper is a ghost?"

"Oh, sure. It's funny now, but as soon as it gets dark, a peeper ghost will become a totally realistic possibility."

"Take the other room, if you want. I don't mind being spied on by Casper."

I'm laughing as we reach the bottom of the stairs, both of us hooking right into the kitchen where the door to the laundry room is located. "You'd probably enjoy it," I say.

"Have you been reading my diary again?"

By the time I pull open the door to the laundry area, I'm having such a good time with my brother that I don't believe what I'm seeing at first. It has to be a joke. Or a television screen playing a grisly reenactment from a Netflix true crime documentary. There cannot be a large, dead man stuffed in between the washer and dryer, face purple with bruises, eyes glassy and unseeing. And there in the center of his forehead is a neat, black-edged bullet hole. It simply cannot be happening. But the bile that spears up my throat is real. So is the ice that hardens me, head to toe, a scream freezing in my throat. No. No, no, no.

"Taylor?" Jude approaches, sounding concerned.

On instinct, I try to push him away. My little brother shouldn't see things like this. I have to spare him from this. My hands prove ineffective unfortunately and before I can summon enough strength, enough wherewithal to prevent Jude from looking into the laundry room, he's there beside me. And then he's dragging me backwards several feet, yelling, "What the fuck?" An eerie buzzing silence descends. The image doesn't go away. He's still there. Still dead. There is something vaguely familiar about the man, but I'm shaking and trying not to vomit and that is garnering all of my concentration. *Oh God, oh God*, what is happening here? This isn't a joke?

"Okay," I whisper. "N-*now* I think we should call the police."

CHAPTER 2

Taylor

I'm wrapped in a blanket, awash in the glow of flashing blue lights. This is not supposed to happen in real life. I'm trapped in an episode of *Etched in Bone*. I'm the innocent bystander who stumbled upon the macabre scene. Of course, the years of therapy I will need to recover won't even be mentioned in the show notes. The pithy hosts won't pronounce my name correctly. But me? I doubt I'll ever forget the sight of that murdered man as long as I live.

Unless...maybe this is a very vivid nightmare?

Nope. There is definitely a huge black bag being wheeled out of the house by medical examiners. Out of the *crime scene* while Jude and I watch it all happen with our jaws in our laps. We're trying to focus on what the police officer is saying from his seated position on the coffee table in front of us, but we have now given him our statements three times each. Not a single detail has changed. And now that the adrenaline of discovering a murder victim is beginning to wear off, I'm getting a strong case of the get-the-hell-out-of-heres.

"It has to be murder, right?" I say, mostly to myself. "He couldn't have shot himself straight on in the forehead like that."

"No," admits the officer—a man in his early forties named Officer Wright who bears a striking resemblance to Jamie Foxx. So much so that I did a double take when he walked through the front door. "It's next to impossible."

"So the killer...they are still out there," Jude says. "Maybe even next door."

The officer sighs. "Well, yeah. Another possibility. And that's going to make our job pretty tough. Damn near all of these places become rentals in the summertime, meaning it's not locals in residence. Could be anyone from anywhere. A visitor of a visitor of a visitor. These rental sites like StayInn.com have become a goddamn nuisance. No offense."

"None taken," I say automatically, watching the final stretch of the body bag disappear out the front door. That's when it hits me. Why the man looked so familiar. "That was the owner of this house. Oscar. I remember now." I fumble for my phone. "His picture is on the listing—"

The officer rests his hand on mine, stalling my actions. "We already know he's the owner. Matter of fact, we know all too well that he lived here."

A different police officer passes by and clears his throat loudly.

Officer Wright's mouth snaps shut.

As soon as the other man has walked out of the house, Jude and I lean forward almost simultaneously. "What did you mean by that?" Jude asks. "You know all too well that he lives here?"

Wright checks over his shoulder, sighs, pretends to be writing something on his notebook. "Someone at StayInn.com should have gotten in contact with you. We communicated at length with them over the whole situation. They should never have let you come here."

"Wait, slow down." Jude drags a hand down his face, visibly regrouping. "What situation are you referring to?"

"We were called here a few nights ago for a domestic disturbance." The officer's voice is low enough that we have to lean even closer to make out his words. At this point, I can basically count the hairs of his goatee. "One of the renters down the block phoned it in. Reported shouting. Loud crashes." He taps his pen against his thigh, checks side to side again. "Turns out, a bunch of girls were renting this place and they came across the peepholes upstairs—"

"Oh my God!" I slap a palm against my forehead. "I forgot about the peepholes."

"You were pretty distracted," Jude says, patting me on the back, but keeping his attention on the officer. "So we weren't the first to discover that little bonus amenity?"

Wright shook his head. "The girl who found them called her father. Big, long-haul trucker type. Well he showed up pissed as hell, understandably, but instead of calling the police, he had his daughter call the owner and bring him over. The father got a few punches in before we arrived to break it up. The girls agreed not to press charges as long as they got a refund and no assault charges were filed against the father. But StayInn.com was contacted about this by Barnstable PD. You should have been informed."

"Yes, we should have." Mentally, I'm already writing a stern email to StayInn.com. It might even include a few choice words, like *emotional trauma* and *legal counsel*...and *account credit*. "Did they actually catch Oscar *looking* through the holes?"

"No." Wright chews on the next part before spitting it out. "But there was a camera. Set up on a tripod."

Without looking at my brother, I know our faces are identical with disgust.

Shaking off the chill it gives me to know a man had been spying on women illegally in this house—and I was about to embark on six days here—I go back to finding an explanation. "I guess the altercation with the angry dad explains the bruises on Oscar's face, but the father of those girls didn't *murder* him, right? Oscar was alive when the whole situation was resolved?"

Wright shrugs. "My lieutenant thinks the father was still revved up after all was said and done. Came back to finish the job. Homeowner gets his ass kicked by one suspect, then winds up getting killed by another? In the same damn *week*? Nah. We don't believe in coincidences. Not that big."

"Yeah, except..."

Something about the scenario is bothering me, though. Not sitting quite right. And I really, really should just stop trying to fit everything together neatly when nothing about this is neat or tidy, but I've always had a hard time leaving puzzles unfinished. However, usually my puzzles come with five thousand pieces, not peepholes and bullet wounds.

Still, my inquisitive nature is the only thing I inherited from my parents. I definitely wasn't born with an ounce of their courage. A fact that they've lamented several times over the years, patting my hand and giving me forced smiles.

That's our little schoolteacher. Always playing it safe.

Jude has been surfing in Indonesia. Skydiving in Montana. He works in an animal sanctuary, mostly with the pandas, but sometimes he actually *feeds lions*. There is a video of him online actually cuddling one of the big cats. Like, rolling around in the grass with the giant creature while he laughs and scrubs the lion's mane. I almost dropped dead when someone emailed it to me. Of course, no one even thought about consulting Jude's big sister about the whole dangerous business, but I'm *not* salty about it anymore. Mostly.

So, okay. Courage is not something I have in large supply. This vacation is one of the most adventurous things I've done in a while. I actually had to chew on a throw pillow when I clicked "book" on this reservation. But something happened inside of me when I walked into the laundry room and saw poor Oscar staring blanky into space.

Or rather...*nothing* happened.

The world didn't end, despite the terrifying circumstances.

I stayed standing, right there on my own two feet. Maybe now...I'm curious about what *else* I can do. Maybe I'm curious if I can help. Be brave like my parents and Jude. Or the hosts of *Etched in Bone*, who infiltrate the scenes of the small-town murders they investigate, asking the tough questions. Can I be brave like that? Am I braver than I've always thought?

Jury is still out, But I *do* have a super strength and it involves overthinking everything to death. Which is what I am doing now. Gnawing on the facts...and finding the plot holes. Perhaps this is not my job, maybe I should focus on finding us another place to stay, but I can't help but feel personally involved, having been the one to discover Oscar's body. I found him. And while it sounds crazy, I feel a certain responsibility toward holding the murderer accountable and completing this puzzle. I'm not sure I can move on from this whole ordeal until the lid has been properly sealed on the facts.

"Officer Wright—"

A wail of grief rattles the windowpanes, followed by a shout of denial. "No! Not my brother! *Oscar?* Oscar!"

Jude and I blink at each other and whip around to face the open front door. At the open doors of the ambulance, a woman collapses into the arms of an emergency medical technician, her head thrown back in a howl of anguish. A voice crackles over the radio attached to Wright's shoulder. "Yeah, we've got the vic's sister here. Can someone send down the social worker?"

"Oh no." The tip of my nose begins to burn and I reach for Jude's arm without thinking, squeezing. "That poor woman. She's just lost her brother. Can you imagine what she's feeling?"

The officer in front of us grunts. "She's probably going to feel a lot different when she finds out what he's been doing."

"Confused, maybe. But still sad," Jude mutters, falling back against the cushions, visibly exhausted. Poor baby never got to finish his nap. I need to find him a safe bed for the night.

"Yes," I agree with my brother. To Wright, I ask, "Are you *positive* Oscar is the peeper, though? The holes—"

I'm cut off once again when the weeping woman stumbles into the house. Using the wall to support herself, she takes one step into the living room, followed by two more, then falls boneless to the couch on our left. My eyes are welled up now and on the verge of spilling, just imagining her grief. If I lost my brother, I wouldn't know up from down. "I'm so sorry for your terrible loss," I offer.

Her attention zips to mine and...

I don't *want* to. But I notice that her eyes are dry.

Everyone experiences grief differently. Paging Amanda Knox. I'm not judging. I just make an entirely casual, non-judgmental mental notation. A cactus could thrive on those arid cheeks.

"Do you mind telling me your name, ma'am?" Wright prompts her.

"Lisa. Lisa Stanley." She pins me and Jude with a look. "Who are you?"

"I'm Taylor Bassey. This is my brother, Jude. We were staying here. Or supposed to be staying here, rather. But we...found Oscar right after we arrived."

"Oh. Well, I'm so sorry my dead brother ruined your vacation," she snaps. Before I can rush to reassure her that we're not complaining, her face crumples. "I'm sorry, I'm just...I don't mean to be unkind. I just can't believe this is happening. They say he was shot! Who would shoot my brother? He doesn't have a mean bone in his body. No enemies..."

No one says anything. But Wright obviously missed poker face training at the academy, because he looks ready to explode.

"What?" asks Lisa, spine straightening. "What is it?"

The world's most uncomfortable conversation ensues while Wright tells Lisa about the confrontation with the renter's father over the peepholes and camera. When he's finished giving the details, Lisa stares off into space. "Why wouldn't he tell me he'd gotten beat up?"

"Probably embarrassed, considering the circumstances." With a sigh, Wright hands us his card and stands up. "Let me know if you think of anything else. If you're looking for a place to hang your hat for the night, there's a DoubleTree in Hyannis. Pool is decent."

"Thanks," Jude says, taking the card. As soon as Wright

has left through the front door, my brother stands. "I'll go call the DoubleTree."

"No need to do that," Lisa interjects quickly, seeming to catch herself off guard. When we only stare at her blankly, she digs in her purse and takes out a large assortment of keys crammed together on a ring. "My brother owns three other rentals on this block. I schedule maintenance for him. Inspect the premises before new renters arrive. Etcetera. I was late getting here to double check this place or *I* would have found him." She lets out a long exhale. "He is...*was*...pretty hands-off with the whole business. A normal guy. Used to deliver mail for a living, before he got into real estate. God love him, my brother was lazy. He delegated. That's why..." She shakes her head a little. "It just doesn't make sense. Oscar wouldn't *spy* on people."

"No. It doesn't make sense," I blurt, before I can stop myself.

"Taylor," Jude says out of the corner of his mouth. "Pump the brakes."

"It's her brother," I whisper back. "I would want to know everything."

"I love you, but please don't get involved in a murder investigation."

"I'm not getting involved. I'm just passing along some specifics."

"Textbook involvement."

Lisa drops down in front of us on the coffee table, occupying the spot where Wright once sat. Elbows on her knees, she leans forward, and up close, I can see the physical similarities she shares with Oscar. Both in their fifties. Slightly hooked noses. High foreheads. Graying hair. But Lisa is more on the petite side, while her brother was...

"Too big. Oscar was way too big to fit into that crawl space."

Lisa's antenna goes up. "The crawl space where you found the peepholes?"

"That's right." I ignore Jude's groan. "No way he could have gotten up there."

"He could have used a ladder, T." My brother joins the conversation with nothing short of reluctance, adding, "Hypothetically, of course," for Lisa's benefit. "It would have been pretty easy to drill those holes from either side. And he didn't *need* to get inside the crawl space. All he had to do was slide in the camera."

"Yes. If he never intended to look through the holes." For a single, fleeting moment, I feel like *SVU's* Olivia Benson. All I need is the overcoat, fathomless brown eyes and Stabler by my side looking broody and fine. "Why did he drill *two* of them?" I split a look between my brother and Lisa. "Those holes were drilled for the express purpose of a person looking through them. If Oscar—hypothetically—only wanted to film his guests, he would have needed a single hole. Not two."

Jude frowns down at his hands for a moment. "You're right. At the very least, it's odd."

"You're saying whoever drilled those holes is small enough to fit in the crawl space," Lisa says slowly, beginning to nod. "A woman, perhaps?"

Don't think about the fact that she still hasn't cried. Not a drop.

"Maybe."

Jude is beginning to get a weird vibe. I can tell because he's doing that thing where he can't stop arranging and rearranging the shaggiest section of hair on top of his head. "We should call the DoubleTree, Taylor. I'm sure Ms. Stanley has a lot of calls to make—"

"The police are already so positive it's the father of the last tenant." Lisa tosses a glance out the window where officers are standing in a huddle at the end of the driveway. "And let's be honest, there is no way they're going to go above and beyond for someone they believe is a pervert, right?" Cogs are turning behind her eyes. "Maybe I should look into a private investigator. My boyfriend is currently deployed, but he grew up with a guy in Boston. Some former detective turned bounty hunter. Someone who could give these locals a run for their money and maybe clear my brother's name in the process."

See? We all grieve in our own ways.

I cry. Lisa avenges her loved ones.

Moral of the story, everyone is braver than me.

"I don't think a private investigator would hurt," I say, finally taking pity on Jude and rising from the couch, letting the blanket slide off my shoulders. "Once again, Lisa, I'm so sorry for your loss." I hold out my hand for a shake. "I wish we'd met under better circumstances."

She pulls me into a hug. "You've given me hope, Taylor. Thank you. I don't want him to be remembered as some sleazebag. I'm going to find out what really happened." Something cold and metallic is pressed into my hand and I look down to find a set of keys. "It's only down the block. Number sixty-two. I insist."

I try to hand back the keys. "Oh, we really couldn't—"

"Are you sure?" She waggles her eyebrows. "It has a clawfooted bathtub."

Am I wearing a sign or something?

"Oh," I breathe. "Really?"

Jude hangs his head a moment, then heads reluctantly for the suitcases. "Number sixty-two, you say?"

On the way out of the house, I stop short at the console table just inside the door.

While I was reading through reviews of the house, I saw pictures of a guest book. Obviously this makes me a total dork, but I was looking forward to writing our own message on one of the pages, for future guests to read. I was going to draw a squid in the margins.

Sliding open the drawer or the table, I spy the white leather book with gold, embossed lettering. *Guest experiences.* I'm not sure what possesses me to take it. To quickly slide it into my purse and cover it up with my hand sanitizing wipes and sunglass case while Jude rapidly shakes his head at me. Maybe I've surprised myself by being so coherent tonight after discovering a body...and I want to know what else I can do. If I have what it takes to solve a mystery and locate the mettle I've always been missing. Or maybe I'm dubious of the police's motivation to inspect this murder beyond their original theory. And let's face it, Lisa's lack of emotion won't stop poking at my sixth sense. I didn't even know I *had* a sixth sense.

Whatever the cause of my impromptu evidence heist, I'll return the book tomorrow after I have a little peek. No big deal, right?

CHAPTER 3

Myles

$\mathcal{I}$ climb off my bike and pop an antacid.

Well isn't Cape Cod just cheerful as hell on this sunny Thursday afternoon?

Little signs hanging from every door proclaiming that life is a beach. Beach life. Life is better at the beach. Seas the day. How anyone can be passionate about a place with so much fucking sand is beyond me. I already want to get back on the road. Unfortunately, I've turned my back on a lot of things, but I couldn't seem to do it with my friend, Paul. Not while he's deployed and unable to fix this mess for his girl-friend in person. Paul once refused to rat on me when I shat-tered a stained-glass church window with a line drive.

I'm here because I owe him one and we grew up together in Boston—but then I'm gone.

Until then, my job is to find Oscar Stanley's "real killer."

This happens a lot in my line of work of bounty hunting.

The family is in denial. Their son violated his parole, but he's trying to turn his life around. Their daughter is on the lam, but only because she's innocent of that drug charge and no one believes her. I've heard it all before and it goes in one ear and out the other. My job is to bring bad people to law enforcement's door and walk away whistling with a check, without having to deal with any of the red tape or paperwork.

This case is slightly different in that there is no bounty to collect. There is no criminal at large. I don't have a name or a face or a prison record at my disposal. All I've got is a big question mark and a favor to return. However, after Paul gave me the rundown on Oscar Stanley and how his peeping Tom ways got the snot beat out of him prior to the murder, I'm inclined to agree with the local PD on this one. The father of that girl came back to finish the job. It should take me one or two days to prove that beyond a shadow of a doubt and get back on the highway, my slate wiped clean of any favors or responsibilities to anyone.

On my way here—to Coriander Lane—I stopped at Lisa Stanley's house and picked up the set of keys I'm holding. Technically, this is a crime scene and there is yellow caution tape across the entrance, but obeying rules isn't really my strong suit. Never has been. That's why I was a shit detective and an even worse husband. Might have been faithful, but loyalty only goes so far when a man leaves out the cherishing part of his vows.

Laughter kicks up down at the beach, voices intermingled with the sounds of Tom Petty. A bumble bee kite dips and whirls in the sky. The smell of hot dogs and burgers carries in thick on the breeze. This is where people come on vacation with their families. To be happy.

I can't wait to get the fuck out of here.

I toss up the keys and catch them in my hand, continuing across the street to the house where the murder supposedly occurred. I haven't seen crime scene photos, but I have the victim's description and it's unlikely that a man of Oscar's stature would have been transported by the perpetrator post-mortem. Furthermore, why would the murderer make it *easier* for the body to be found? No, this was a crime of passion. Anger. Cut and dried.

Get this over with.

I'm halfway across the street when I sense eyes on my back.

Slowly, I peer back over my shoulder and find a young woman, brownish-blonde hair, maybe in her mid-twenties, watering a flowerpot on the front porch of a house. She's completely missing the pot, though. Water is pouring from the spout straight down onto the floorboards, splashing up onto her bare calves. And she doesn't seem to notice at all.

"Can I help you?" I bark in a hard tone.

She drops the can with a loud clatter, spins on a toe and runs head on into the front door, bouncing right off the damn thing. Even from a hundred yards away, I can see the canaries spinning around her head. *That's what you get for being nosy.*

I dig another antacid out of my jeans pocket, pop it and continue on my oh-so-merry way across the street, ripping the caution tape off the front door and letting it flutter to the ground. I'm halfway over the threshold when I hear footsteps approaching from behind. Nimble, girly ones. In the reflection of the storm door, the nosy neighbor approaches. And boom, I'm already annoyed. "Listen, you want to call the cops?" Scowling, I turn around partially to face her. "Be my..."

It's extremely weird, the way I just sort of forget what I'm saying.

This has never happened to me before. Every word out of my mouth has a purpose and whoever I'm talking to better damn well listen. I just...don't really know why I was planning on being so mean to her is all. Didn't she just run into a door? That had to hurt. Plus there are water splatters all over her legs and she is...

Facts are facts. She's cute as a button.

I don't look twice at cute women. *Anything* cute, really. That would be like a tractor admiring a dandelion. Looking might seem like a fine idea, but tractors are built to mow down dandelions. It's what they do. So there isn't very much use in me noticing the way freckles just kind of...scatter all the way from her nose down her neck. To her tits. Which are tied up in a bikini top. A pink one. The color alone makes me feel guilty for looking, but hell, they'd fit right into my hands. A lot of her would. Those hips. Her knees. The sides of her beautiful face.

Christ. The top of her head barely reaches my chin. What the hell is the matter with me?

I clear my throat. Hard. "As I was saying, you want to call the cops, half pint? Be my guest. They know I'm here."

"Half pint?" she gasps. Sputters. Pushes a big hunk of hair behind her ear so I'm impacted by the full force of her eyes. Green ones. Fuck. "I'll have you know," she continues, "that I'm the tallest one at my job."

"You either work alone or you're a kindergarten teacher."

A split-second's hesitation. Subtle shift from right to left. "Wrong."

I wink at her and she bristles. "I'm never wrong."

Is that a flush creeping up her neck? God, she has to be eight or nine years younger than me. Mid-twenties to my mid-thirties. So I'm definitely not noticing the spot where her bikini strap digs into her shoulder, ever so slightly. Just this side of too tight. I'm definitely not thinking of tucking my finger beneath it and dragging the little strip of material down her arm. Unwrapping her like a birthday present.

Jesus, I need to get laid. That fact wasn't obvious until right now, when I'm lusting after this stranger in the heart of Middle Class Vacationville wondering what her nipples would look like in the sunshine, all licked up in my spit. She's probably married. Single girls in their twenties don't vacation in Cape Cod. Provincetown, maybe. But not this family-oriented section of Falmouth. So why isn't she wearing a ring?

She notices me looking for one.

Dammit.

In response, her posture changes. Her hands drop to her sides and she shifts left to right, unconsciously tossing her hair back over her shoulder. Kind of like she's only now, this very second, becoming aware that I'm a man and she's approached me in a bikini and ridiculous cut-off jean shorts that cover only slightly more than a pair of panties. And that I'm interested enough to wonder if she's already got a man waiting for her in that saccharine sweet house with heart shapes cut into the shutters. She's figuring all of that out and hiding none of it on her spectacular face.

Great. We've gone from beautiful to spectacular.

She's definitely married, you idiot.

Do your job and get gone.

"Go water your flowers. I'm busy."

"I know. I was just..." Her hands flutter around until she folds them at her waist. "Well, I was just wondering if you had any theories yet."

"I just got here." I tip my chin at the bike. "You saw me arrive, right?"

"On your death trap. Yes. But I assume you've gotten some kind of advance...dossier. Or case file. Right?"

I give her a narrow-eyed stare, hoping she'll cower and slink away like everyone else who is unlucky enough to be on the receiving end of this look.

"Fine. Be coy about it, Mr...."

"Don't worry about my name."

That throws her off for a second, almost like she's disappointed. But finally, she shrugs. "I just thought you might like to speak with me." With a prim little once-over, she turns and heads back across the street. "Since I'm the one who found the body and all."

"Come back here."

"I don't think I will."

"Half pint."

"*I* have a name."

"Come back here and tell it to me, then."

What in God's name is wrong with me? Am I really following this young woman, who is *definitely* married, probably to someone named Carter or Preston, across the street? I should be in the murder house taking pictures, checking for blood spatter or missed evidence. I should not be suddenly desperate to know this woman's name. But hell if I can stop following in her wake when her ass moves like an ass *ought* to move. *Damn.*

She spins on a dime and I almost mow her down, just like a tractor always does with a dandelion. We end up toe to toe, only I'm a good ten inches taller, so her face is tipped up to the sky and blanketed by sunshine. Something flips in my chest. Something I really don't like.

"You found the body," I say, trying my best to stick to the job. That's what this is.

Get in and get out. No entanglements. That's what I do. It's what I like.

Her gaze drops to my mouth for a split second, but it's enough to make my briefs feel like an XL instead of an XXL. "Uh-huh."

Why does my skin turn clammy thinking of her around a dead man? A recently murdered one? She shouldn't have to see something like that. Not this woman who waters flowers and runs into doors. "Tell me you got out of the house immediately. In case the murderer was still on the property."

"Oh." She scrunches up her nose. "No. We...did not."

We. There it is. I grunt, because It's not a good idea to speak with my heartburn acting up. That's what's wrong with me. That's why everything south of my neck is off-kilter. "You and your husband."

"Me and my brother."

Where did my heartburn go? It must be coming in waves. "You're here with your brother," I confirm, wincing over the thread of relief in my tone.

She nods, eyes serious. "Who discovered the body is very important information. It probably should have been in the dossier."

Now I have the damnedest urge to smile. Obviously I need my head examined. "We don't call it a dossier, half pint."

Curious head tilt. "What do you call it?"

"Notes. Boring old notes. And that's what this case is going to be. Boring, fast, open and shut. Dude was spying on a bunch of girls and got caught. Dad lost his temper. Physical altercations end in death a lot more often than you'd think. Either someone loses the fight and wants payback. Or one of them can't let it go. That's what happened here."

"But you were hired by Lisa Stanley? Oscar's sister?"

"Technically, yes, though I'm doing her boyfriend a favor."

"Did you *speak* to her? Didn't she tell you about the issues with the peephole theory?"

My head falls back on a gusty sigh. "You're one of those amateur sleuths aren't you? You've watched a couple of sensationalized documentaries on Netflix and now you think you're an honorary member of law enforcement."

"Podcasts are more my thing, actually—"

I send a groan toward the clouds.

"—but that's not relevant. I've *always* liked to leave things neat and tidy. For instance, there is a loose thread on your shirt and I am dying to trim it off." She wiggles her fingers at it and I come very close to stepping forward to give her access to the thread, just to get her touching me. "There is no reason for two peepholes if filming the guests was the goal. Only one would be necessary. Someone had to have spied with their two eyes at one time. And Oscar Stanley could never have fit into that crawl space."

"Maybe he drilled the holes first, then realized he'd miscalculated his ability to fit." Chewing on her lip, she says nothing. "There isn't always a rhyme or reason to a person's behavior. And a lot of time, people just make mistakes. Sort of like me taking this job." I make a shooing motion with my hand. Seriously, I need her to go back to her cookie-cutter vacation house across the street because she's fucking with my peace of mind. I'm starting to notice things about her. A little mole beneath her navel. The way she sucks in a breath before she starts speaking. Her apple orchard scent. "Run on home. I've got this covered. Like I said, I'm going to wrap this up quickly."

After a moment, she nods and begins to back away.

And it's like she's pulling my stomach along with her.

The odd sense of loss doesn't make any sense. *Ignore it.*

"Okay," she murmurs, adjusting her bikini strap. "Well, when you need the guest book, I have it in my luggage."

"Uh-huh," I say. I'm half turned when I realize what she said. "Wait a second. You took the guest book from this house?"

She keeps walking, that sexy butt ticking side to side. "Let me know if you need it."

"You can't just take evidence from a crime scene."

"What was that?" She cups a hand around her ear. "Sorry, I can't hear you over the ripping of caution tape."

"Don't be a smartass," I growl. "I'm a professional."

Stopping at the bottom of her porch stairs, she cocks a hip. "Neither one of us is qualified to collect evidence because we're not police officers. Lisa said that you're a bounty hunter, correct? And I'm a second grade teacher."

A second grade teacher.

I was mostly right. That's why she's the tallest at her job.

She must know what I'm thinking, because she gives me a grudging smile.

Before I can stop myself, I smile back.

I smile back.

It drops faster than a bowling ball. "Give me the guest book, half pint."

She's jogging up the stairs now, like she doesn't have a care in the world. "Only if you keep me informed of any developments," she calls over her shoulder.

Time to face facts. I am a big, nasty motherfucker and

this freckle-faced teacher couldn't be less scared of me if she tried. "*Not a chance in hell,*" I shout back.

She gives me a pinky wave and shuts the door.

The absence of her is like a cloud passing over the sun and the fact that I notice her being gone so profoundly does not sit well. I've known her for ten minutes. She's deliberately withholding something that might make my job easier. And most importantly, she's not my type. She's not even in the *stratosphere* of my type. Every once in a while, I take home an age-appropriate woman, usually a divorcee like me, who shares my disdain for romance, true love, happily ever after. Disney sells that shit to females from age zero and men have to cope with those expectations our entire lives. Nope. Not me. One look at that woman and it's easy to see her expectations are on the fucking moon. Bring her flowers? Not enough. I'd probably have to plant her a garden and waltz in it with her beneath the stars. She's the marrying type—I can guarantee that based on the fact that she's vacationing in Cape Cod and not the Jersey Shore or Miami. She's not a one-night roll in the hay and that's what I like.

I'm not interested in anything else.

Doing my best to put the green-eyed menace out of my mind, I kick open the door to the house and stomp inside. The scent of decay lingers in the air, but not strong enough to require a face covering. Nice place. Not the kind of rental that would put a person on guard against peepholes or hidden cameras. First, I head to the laundry room, camera app at the ready. Blood spatter on the wall indicates the victim was shot in this location, as does the black pool of bodily substances on the ground. Perp would have likely entered through the back door of the house, so I go there next. Lock is intact, not broken, but that doesn't mean anything. It could have been unlocked at the time of the murder. No breaking and entering required.

I make my way upstairs to the master bedroom, and irritatingly, I find myself wondering if I'm looking at the bed where she planned to sleep. Damn thing would have swallowed her up. Now if I was sleeping in it with her...

A pulse travels through my dick at the thought of it. Us in bed together. She'd have to ride me, though. I couldn't just get on top and go for broke. Not with our size difference. I'm not gentle in bed and she'd...she'd need that. Tenderness. Wouldn't she?

"She's sure as shit not getting it from you," I mutter, scrubbing at the back of my neck, unable to find the itch that's plaguing me. I'm probably just unsettled because there is a piece of evidence I should have at my disposal and someone has stolen it. Right out from under the noses of the cops, too.

Huh.

She might come across innocent, but she's got a rebellious streak, doesn't she?

Don't think about that. Don't think about what that streak might lead her to do.

Like hook up with a rough, unmannered bounty hunter while on vacation.

"Not my type," I rasp, raising my camera to get a shot of the peepholes—

I stop. Tilt my chin and lean closer.

The woodgrain at the edges of both holes points outward, toward the bedroom

The holes were drilled from inside the crawl space.

"Goddammit."

Oscar Stanley was a big man. It would have taken serious maneuvering to drill those holes without physically being inside the crawl space. And yeah, fine, why would he need two holes unless he planned on looking through them?

I'm nowhere near abandoning the cut and dried theory that Oscar Stanley is a peeping Tom who spied on his guests, but the woodgrain is throwing me off a little. Despite wanting to wrap up this job as quickly as possible, I am not and will never be the type to leave questions unanswered or close a case with the finger pointed at the wrong suspect, all in the name of expediency.

According to Paul, the cops already spoke to the father—Judd Forrester. He denies shooting and killing Oscar Stanley. Only admits to the fistfight days before. But I need to speak with him myself to determine whether or not he's telling the truth.

Beyond that...

Who else had—or has—access to this place?

"I don't know, do I?" I grit out, striding down the staircase. "Because I don't have the goddamn guest book."

When I open the front door of the house, she's watching me from the front window of her house, lip caught between her teeth. She starts to duck out of sight, but I shake my head, crooking my finger at her. Now it's her turn to shake her head. I keep going until I've climbed the porch and knocked on the door.

"Are you going to keep me informed?" she calls through the door.

"No."

"I'd really just like to be kept in the loop."

"Nope."

"Please?"

I'm about to state my intentions to kick the door off the

hinges, but my mouth snaps shut on the word "please." I don't know why. It's just a word. But coming from her, it makes me sweat. Who says no to this woman? Especially when she asks in that hopeful princess voice? Me continuing to say no is disappointing her. I can hear her growing less and less optimistic and...that doesn't sit right. In fact, disappointing her is like broken glass digging into my stomach lining. Am I going to say yes *just* to make her happy? Hell, I don't know. But I find myself very unwilling to do the opposite.

"Why?" I say, crossing my arms. "Why is this so important to you?"

A tick passes and then the door opens. Slowly. There's her face, appearing in the opening, and I won't acknowledge how my ribcage seems to shrink-wrap around my heart, throwing off the steady beat. Damn, she is a beautiful woman. Soft. The kind of woman who makes a man want to be a hero.

Other men. Not me, obviously.

She looks back over her shoulder—to see if her brother is around? When she faces me again, she speaks in a reluctant whisper, forcing me to lean forward. Forcing me to count the flecks of gold in her green eyes. "I'm not very brave," she says quietly. "I'm really sensible and I always play it safe. But I saw a dead body and I didn't vanish into dust. I stayed calm and I called the police. I found blankets for me and Jude, gave a detailed statement to Detective Wright. I haven't thought a lot about how I would react in a terrible situation like that, but I thought I would cry or hyperventilate or die of fright. *Definitely* thought I would pack up and run home. But I didn't. I surprised myself by sticking it out. And I guess I just want to see what else I can do." She blinks up at me, the dark fringe of her lashes seeming to sweep down and up in slow motion. "Does that make sense, bounty hunter?"

She still doesn't know my name.

Keep it that way.

Because I'm about to ask if she, perhaps, needs a blanket *now*, too? So if she said my name, I would be fucking toast. Somehow I know that like I know my way around a Harley. Because I'm not going to lie, her explanation seems to have opened a trap door in my belly and all of my irritation is falling right through it. Gone. I'm mostly wondering who the hell told her she wasn't brave. That would be a satisfying person to kill. "You aren't backing down from my scary ass, are you?" I cough into a fist, glancing off down the block. "Seem pretty brave to me."

When I look back at her, she's smiling at me.

Not a grudging one. A big, unrestrained one that punches me square in the jaw.

"Uh..."

"You're not scary at all," she informs me brightly.

"*Yes, I am,*" I shout back, because it feels totally necessary. Like I'm acting out of self-preservation here. *Am I?* What has happened to me in the last thirty minutes?

"Taylor, who are you talking to?" Following the newcomer's muffled question, footsteps approach behind her and a man appears, grinding a knuckle into his eye socket and yawning. When he opens his eyes and spots me in the doorway, he jolts backward with a startled curse.

"Jesus fucking Christ."

"See?" I tell her, caught between satisfaction and... embarrassment, an emotion I am very unfamiliar with. It has never existed for me. Until now, apparently, when this woman is about to realize I'm the beast and she's beauty.

But she just goes on smiling. "Do you want to come

inside and look at the guest book?" She pushes the door wider. "I just made lemonade."

I'm giving up too much ground here, so I say, very pointedly, "Do I look like I drink lemonade?" I step inside the house and they both back up, the brother—Jude, I believe she said—edging toward his sister protectively. "I'll take a beer."

"Okay," Taylor says, nudging her brother in the ribs. "He's going to let us help solve the murder case!"

"I didn't say that—"

But she's already skipping off toward the kitchen.

What in God's name have I gotten myself into?

CHAPTER 4

Taylor

I hand the bounty hunter his bottle of beer and he grimaces at the label.

"Sorry." I take the chair across from him in the living room. "It's all we have."

"Peach-flavored beer." He turns it over and reads the nutrition facts, as if he suspects we're playing a practical joke on him. For once since the hunter arrived, he's not inspecting *me* very closely, so I use the opportunity to return that scrutiny. Based on appearances alone, this man might have just walked out of a criminal underworld. If the permanent scowl on his face didn't scream *villain*, then the long, unkempt hair and poorly scrawled tattoos do the trick, as do the scars on his knuckles and the side of his neck.

And then there is his attire. Filthy boots covered in suspicious substances, jeans and a black T-shirt in dire need of washing—or burning—and worn, brown leather cuffs on his wrists.

Sitting on the fluffy white couch and frowning down at the peach-flavored beer, the giant—at least six foot five—man looks comically out of place. He belongs in the back room of a roadside bar playing pool and inciting violence and causing general mayhem. He's been plucked from that sketchy scenario and dropped into yet another nautical-themed living room, surrounded by tasteful reminders of the ocean and throw pillows covered in little ship wheels.

For all intents and purposes, he should be terrifying.

He might be. If it weren't for a few little clues that he is, in fact, the opposite of scary.

In regards to *me*, anyway. I'm sure everyone else's terror is warranted.

When I informed the bounty hunter that I'd discovered the body, he turned white as a ghost. Looked like he was preparing to toss his cookies right there in the street. For that fleeting handful of seconds, his scowl dropped and he shifted straight into protective.

Tell me you got out of the house immediately.

In case the murderer was still on the property.

He was worried about me. How unexpectedly heart-warming.

And I would be remiss if I didn't take into account his smile.

Upon finding out that he was correct and I am, in fact, a teacher, we shared a smile across the street and I'm still feeling...kind of jumbled over it. When this man smiles, he's actually quite handsome. His teeth, though white and straight, look like they could chomp straight through a leather belt or crush a rock, but yes, when he smiles, he's undeniably attractive. His own brand of attractive. Not the classic kind. Not like the men I usually go on dates with. Tidy businessmen with neat fingernails and upward mobility in their line of work. They are searching for the right partner with whom to purchase a starter home and eventually have children. It's all outlined in our dating profiles. Serious prospects only.

I wonder if the bounty hunter has an online dating presence.

He'd probably be flashing the middle finger in his profile picture.

All the right women would match with him. Adventurous souls who desire to tear down the highway on the back of his motorcycle and...who knows. Eat fresh clams at some hideaway that only the local baddies know about. Or something.

My last date was at the Cheesecake Factory.

I don't realize I'm frowning at the bounty hunter until he raises an eyebrow at me.

"Have you ever been to the Cheesecake Factory?" I ask him.

"The what?"

"I knew it." I force myself back to a pleasant frame of mind, gesturing for Jude to sit down. He's still caught halfway between the kitchen and the living room, as if undecided about whether or not to call the police. "Well. Would you like to share your first impressions of the crime scene?"

He sets down the peach beer on the distressed white coffee table, sliding the offending drink away with the tip of his finger. "No, half pint. I would not." He clears his throat. "Anyway, you two are technically both suspects until I rule you out. Wouldn't exactly be wise to give you the pertinent details."

"*Suspects?*" I sputter, incredulous. "But we have alibis. We weren't even in Cape Cod yet when the murder took place."

"How can you have alibis when time of death hasn't been determined?"

My mouth snaps shut. I need to start paying closer attention to *Etched in Bone.* Working on my lesson plans at the same time has clearly led to some important lessons being missed. "I suppose I made an assumption based on the smell of decomposition."

"Guess we'll see. Barnstable PD is pulling toll bridge footage to make sure you didn't get here sooner." The bounty hunter rolls a shoulder. "Where is the guest book?"

Now that he has shocked me by calling us suspects, I feel a strong urge to return the favor. To surprise him. Let him know he's not just dealing with a bumbling podcast junkie. I'm a pandemic-era teacher, dammit. That basically qualifies me for a presidential run. A little caught off guard by this new glimmer of self-confidence, I sit up straight. "Did you happen to notice the wood grain of the peepholes?"

His head comes up fast. Ha! So he *did* notice. And while his gaze is drilling into me, curious and irritable, *I* notice his eye color is a lovely mixture of brown and mossy. Why do I find that combination so pleasing and hard to look away from? "You've been back over there since the night you discovered the body, haven't you?"

"Of course she hasn't. It's surrounded by caution tape," Jude points out, mid-yawn.

"Yes, and I replaced it exactly as I found it," I explain, hoping my cheerful tone will make it sound altogether less illegal. "That's more than I can say for some people."

Jude leans a shoulder against the wall, expression dazed. "You really went back over there without telling me? *Alone?*"

He studies me closely, half impressed, half horrified. "That's not like you, T."

Suddenly I'm jumpy. "I know." Now they're both looking at me like a bug under a microscope. My brother is totally right, this is not like me. Do I love a riddle? A mystery? Yes. I love wrapping up debates or discussions with a resolution. No open ends. But those qualities are usually applied to a game of Clue. I am not the type of person who breaks into a crime scene. What I told the bounty hunter is true, though. I surprised myself when I discovered Oscar Stanley's body. A foreign sort of calm permeated my blood, settling the flow and I started operating on the high wire of adrenaline. I'm extra awake. Noticing every detail. I don't want to lose that feeling. I want to keep exploring the boost of confidence it gave me to be so...hardy.

Maybe this will be short-lived.

Maybe I am just play-acting as a brave person.

But I would like to know one way or the other.

"Sorry, Jude. I'll tell you next time."

My brother stares without blinking, amusement making his eyes twinkle. "*Next* time?"

"There isn't going to be a next time," states old gravel-voiced party pooper, aka the bounty hunter. "Give me what I need so I can leave."

I ignore him, still speaking to my brother, because we weren't finished. "I promise not to let this interfere with your vacation. I want you to go home relaxed."

"We both need to relax, all right?" Jude says softly. "Not just me."

"I know, it's just...that."

"It. Yeah, I know."

Silence lands in the room. The bounty hunter treats

both of us to a frown. "Are you two talking in fucking code or something?"

Jude chuckles. "That's probably what it sounds like." He pushes off the wall and moves into the living room, dropping down onto the opposite end of the couch from the hunter, ankle thrown over knee. "My sister used a big chunk of her savings—despite my protests, I might add—on this vacation because I lost someone close to me."

The surly man sort of chugs through an apology. "Sorry."

That word appears to taste like old bathwater in his mouth.

"It's fine. It was time," Jude sighs, looking down at his hands. "Bartholomew made it all the way to twenty-two."

The bounty hunter's frown deepens. "Twenty-two?"

"Bart was a panda. I'm a panda caretaker."

"You're more than that," I say, trying and failing to keep the pride out of my voice because I don't want to embarrass him. I'm the queen of embarrassing my brother. When they called his name at his college graduation, I leapt onto my chair and screeched louder than anyone. I was sobbing so hard, I knocked over a tuba player and twisted an ankle trying to get down. Never stand on a cheap plastic chair in high heels. "Displaced or abandoned pandas are brought to the animal sanctuary where Jude works. Some of them are so young they haven't learned to survive on their own yet. So Jude dresses like a panda and teaches them."

"You dress like a panda?"

"Yes. Teach them how to forage, eat and climb, socialize with the other pandas." Jude winks at the man on the other side of the couch. "The suit looks great on me."

"Bartholomew was sort of the...unofficial forest dad, wasn't he?" I dab at the moisture in my eyes. "He was sort of disagreeable, like you, bounty hunter, but once Jude taught the newbies the ropes, he started to warm up to them."

"Hate to break it to you, but none of that heartwarming shit is going to happen here." Our guest appears to be contemplating the peach-flavored beer out of pure desperation. "I'm a bounty hunter and you are some of the weirdest people I've ever met." He's silent a beat, then looks at Jude. "Do you actually eat the leaves?"

Jude grins. "I don't swallow."

The bounty hunter does a double take at that, then abruptly points at me. "Guest book. Now."

"Okay, okay. It's upstairs." No one has ever risen from a chair more slowly in their life. "I'll just go grab it now. But while I'm still here in the living room..." One step toward the staircase. Pause. "You don't seem quite as sold on the original trucker dad theory anymore."

"I'm just performing my due diligence." He scratches his upper arm absently, giving me a more complete look at his tattoos. Wow. That skeleton has fireballs for eyes. "The working theory stands, though. As far as we know, no one else had a motive to murder Oscar Stanley."

"See, that's what *I* thought."

"But then we lived on this street for two days," Jude drawls.

"And we met some of the permanent residents. You might say one of them stood out." I wiggle my fingers in my brother's direction. "Show him, Jude."

"I don't want to be shown anything," gripes the bounty hunter.

I shush him.

He gapes at me.

Jude's finger moves across the screen of his phone, locating the music streaming app. He hits play on the first song on his list and Bleachers begins to drift through the Bluetooth speaker situated on the fireplace mantle. After a nod from me, he cranks the volume—and right on cue, there is a loud crash outside. A door slamming. And then the side of our rental house is being bashed by the handle of a broom.

"That would be Sal," I inform the hunter. "Our neighbor. He also does this when our tea kettle whistles and when I…" Great. I'm blushing. "When I sing in the shower."

Do I detect a slight lip twitch from the big tattooed meanie?

That burgeoning smile disappears when Sal begins his tirade.

"Keep it down in there. I can hear your music through my walls! This is supposed to be a quiet community and you fucking renters are ruining it! *I'm sick of this shit!*" That's when he really starts to wail on the house. "I'd like to kill the bastards who allow this. What about my right to peace on my own property, dammit?"

Jude turns off the music, tosses the phone up in the air, catches and holsters it in his pocket like a Wild West gunslinger. "You should hear Sal when Taylor sings anything by Kelly Clarkson."

"Something about 'Since You've Been Gone' just triggers him," I add with a shiver. "Then again, it might just be my singing. I sound like a choking cat."

"No, you do not," Jude argues. "You're amazing."

My eyes are moist again. "Thank you."

The bounty hunter drops his head back and sighs at the ceiling. "Jesus Christ."

I take one more very slow step toward the staircase. "Aren't you going to say anything about Sal?"

"I've made a mental note," he responds through his

teeth. He looks like he's about to say more, but apparently Sal isn't finished.

From outside the kitchen window, our temporary neighbor yells. "Tell that bitch to close the window when she sings, before she breaks every mirror in my house!"

I've never seen anyone move so fast in my life.

One second, the bounty hunter is there. A dangerous glint occupies his eyes. So dangerous that it actually makes me shudder. And then he's on his feet, storming out of the house and down the front porch. Sal makes a muffled exclamation followed by something low and unintelligible from the bounty hunter.

Jude and I stare at each other, jaws in our laps.

"What's he doing?" whispers my brother. "Who *is* this guy?"

I don't have a chance to answer because our guest is stomping back into the house, slamming the door behind him loud enough to rattle the hinges. "Guest book. Now."

I run for the stairs and take them two at a time.

On the top one, I stumble a little bit. When I glance down the steps to determine whether or not anyone saw me, I give a closed-mouth scream. The bounty hunter is right behind me and I didn't even hear him move. Glowering, he wraps his gorilla-sized hands around my waist and lifts me back onto my feet. "Move."

"Okay," I whimper.

He follows me down the hallway and into the master bedroom. My heart is bouncing back and forth between my ear drums and my jugular. My bikini top and cut-off shorts were appropriate downstairs as we are mere steps from the beach and this is Cape Cod, but now? In this plush, inviting —nautical-themed, of course—bedroom, I am suddenly feeling very underdressed and exposed, goosebumps launching to attention on every inch of my skin.

In my self-consciousness, I get defensive. "You don't have to shadow me." I kneel in front of my suitcase and frown at him over my shoulder. "I'm getting the book."

From my position on the floor, he towers over me like a skyscraper. "You were stalling."

I shuffle aside the sudoku puzzles I brought in search of the guest book. It would be much easier if I opened the suitcase, but my fancy panties are in the mesh side pocket and I think if this man saw them, I would die. "What did you say to Sal?" I ask.

"Don't worry about it."

"Uh...Taylor. Are you okay up there?" Jude calls from downstairs. "I'm coming up."

"No, it's fine," I call back. Do I have a sort of weird—possibly misplaced—confidence that this man won't hurt me? Yes. Is he a wild card where everyone else is concerned? Yes. The last thing I want is Jude putting himself in jeopardy. "We're just talking." I wet my lips, searching for a way to reassure my brother. "Jude. *Coconuts.*"

"Be a little less obvious about giving a code word, half pint," mutters the bounty hunter, his knees hitting the ground beside me. Before I can stop him, he's thrown open the top of my suitcase. And there they are. My frilly red panties. Right there in the dead center of the case, impossible to miss.

Don't panic.

Maybe he'll do the polite thing and ignore them.

"What are those?" he asks, jabbing them with a blunt finger.

"They're...you know what they are!"

He glances between my suitcase and the dresser. "Why didn't you unpack them like everything else?"

My face is a deeper shade of red than the panties now. "I didn't...know if I was going to need them."

Understanding dawns. "You brought them in case you meet someone."

I stay staunchly silent. After some very brittle digging, I hand him the guest book. Only now he doesn't seem as interested in taking it and leaving. He's watching me from beneath those thickly drawn eyebrows. "You have a pair of hook-up panties?"

"No. I don't," I blurt. "I'd have to hook up in them at least once to call them that."

Why?

Why did I say that?

Can I please fast forward to the end of my life now?

"You date, right?" He's not letting this drop? Mere moments ago, he was dying to get out of here, now he looks like he's settling in for a conversation? "You must date constantly."

"Why would you assume that?"

He rolls his eyes. "Oh, we're going to play games?"

"Games?"

"You're going to pretend you don't know you're beautiful to get a compliment out of me. Is that how this is going to go, half pint?" His laughter is strained. "It's not happening."

I'm not going to point out that he just referred to me as beautiful.

Meaning he *already* complimented me.

That would be childish.

"I date, yes. But I wouldn't call it constantly. More like...occasionally."

Is there a slight sheen of sweat on his forehead that

wasn't there a moment ago? "And you've never gotten to use your hook-up panties."

"Stop calling them that." I smack him hard in the shoulder and he doesn't even flinch. "I'm not a virgin. I'm just...I'm picky. Unforgivably picky. It's why I'm going to end up alone."

He processes that with an unreadable expression. "Let me guess. You want a man who wears a suit and argyle fucking socks to work and reads the finance section of the newspaper at breakfast while mumbling 'yes dear, no dear' like a robot."

"That's a pretty bold assumption."

His upper lip curls. "Am I wrong?"

It's the challenge in his eye that pushes me past polite into uncharted territory. Maybe discovering poor, dead Oscar brought me to this place, too. A place of clarity. I'm not sure. But as I kneel on the floor beside this behemoth, I hear echoes in the back of my mind. People throughout my life, college friends, colleagues and especially my parents, telling me I'm sensible. That I always play it safe. Even my second graders like to point out my idiosyncrasies. Giggling over the way I check the temperature of my coffee with a pinkie before sipping—even after five or six gulps. Just to be sure. Sending out search parties for kids who take longer than five minutes in the bathroom, like a nervous nelly. And I'm not claiming that my recent proximity to murder has transformed me into the new Lara Croft or anything, but I've felt bolder and more in charge in the last two days than I've *ever* felt before.

This bully isn't going to knock me back a step.

Besides.

I haven't always *wanted* to play it safe. Not in every aspect of my life.

I've always had a little...or maybe *not* so little...desire for some added...zest.

"I guess I wouldn't mind the suit and socks and finance section type of man. No, that would be fine with me. As long as he doesn't treat me like porcelain in bed." Lord, it is incredibly satisfying to witness the smirk fade from his face. Take *that*, muscle head. "That's where the pickiness comes in. It seems I can't have both. On one hand, I'd like a man who makes a good living and wants a family someday. On the other, I'd like to be manhandled once in a while. Just sort of thrown down and told who is boss, you know? Is that so much to ask? But on the three occasions I've dated a man long enough to...to do...*it,* they insisted on treating me with respect in bed. It was incredibly disappointing. Zero stars. Would not recommend."

That sheen of sweat is a lot more obvious now.

Along with his utter shock.

I *like* the bold new me. I've just rendered a bounty hunter speechless!

And I still have four days left of this vacation!

"There." I pat his massive shoulder. "You have your book. Time to go."

"Book?" he rasps.

"The guest book." This is the best day of my life. "The one you're holding."

"Right."

"You *might* be interested to know that prior to the group of girls who stayed there last week, no one had rented the house since last summer." Using the edge of the bed for balance, I climb to my feet. "Because Oscar himself had been living there for a full ten months."

"That so?" the bounty hunter murmurs. He is staring at my belly button like it's the one speaking. I could pretend I don't like his attention on me, but I think that ship is leaving port at full speed. I found him attractive before, despite his wildly rude personality. Now, in the setting of the bedroom, having given him very personal details about my sexual longings, intimacy builds between us. Potent. Visceral. And I can't help it, there's no way to stop my body from responding to him. Because this man is *definitely* not the one I'm searching for to settle down with. But I bet he'd give me that elusive physical excitement I can't seem to track down for the life of me. Or at least come close? I'm starting to think animal attraction, paired with actual love and respect, only exists in scripted movies and romance novels.

His gaze travels down and lingers on the zipper of my shorts, inching lower to the apex of my thighs. He wets his lips. The air in my lungs evaporates. Oh God, what's going to happen? Nothing. Nothing can happen. Right? It's daytime and my brother is downstairs.

Apparently I'm the only one making a mental pro/con list, because the bounty hunter reaches out and grips the waistband of my shorts, the heat of his touch searing my hips, and he drags me forward. Fast enough to make me stumble a little. His hot breath curls in my belly button and I reach for his hair, tangling it around my fingers, exhilaration pouring through me like a mile-high waterfall. And then *he licks me*. He licks across my exposed belly from one hip to the other. Then bites down on my abductor. Hard enough to make me gasp.

"I'm Myles," he says hoarsely. "That's my name."

"Myles," I whisper, my knees seconds from giving out.

"Taylor," calls Jude from downstairs, beginning to sound alarmed. "You good up there?"

"C-coconuts," I try to say, but it comes out sounding like gibberish—and that gives the bounty hunter pause. With a rocky sigh, he rises to his full height and looks down at me through narrowed eyes. He takes my chin in his hand and tilts it up, scrutinizing every inch of my face. "You might feel unsatisfied after being treated with kid gloves. But...at least there was affection there. I don't have any of that in me. None. Trust me, you'd feel a lot worse after us sleeping together. Being respected is better than empty sex. That's what I'd give you."

"Maybe that's what I want."

His pupils dilate a touch more and he steps closer, eyelids drifting down, his fingers sliding up into my hair and gently fisting my hair. "And goddamn, I'd like to provide it. That mattress would never be the same if you put on those red panties for me. But it's the worst idea I've had in years, and believe me, half pint, that's saying something." With a visible effort, he drops his hand from my hair and backs away, dragging a shaking hand down his open mouth. "Stay out of trouble, Taylor. I mean it."

Does that mean he's not coming back?

I nod absently, trying to hide my immense disappointment that he's no longer touching me. My body is hot and exposed and I'm twisted up in knots in the most intimate of places. And he's leaving. My brain tells me there is no other choice. He's right. I can't just have a fling with a bounty hunter. A mean one who looks—and acts—like he just escaped hell, no less. Maybe I'm overestimating my ability to have a wild fling? Maybe I'm just on a high from this new courageous behavior, but I'm not *actually* built for meaningless sex?

"The neighbor won't bother you again. Sing Kelly Clarkson as loud as you want." He looks like he feels stupid for saying that, cursing under his breath and wheeling around on a booted heel to leave the room. A moment later, the door slams downstairs. Without thinking, I cross to the window and look down, watching Myles climb onto his bike —a Harley Davidson, I notice now—and strap a helmet on. He looks up at me and kicks the engine to life, and God help me, I have to cross my legs, the ensuing clench of my sex is so intense and prolonged.

Finally, he breaks eye contact and roars off down the street.

I drop down on the bed and stare blankly into space, willing my libido to shrink back down to the usual, reasonable level. Something is off in the room, but I don't quite realize what it is for several moments. Not until Jude walks in to check on me and I automatically reach for the suitcase lid to close it, so I don't have to explain my frivolous purchase twice in one day.

And that's when I realize the red panties are gone.

Myles's business card sits in their place.

CHAPTER 5

Myles

I'm missing something.

Not quite sure what it is, but I'll know when I see it.

It's just after sunrise on Friday morning and I'm back at Oscar Stanley's house. Last night, I took a ride to Worcester to lay my own set of questions on Judd Forrester, the trucker who assaulted Stanley, but he was on a long-haul job and won't be back until late this afternoon. From my motel room last night, I made a preliminary timeline, ran a few background checks on the neighbors on Coriander Lane and any known associates of Stanley from the postal service—though he mostly kept to himself. I went through the guest book and determined that yeah, Taylor was right, Stanley had been living in his own rental for ten months prior to the group of girls arriving. No prior issues with any renters. All stellar reviews.

There's just something...off. Can't put my finger on it.

Tossing an antacid into my mouth, I circle the living room, my eyes straying toward Taylor's place. Not for the first time. Far from it. A few more trips to this window and I'm going to wear a path in the floorboards.

Half a day has passed since I licked that smooth, sun-kissed belly of hers and my cock is still standing at half-mast for it. God, she tasted like a candy apple. Of course I bit her.

I bet she'd have wrapped around me like hot caramel, too.

Stop thinking about how she whispered your name. Trembled. Definitely don't think about how you've been carrying around her panties since yesterday.

Damn. How did this woman get in my head so fast? Because that's where she is. Might as well admit it. If I was just in heat, I'd have tossed her up onto the bed yesterday and given her exactly what she asked for. *I'd like to be manhandled once in a while. Just sort of thrown down and told who is boss, you know?*

Fuck.

Shocking me isn't an easy thing to do and I did *not* see that coming.

The nosy little schoolteacher wants it down and dirty.

Walking out of the room after she admitted that to me? Hell. Pure, torturous hell. Because down and dirty is the only way I know. But this intuition of mine? Apparently it doesn't only operate on crime-related matters. No, my gut told me to get out of that bedroom fast or I'd never want to leave—and that just isn't happening.

There is a crime to solve here.

Keep your damn head in the game.

If my past has taught me anything it's that distractions lead to mistakes. I have firsthand knowledge of what can happen, the lives that can be destroyed, when a detective takes his eye off the ball. I may have turned in my badge three years ago, but for all intents and purposes, I am an investigator on *this* case. I'm handling *one* job for an old friend. If I can't wrap one single case up without a blunder, I never should have graduated from the academy.

Focus.

With a final glance across the street, I go out back to the shed. Look for the tool used to create those peepholes, hoping to get some kind of idea how long they've been there. But there's nothing. Nothing but beach chairs and a flattened bike wheel. A box of mouse traps.

I go back into the house and immediately stop short.

Humming.

Someone is humming. A woman. And I have a pretty good idea who it is.

The fact that my stomach tightens like a drum doesn't bode well for my concentration.

Rounding the corner into the living room, I find Taylor on hands and knees, using the flashlight app on her phone to search beneath the couch. "Looking for something?"

A scream rips out of her. Thankfully, it cuts off somewhere in the middle when she catches sight of my reflection in the window behind the couch. Hand pressed to her heaving chest, she twists around and slumps back against the blue and white striped furniture. "I didn't see your bike outside."

"I parked it down the block."

"Why?"

"So you wouldn't see it and scurry over here to bother me."

That's a bald-faced lie. I stopped for coffee down the

street and it was a short walk to the house from there, not worth moving the bike over.

"Oh," she says, her mouth turning down at the corners. "I see."

I almost tell her the truth. Almost. Just to get her to stop frowning. Who am I becoming?

Definitely not the kind of person who wants to tell her she looks pretty in her blue jumpsuit thing.

"What are you doing over here, half pint?"

She purses her lips in lieu of answering me. "Why are you so determined to make us enemies? Do you truly find me annoying or were you stung badly in the past by another WASPy girl from Connecticut and you're taking it out on me?"

"I truly find you annoying."

I'm lying again. I actually think she's pretty goddamn funny. And persistent.

Gorgeous as fuck. Can't forget about that.

"Thank you for being honest." She stands up, dusting off the seat of her shorts. Which are connected to the matching top. What are those called? Rompers? What is the easiest way to get one of those things off? "Did you know a lot of friendships are formed because two people share a common enemy? That's us. We're united against whoever murdered Oscar."

"I work alone. We are united in nothing."

"Okay, but we both want the same thing. We have a commonality. My students form bonds over their dislike of homework. Eventually they realize how many other things they have in common." She gives a brisk clap of her hands. "Let's do some morale building. On three, let's both say something we dislike."

I can imagine her in front of a class, commanding attention. Colorful and engaging and creative. She's probably amazing at what she does. "I don't want to play—"

"One. Two. Three. Scream sneezers."

"I said I didn't want to..." A laugh scales the insides of my throat, almost making its way out of my mouth. "What was that?"

"Scream sneezers. People who feel the need to make such a huge, loud production out of their sneeze that everyone loses ten years off their life. I dislike that very much."

"You can't just say you *hate* it, can you?"

"I don't allow the word 'hate' in my classroom."

"We aren't in your classroom," I point out.

Though I would like to see her there.

Just a glimpse, for no particular reason.

"I have to stay in practice." She skirts the coffee table in my direction and I spy tan lines on her shoulders, peeking out from beneath her tank top straps. Making me wonder where else she's got them. Her hips? Breasts? Bet there's a low triangle between her thighs. Shit. "I bet you have to be really mean to be a bounty hunter. You're definitely keeping in practice for that, aren't you?" I don't answer her. Mainly because the scent of apples is growing stronger and it's hindering my ability to make words. "Do you like your job?" she asks.

"It's just a job."

"A violent one. A scary one."

I can't disagree with that, so I nod, wondering where she's going with this. Waiting for the next word out of her mouth like a reward, when I should really be carrying her over my shoulder back to the house across the street and ordering her to stay put.

"Do you ever track someone down and want to let them go?"

"No."

"Never?"

"Once." Did I just say that out loud? I had no intention of telling her this. Or anything. The plan was to be as rude as possible until she left and went somewhere safe to enjoy her vacation. As far as possible from a murder investigation. "I let someone go once."

"Really?" she whispers, like we're sharing a secret.

I shouldn't want this sense of not being alone. Normally I don't mind it. The loneliness and solitude. Hell, I welcome it. But I must be having a moment of weakness. Or maybe I'm tired from reading through internet searches galore last night. Because I find myself...*talking* to this teacher. The way I haven't talked to anyone in a long time. Years. "Mother of three. She... was afraid to show up for her court date because the father of her kids was threatening to be there. Make trouble, take off with the kids. Make her pay for leaving. Someone probably brought her into the cops eventually, but I couldn't do it."

"What did you do with her instead?"

"Nothing." She stares at me until I feel forced to fill the silence. "I don't know what happened after I took them to the shelter."

Her eyes soften to a different kind of green. Like something out of a tropical fucking rainforest and I find myself leaning way too close, trying to determine the shade. Why is she looking at me like that? I mean to sound callous and dismissive. Not to make her happy with me. "What is teaching like?" I growl, purely to get the focus off myself.

Not because I want to know things about her.

"I love teaching," she says quietly. "And I've only had to

turn in one of the kids to the police over a missed court date."

I laugh and grunt at the same time. It's a terrible, gravelly sound, but it makes her smile. A smile I'm looking at way too closely. Sidling in, wondering what it'll taste like. Wondering how rompers come off or if they just get ripped down the middle or what.

"See?" she murmurs. "You laughed. I can't be so bad to have around. Let's try again. Name something you dislike on three."

I knew it. She was lulling me into a false sense of security. "No," I bite off.

"One, two..."

"Allen keys," I half shout.

At the same time, she says, "People who crowd the drink pick-up counter at Starbucks and stare impatiently at the poor barista as if they aren't trying their hardest to hurry. Honestly, it's—" Her eyes widen on an inhale. "Wait, did you say Allen keys? I dislike those, too! I have a junk drawer full of them because I feel guilty throwing them away! This is good. Just a couple of co-investigators having a bonding sesh."

"None of that last sentence is remotely true." Her crestfallen expression is like having an alligator jaw clamped around my middle. Before I can talk myself out of it, I find myself softening my tone. Stepping closer. Inhaling apples like I'm storing up her scent for the winter. "Look, something feels weird about this case and I don't...like...you around that. So."

Taylor blinks. "You don't like me around what?"

She's prodding something I don't want prodded. "Danger."

How can she look so confused when I basically just

showed my hand? How much more clearly can I spell out that having her around potential threats makes me queasy? "I'm a consenting adult. *I* choose my own risks."

"No." I shake my head. "Nope."

"You're very difficult to bond with," she says, sounding like she's being strangled. "Fine." Before I register her actions, she's moving away from me. Taking her apples smell along with her. "I'll get out of your way for now..."

As she walks toward the door, she crosses a floorboard and it's subtle, *very* subtle, but one end of it lifts, as if it's not attached at the joint. Unfortunately, Taylor sees it, too.

We both lunge for the loose piece of wood at the same time, prying it up together...

And revealing a thin, white envelope.

Taylor

*S*hock knocks me backwards onto my butt.

Who finds a loose floorboard with a hidden envelope on the other side? In real life?

This doesn't even happen on *Etched in Bone*.

Unless it *does* happen. And the public never finds out, because the person who finds a hidden letter is definitely the next victim. Are we going to open this envelope and find some taunting, Sam Berkowitz-style ramblings?

"What the hell..." Myles mutters, reaching down and plucking the envelope from its hidey hole. And he doesn't manage to hide his concern when he looks at me. "You should really go, Taylor."

He's probably right.

This is getting creepy.

I discovered a body thirty yards from this spot and if I'm being honest, something hasn't felt right since the moment I clocked the peepholes. I'm supposed to be on a relaxing vacation with my brother, but instead I can feel myself sinking deeper into the unfamiliar.

But I'm not freaking out. I'm just a little scared.

And once again, the world isn't ending.

Maybe I have the same fortitude as everyone else. Or more.

I'll never know if I run away now. I'll go back to being safe, reliable, routine-oriented Taylor on her hunt for a safe, reliable, routine-oriented life partner. Or I could stay here and find out what's in the envelope.

Of course I have to stay.

I might even have to send an email to *Etched in Bone* about this. Unless it's a grocery list that accidentally slipped through the cracks of a loose floorboard? Something tells me that's not the case. And when Myles slips out a piece of paper, unfolds it and scans the contents, his mouth flattening into a grim line, my theory is confirmed.

It's definitely something.

Myles starts to tuck it into the pocket of his shirt without showing it to me—and uh-uh. That's not happening. Now that I've made the decision to stay and investigate, he's not depriving me of the opportunity to process new evidence. I make a lunge for it, across his lap. He's not expecting it, either. Neither would anyone who has ever met me, but I'm pretty sure my students would be cheering their little faces off.

I pluck the letter out of his blunt fingers in mid-air—a move that I didn't *really* think through. Not all the way.

Because I land face down across his thighs with an *oof*. Knowing I probably only have three seconds before he wrestles the letter back, I scan the hastily scrawled words on the sheet of paper as quickly as possible.

> *You're going down with me.*
> *They're all going to know who you are.*
> *I've known all along, but it won't be my secret much longer.*

I've only just finished the final threatening line when Myles moves, reaching over the top of me to steal back the letter and I twist to the right, free falling from my position on his lap. With a curse, he tries to catch me, sliding a burly arm beneath me to cushion my fall—and that is how I end up on my back, face up, with two hundred and fifty pounds of muscle on top of me. I must be operating on pure pride now, because I make a silly attempt to hold the letter above my head, out of his reach, arching my back to extend as far as possible.

Reach, *reach*—

His groan rends the air.

I'm breathless, halfway to laughing, because me trying to keep *anything* from this mean, professional hunter of humans is comical, but...suddenly there is nothing funny about our positions. Nothing whatsoever. His hips weigh down on mine, fastening me to the floor. A telltale ridge grows between us with every panting breath we exchange. I look down between our bodies, reluctantly eager to catalogue our size difference. How he looks on top of me. I think

I know what I'm going to find, but the actuality of what I see is staggering.

My breasts are almost free of the romper. Free of the bikini top I'm wearing underneath. The neckline has been tugged down in our struggle and I'm all but exposed, my nipples on the verge of making a very enthusiastic appearance. Yes, *enthusiastic*, because they are rock hard and throbbing with more and more awareness the longer this man, this huge, visibly frustrated man, keeps his weight on top of me. It's not just our size difference that occurs to me in this moment. It's the fact that he's older, by at least eight years. Undoubtedly more experienced with sex. Intimacy. And he's dangerous. Mean and dangerous and I'm underneath him, tempting him. Giving him a stone solid erection.

"I'm going to get up now," he says, breathing hard.

"Okay," I whisper, dropping the letter.

When I do that, when I let go of the piece of paper, there's no longer something to fight over. He's just a man on top of a woman, holding her wrists. Fastening them to the hard ground. Looking like he's contemplating eating me whole. In one big bite.

My body wants that.

It's thrumming, anxious, begging me to open my thighs around his hips and lift, tease, do whatever I have to do to make him touch me. Make him use his strength on me. Now.

"Please."

"Please what?" He hooks a finger in my top and tugs it lower, that final inch that reveals my pointed nipples, a groan rumbling deep in his barrel chest. "Suck these beautiful-ass tits? Goddamn, I knew they'd have those little triangle tan lines on 'em. *Fuck.*"

I'm intoxicated in a blinding instant.

He just...

Talks like this.

All the time. Bluntly. Even crudely. But he's...complimenting me? I don't understand why the gravel delivery of such abrasive words should make my hips writhe impatiently beneath his entrapping ones. I'm bowing my back even more dramatically, wanting him to perform the act he spoke about in such explicit terms. Yes, *yes*. What he said is what I want.

"Please."

His long hair falls around his face and I can barely make out his features. Only enough to know they're tight. That his lips are open and parted. Eyes dark.

Briefly, he lets go of one wrist and removes the gun from the back of his waistband, sliding it away carefully on the floor. Then, he lifts the same hand slowly. Slowly. Lets it hover just above my naked breasts. And my tummy tangos excitedly. Hollows and heaves, waiting to see what he'll do. Where he'll touch. All because he lifted a hand. I'm holding my breath, a whimper ready to break free. I'm shaking. I'm *shaking*. Waiting for the contact is borderline excruciating. "Never seen anything so hot in my life. Hot—and hot for it. Aren't you?" Tongue perched in the center of his bottom lip, he lowers the pad of his index finger to one of my nipples, barely touching it, and he slowly grazes a light circle. "Yeah, you are."

I choke on a moan, the end of it releasing long and loud, my body tightening and melting all at the same time beneath him. I don't know what comes next or exactly what I want. I just know I need it now. Immediately. And I don't want to think. I want him to think and decide for me. For us. All day long is for thinking and deciding. Right now I just want to be hijacked.

He traces that fingertip over to my other nipple, circling it with the same light, torturous treatment. "You want that pretty little mouth kissed?"

"Y-yes."

"Now say it again without stuttering, baby."

"Yes."

That hand. That hand he's using on me so lightly continues its gentle journey up, up—and then it wraps firmly around my throat. So unexpectedly that I gasp, the flesh between my legs growing pliant, so tender, thighs falling open naturally. As if they haven't been given a choice and he rocks into them once, easy, laughing without humor at whatever he feels.

His mouth dips toward mine. I moisten my lips in preparation.

A car door slams outside.

No. Through the sudden lust haze in my brain, I realize it's more of a sliding van door. In the driveway of the house. That loud sound is followed by more vehicle engines cutting out and the peppering of excited voices. Footsteps. High heels and more muted ones.

"We'll set up over here. Let's make this quick," says an older female.

Myles drops his head forward with a curse, then rolls off me. Stands. Adjusting the protrusion in his jeans before reaching down and helping me up. Until he squeezes my hip and touches our foreheads together, I have no idea how badly I'm craving that show of...what? Comfort? But the second I have it, a twitchy feeling in my stomach settles. He looks me in the eye until I nod—and I barely know why I'm nodding. Only that I liked him holding me down, hand on my throat, but it woke me up to such a degree that I need his eye contact and softer contact to come back down. With my nod, I'm communicating something important to him that doesn't need to be spoken out loud.

Weird.

We cross the living room to the window together, finding a group of people standing in front of the house. A dark-haired woman dressed in a smart, plum-colored pantsuit. A young man with a clipboard and a camera crew.

"What the fuck now," Myles mutters.

He strides to the front door and starts to exit, before drawing to a halt and pinning me with a look. "You stay put."

"No."

With a rumble of unpleasant words, he vanishes through the doorway. After making sure my clothing is fixed, I jog into the front yard behind him. Five heads have swiveled in our direction. Clipboard Guy stares, pen poised over the surface of his notes. Pantsuit woman's smile appears to be frozen to her face. The camera crew continues what appears to be their mission to stage a mini press conference, complete with a glass podium on wheels.

"What's going on here?" Myles demands to know.

"I could ask you the same question," responds the young man. With an amused glance in Pantsuit's direction, he wedges the clipboard beneath his arm and approaches us with a hand extended, which we take turns shaking. "I'm Kurt Forsythe, the mayor's assistant." He smiles over his shoulder, then directs that smile at me, where it broadens. "Surely you know the mayor, Rhonda Robinson."

"We're from out of town." Did Myles just edge closer to me? "You getting ready to film something?"

Kurt tilts his head. "Do you own this property?"

The assistant poses the question in such a way that he obviously already knows the answer. Myles doesn't bother responding. Just crosses his arms and regards Kurt like a flea.

"No, I didn't think so," the assistant says, taking a not so discreet step back from the bounty hunter. "Erm. Do you mind me asking what you're doing here?"

"I've been hired by the family. Privately. To investigate the murder of Oscar Stanley."

"I'm on vacation," I say. "And also helping him investigate."

Myles is already shaking his head. "No, she's not."

Kurt splits an amused look between us. "Interesting."

"You're a renter?" calls the woman in plum. The mayor, apparently. "You might want to cover your ears for this," she says, giving me a wry smile. "I'm about to come for you." She places her hands flat on the podium and nods at the cameraperson. The lighting person gives a thumbs up, followed by a red light blinking to life on the camera itself. "Good afternoon, residents. I know we're all shaken up by the recent events that have transpired on the shores of our beloved community. A life was taken and my office wishes to extend heartfelt condolences to the family of the deceased, Oscar Stanley."

The mayor adjusts her stance.

Kurt releases a gusty sigh, regarding his boss with visible pride.

"My office hears your concerns. They are *more* than valid," continues Rhonda. "This unfortunate loss of life is part of a much larger problem, however—vacation rentals. The competitive discord they create and the disruption they cause to our daily life. This is an ongoing problem on the Cape and my promise to *you*, since the beginning, has been to regulate this market from taking over our Falmouth neighborhood and turning it into a party zone. Today, I want to reassure you that I am renewing my efforts to curb these noisy nuisances so that we can get back to enjoying our quiet summers with family and friends—it's the Cape Cod way."

A long pause ensues.

The red camera light turns off.

The mayor's smile drops as the podium is removed in an efficient rush.

"That was perfect, mayor," Kurt calls, flashing her an OK sign.

"Let's have that up on the website immediately, please?" Rhonda says, now scrolling through her phone. "Send it to the local news and ask them for the six o'clock spot."

Kurt is taking notes on his clipboard. "Already on it." He turns to us—me, actually—grinning in a more relaxed manner than before. "I have to make sure the mayor makes it to her next appointment." He rubs his eyebrow with the eraser of his pencil, shooting Myles a fleeting glance. "So you two are just co-workers or...?"

"Beat it, Kurt," Myles interrupts, making a shooing motion.

A literal shooing flick of his wrist.

Without another word, the assistant turns on a heel and rejoins his boss.

"That was extremely rude."

And I didn't like that show of possessiveness at all.

Not one bit.

Right.

"If you're still surprised by my rudeness, sweetheart, that's on you." Through narrowed eyes, he watches the major, Kurt and the film crew climb into their respective vans and cars. "I have to get to Worcester to question Judd Forrester." He notices my blank look when he looks down at me. "The father of the girl who assaulted Oscar Stanley."

"Right." I guess we're just going to ignore the fact that we almost made out on the floor a few minutes ago. The floor. The *letter*. The unlikely discovery we made before we almost kissed comes back to me in a deluge. "Do you think that threatening letter is from Judd Forrester? Do you think he wrote it to Stanley?"

"I don't know." Myles reenters the house with a heavy stride and I follow, watching him stoop down and pick up the letter where we left it on the floor. He straightens and turns, his eyes dancing across my neck, my mouth. Then away with determination. But not before my erogenous zones shriek for attention. God. What is this voltage between us? Is it normal? "But since Oscar lived in this house for almost a year, it seems more likely he would have known about the loose floorboard. Or even created it. Therefore..."

"The letter was written *by* Stanley? Meant for someone else?"

"That's what I'm thinking."

"Which might also mean...the camera wasn't left here to record the guests at all. It was here to record him."

"Yeah. He was targeted for a reason. A target for murder." His eyes move over the three threatening lines of the letter. "Might have even made himself one."

CHAPTER 6

Myles

"I didn't kill that guy. Swear to God." Judd Forrester swipes sweat from his brow. "Believe me, I wanted to. I came this close. But he was breathing when I left."

For once in my life, I wish my gut feelings weren't so stubborn. Intuition is telling me this man didn't kill Oscar Stanley and, shitty as it sounds, I wish he had. That would make wrapping up this case and moving on a whole lot easier. As soon as Forrester opened his mouth, unfortunately, a little voice whispered in the back of my head *you're not going anywhere yet.*

I left Taylor's place about two hours ago and rode a couple more to Worcester. The chief of police over at Barnstable PD—the department on the Cape that responded to the crime scene—is extremely reluctant to give me any information pertaining to the case. There isn't a single cop alive who jumps for joy when a bounty hunter, or in this case a freelance investigator, rolls into town and starts digging into the same crime with a lot less red tape to deal with, but it sure as hell lights a fire under their asses.

It took a promise yesterday to share any information I stumble across for the chief to spill the news that Forrester made bail. Tracking the man down was up to me, though. The chief drew the line at sharing Forrester's address. Thank God I have the internet for that. And when those searches don't pan out, I can still tap my contacts in Boston. I guess I can't be too mad about the police keeping me out of the loop, since I'm not sharing the threatening note Taylor and I found. I'll share it with them eventually. But there's no harm in getting a hard start holding the new piece of evidence, if it turns out to be relevant.

I attempt to refocus on the man sitting across from me. The fact that Forrester made bail so fast should have told me they didn't have a lot of evidence that he killed Oscar Stanley. Needed to see it for myself, though, so I could confidently cross him off the list of suspects. I'm not quite ready to do that yet. Not when he had motive and opportunity. But the honesty ringing in his voice is causing my heartburn to act up.

There's potential meat to this case. Meaning, I'm not getting away from Taylor any time soon. And I really, really need to get away from her. I'm sitting here, sure, but my mind is on her. Her safety. I know damn well what happens when I get emotionally involved in a case. Last time that happened, the outcome was so unacceptable, I turned in my detective's badge. Like it or not, Taylor Bassey is involved in this situation. Hell, I haven't even been able to eliminate her or Jude as suspects yet. She's going to be in the periphery of this investigation and she is a too beautiful, too interesting distraction that I cannot afford.

And I don't like the way she makes me feel.

I don't need her surprising me or challenging me. I just want to remain an impartial observer of life. A blow-in. Just passing through. I haven't even spoken to my parents or brother in three years, because attachment to anything and anyone after what happened on my final case with the Boston PD? It fucking hurts. I hate the weight of attachment sitting on my chest. Connections to people are nothing but responsibilities—and I don't want them. I don't need people around to be disappointed when and if I fuck up. And in this line of work, fucking up is inevitable, right? People die. They go missing. God help a man if the victim ends up being someone he's started caring about. So yeah, I don't need my head muddled by a woman or I'll lose sight of my job here. To solve a murder.

Then I can get back on my bike and get the hell out of here.

The sooner the better.

I lean sideways in my chair to access my pocket, taking out the letter found beneath Stanley's floorboards and I lay it on the table in front of me. Forrester doesn't react. There's no recognition there, but I ask anyway. "Do you recognize this envelope?"

"Nope."

I take out the letter, unfold it and smooth it out, not taking my eyes off him once. "Did you send this to Oscar Stanley prior to murdering him?"

"No! Jesus, I told you a hundred times, I didn't kill that piece of shit."

I replace the letter in my pocket. "Do you own a firearm?"

He hesitates. Wets his lips and looks around.

That's a yes, but he's reluctant to share.

The cops must have asked him this question, right?

Why does it seem like the first time he's answering this question?

"Look, I don't have the authority to fine you for not having permits. Just tell me how many." I click open my pen. "And what models."

I already have information on his registered weapons, but what he's *actually* holding could differ. Drastically. There's always something extra hiding somewhere.

Sighing, he rubs at his eye sockets. "Couple of thirty-five millimeters for hunting. A Glock for protection. Nothing crazy."

He's not looking me in the eye. "And which one doesn't have a permit?"

A bead of sweat rolls down the side of his face. "The Glock," he sighs.

"Mind if I take a look at it?"

"I loaned it out to a buddy," he says. Too quickly?

Even though Forrester is acting shady, there is something that doesn't place him at the scene for me. He doesn't have an alibi—claims to have been home alone. But there is something cold and precise about a bullet in the center of a man's head that doesn't speak to this man's temperament. There are two dozen pictures framed on the walls depicting his hunting accomplishments and in every single one of them, he's surrounded by friends, antlers in one hand, a can of beer in the other. When he beat up Oscar Stanley, he had an audience, too. His daughter and all of her friends.

Forrester wouldn't be satisfied with a quiet, solitary killing. For my money, it doesn't fit, even if I can't quite cross his name off the list yet.

We go over his story one more time, me searching for those subtle changes that can often break a case open, but he's firm on details and getting impatient with me in his kitchen. It's late afternoon by the time I get on my bike and head back to my motel on the Cape. With evening turning the highway into a sea of headlights, I try and fail not to think of a certain brunette with green eyes. Not a simple feat when her frilly red panties are burning a hole in my pocket.

Walking into my rented room a while later, I take them out, laying them flat on the nightstand. Smoothing the see-through panels that run vertical at the hips. Just a peek of skin.

Does that mean she's a tease in the sack?

Yeah.

Yeah, I bet she'd work me up good before letting me drag these off. Fill her up tight.

What the hell am I doing carrying around her underwear?

These urges Taylor has woken up inside of me in such a short space of time...they're not typical for me by any means. I'm not the jealous type, but I didn't like the asshole assistant smiling at her. I've never been possessive, but when she was underneath me...I could feel her wanting to be dominated. She liked my hand on her throat. She liked being pinned. And the way she turned to me for reassurance after all of it? I have no experience with soothing women. That idea would have been laughable as recently as this morning. Still, I somehow knew exactly what to do. For Taylor. Like we communicated without saying a word.

Meanwhile I couldn't even communicate with *actual* words in my first disastrous marriage? Jesus. Nah, I must have imagined those tugs of intuition with Taylor.

No way I'd be good for her. I'd be in it for the fucking.

She's the kind of woman who emotionally invests in everything. Crying over pandas and shit. Christ. Thinking about her in red lace panties is the last thing I should be doing, because I'm not just fantasizing. Not just thinking of how good the sex would be.

I'm thinking of her...

Smiling up at me.

Telling me how good I'm making it for her.

I'm thinking of her fingers in my hair and all over my back.

I'm thinking of...the trust in her eyes.

"Nope. No, no, no." I swipe the panties off the nightstand and shove them back into my pocket. "Going to return them. You are giving them back."

So she can wear them for another man?

Suddenly, my jaw feels like it's about to snap.

Which is why when my phone rings, I am too distracted to look at the caller ID. I simply thumb the green button and bark, "This is Sumner. What do you want?"

"Hello, Myles Sumner." Taylor's exhale in my ear turns a slow crank in my belly. "Shouldn't a bounty hunter have an intimidating nickname? Like Hellhound or Lone Wolf?"

"Only if they're an overinflated asshole." Hearing her voice in the middle of the mental tug-of-war she inspired isn't doing great things for my patience. But I'm not impatient with *her*. I'm annoyed at myself for being so damn relieved to hear from her. "Why are you calling me, half pint? I'm busy."

"Oh." A long pause ensues. I can hear the ocean in the background. Waves. Louder than they sound from her rental house. Is she on the beach? I don't know, but the longer the silence stretches, the guiltier I'm feeling for being so abrupt with her. If my guilt isn't a red flag that this woman has the ability to make me feel shit I don't want to feel, what is? "Well I don't want to interrupt whatever you're doing..."

Thinking of you in red panties.

Thinking of you moaning, telling me my dick is the perfect size.

"I'm working a case, Taylor."

"Right." She sighs and another arrow of guilt nails me in the stomach. "So I should just bag the murder weapon myself and bring it to the police?"

My brain snaps into focus like a rubber band. "*What?*"

"Sorry to bother you—"

"*Taylor.*"

"Hmm?"

"Where are you?"

"I'm on the beach, maybe a quarter mile from our house?" The wind carries her words away slightly and I don't like it. I don't like her standing on a windy beach in front of a gun, especially after the sun has set. Not without me there. "Jude met some surfers today and they invited us over for burgers. They have a really good view of the ocean and it looked so beautiful, so I brought my drink down here. I was just going to get my feet wet, but I started walking. I saw something shiny in the brush. Before you ask me, I haven't touched it."

I'm already halfway out the door of my motel room, keys in hand. "Do you know the name of the street you're on?"

"No. We walked here on the beach. We didn't drive."

Why is my skin suddenly layered with clammy sweat underneath my T-shirt? "Call your brother and tell him to come wait with you until I get there, Taylor."

"Oh no." Her tone suggests that whole idea is preposterous. "I don't want to interrupt his good time. He's *finally* beginning to relax. Myles, losing Bartholomew has been very hard on him. This would only stress him out again."

"Ahh. God forbid we get stressed." I switch to Bluetooth on my jog through the parking lot. "There hasn't been a murder or anything."

She sniffs. "You should know that sarcasm makes me shut down. There was a very sarcastic bully who lived next door to us growing up. He called me Shaquille O'Neal in front of the whole neighborhood. All because I was short. I couldn't walk by without him demanding I dunk on their hoop in the street. To this day, I cry every time I see Shaq, which is very unfair. By all accounts, he's a lovely man."

My teeth are grinding together.

To keep from growling or laughing, I have no idea. I've lost my fucking mind.

Now I'm also roaring out of the motel parking lot at fifty miles an hour, skidding sideways on the main road and correcting my bike in the direction of Coriander Lane. "Did you walk east or west on the beach?"

"What am I? A compass?" I can picture her wrinkled nose. It makes me ride faster. "We walked down the staircase that leads from the end of our block down to the beach. And we hung a right. Does that help?"

"Send me a pin of your location."

"Oh yeah. I can do that." My phone buzzes in my pocket a moment later and I pull over long enough to map a route to the closest block to where she's waiting on the beach. "Do you have all of the necessary equipment for evidence collection?"

Do not even think of smiling. You're on a slippery slope. "Yes, Taylor," I sigh.

"Fabulous. Then I'll see you in a while—"

"Oh no." My hand tightens on the handlebars. "Don't you dare hang up."

"Why?"

"Because you're alone in the dark and there might be a murderer in the area."

"Are you worried about me, Myles? Not only am I out here alone and defenseless. But I should mention that my emergency stash of panties has been mysteriously depleted. I'm worried we might have *two* criminals on our hands. A murderer and a panty thief. This has to be some kind of record for Cape Cod."

"You're very funny, half pint." Red lace. My thumb pressing through the material *right there*, rubbing until she's wet. *God.* "You just found the potential murder weapon and you want to discuss underwear?"

"I just find it curious that *you* are clearly a thief and yet *I* am a murder suspect."

"I don't suspect you. There just hasn't been cause to eliminate you yet. And if you want to get technical, miraculously finding the murder weapon doesn't exactly exonerate a person."

"I wish I hadn't called you."

That statement definitely shouldn't make me feel like I swallowed a lit candle, right? "That's fine, Shaquille," I say, to play defense against the burn. "Just don't hang up."

She gasps.

The sound of the ocean immediately cuts out.

"Great." The guilt is back. Thicker than ever. "She hung up."

With a gritted curse—and my nerves running loose in every direction—I pick up speed.

CHAPTER 7

Taylor

I don't even look at Myles when he arrives.

Continuing to stare straight out at the ocean, I point wordlessly toward the hill where I spotted the gun earlier, chin raised. As soon as I hear the evidence bag open and I'm confident he has found the weapon, I sail in the direction of Coriander Lane and our rental house. I've already texted Jude to let him know I'm heading home, though he probably won't see the text for an hour. When the conversation interests my brother, the way it was at tonight's impromptu get-together, he becomes thoroughly absorbed and forgets to look at his phone. It's another one of the things I love about him. His ability to give someone his undivided attention and make them feel like they are the only human being left on planet earth.

Speaking of very few beings being left on earth, if Myles

and I were the last people in existence, that would spell a very tragic end to the human race.

Not only does he refuse to eliminate me from his list of suspects, but his lack of gratitude is unspeakable. The only reason I didn't call the Barnstable PD is my concern over their apparent unwillingness to look at anyone but Judd Forrester. Well, next time I discover a murder weapon, I am going straight to them. I've already mentally deleted Myles Sumner's number from my phone. Poof. What bounty hunter?

I can't *believe* he called me Shaquille.

"Taylor," says the bounty hunter from behind me. In his deep, dumb, sexy rasp. "You're really going to ignore me?"

I don't respond.

Take that, bucko.

"I act like an idiot when I'm worried," he says, making me frown. "You're right, I was worried about you. Can you slow down now?"

If anything, I walk faster, alarmed.

I'm not sure about this...swooping sensation inside of me. It starts at my chest and scoops down into my stomach, moving things around. Things I wasn't expecting Myles to jostle. I've never been jostled before and I am very wary about this man—who just poked fun at my childhood trauma so cavalierly—having that power over me.

"In case you haven't noticed, I'm not exactly the sensitive type. That's one of the reasons I'm divorced."

Oh, *damn*. Now I'm curious.

He's divorced. This little nugget of information is like an untied shoelace. My fingers are itching to make a bow. There is no use pretending I'm not dying to know more about this surly, antagonistic man, is there? A few questions won't hurt, as long as I'm casual about them, right?

My steps slow down, ever so slightly.

"Well?" I cross my arms tightly over my boobs to offset my concession. "What are the other reasons you're divorced?"

Behind me, he grunts. Silence stretches.

"Before I started bounty hunting, I was a detective. Boston PD. Like my father and brother. It's the family business." He clears his throat. "My brother and I....we were spitballing about retiring early. Opening a private investigation firm. I was getting ready to file the paperwork with HR, but I wanted to tie up the Christopher Bunton case. A kidnapping. I...don't know. This kid, the one who'd been taken, reminded me of a childhood friend. My best friend, Bobby. He was sick when we were kids. And he didn't make it."

I slow down a whole lot more, my arms dropping to my sides.

"Paul, the guy who hired me to do this job? We both knew Bobby. The three of us were best friends as kids and that's probably why I felt...I don't know. Responsible. When he called and asked me for help following up on Oscar Stanley's murder."

"Oh." I let out an exhale that does nothing to ease the mounting pressure in my breast. "I didn't realize. I didn't think about how you knew Lisa's boyfriend."

"It's fine. Anyway, this kidnapped boy looked just like Bobby. I got too invested. I stopped going home. This case...I was obsessed with it and that's the kiss of death for a detective. When you stop being objective and let your emotions start making decisions for you. And I fucked it up. The case and the marriage." He laughs, but there is no humor involved. "When I got home one day, the place was empty, like I kind of suspected it would be. Got the divorce papers maybe a month later. I'd been so checked out, I couldn't even remember the last time we'd spoken."

There are a lot of blanks to be filled into the story, but his curt ending tells me he's said all he's willing to say. "I can't imagine you proposing to someone."

"Why not?"

"I don't know. Because it's a vulnerable moment. Waiting for an answer."

"You're right. I don't do vulnerable well. Or relationships." Once again, the silence drags out. So long that I turn and look back over my shoulder to see if he's still following me. And oh, he is. His intense eyes are trained on me in the darkness. "That's why I'm just here to work the case, Taylor. Not chase you down the beach while you pretend to be mad."

Caught between outrage and embarrassment, I whirl on him. "*Pretend?*"

Myles keeps coming. He walks until our bodies collide, pressing chest to thigh, his mouth hovering a breath above mine. "That's right. I'm calling you out. You couldn't be strutting that ass any sexier in front of me if you tried."

Red bleeds in from the edges of my vision. "In other words, I'm asking for it?"

"I wouldn't lay a *hand* on you without permission, Taylor. You're asking for it?" He shakes his head. "No. I'm asking *you* to stop offering."

"I'm not," I murmur, trying so hard not to be turned on by how he surprises me. How he's restraining himself despite the fact that his erection is spearing me in the belly. "I'm not offering you anything."

"Really?" he drawls. "Whose fingers are those unbuttoning my jeans?"

Those would be mine.

I'm literally trying to twist the metal button free of its hole.

I draw my hands back like they've touched a hot stove. Which isn't so far off considering the heat radiating from his hard stomach. His mouth. Eyes. All of him. I've never experienced this. Irritation and lust at the same time. It's itchy. It's consuming—and most definitely misplaced. "Are you implying that I'm sending mixed signals? Because you're standing here asking me to quit offering you...physical pleasure—"

"Sex, Taylor. It's called sex."

"And yet, you stole *my* hookup panties and almost kissed me this morning. Who is the one sending mixed messages?" His jaw grinds so dramatically, I can hear it creaking, but he says nothing. "Going to bed with you would be a disaster. You have the emotional availability of a banana."

"There it is. 'Emotional availability.'" His expression shifts to smug satisfaction. "You see? You're lying to yourself about wanting a hard, sweaty roll in the hay. You are a relationship girl. You are a spring wedding bridezilla waiting to happen."

My gasp echoes down the beach.

I shove at his chest, but I'm the one who ends up stumbling backwards, due to him being built like a Mack truck. He ends up steadying me by the elbow. "Take back the bridezilla part."

"The rest of it is true, though?"

"I never lied about wanting to settle down. There's no shame in wanting a husband and a family and matching shirts at Disneyworld. If you remember correctly, I said I wanted the hard, sweaty rolls in the hay, *as well*. These things shouldn't have to be mutually exclusive."

Lord, the man appears to be chewing on burning plastic.

"Maybe they're *not* mutually exclusive. But there is nothing about you that even...hints to a man that you'd like to be manhandled. Not remotely."

My interest is piqued. I hate giving him the satisfaction of wanting to know more, but my gut tells me he's on to something. Something I might not want to know, but could be valuable insight, nonetheless. "What does that mean?"

"It means you shocked the hell out of me and I'm a trained detective. You're not giving off the...I don't know. Wildcat vibe?" Slowly, he begins to circle me. "When I saw you, my first thought was, she's cute as a button. I've since amended that evaluation. A lot. But the men you're hunting for—"

"Hunting," I snort.

"If they're in the marriage market, they're only half as smart as me. At *best*. You're expecting too much from them. All they see is the wholesome girl next door, like I did."

"You're saying I need different energy if I want to find a gentleman in the streets who also happens to be a freak in the sheets. Do I have that right?"

Having completed his circle, he comes to a stop in front of me, opening his mouth and closing it, as if the conversation is getting away from him. "I'm saying you're marriage material. I'm saying you are a girl who demands respect..."

"And none of the *dis*respect I'm looking for." Half in a daze, I turn and sort of float down the beach, considering the conversation from all angles. Is Myles right? Am I expecting too much from the men out there? How would they know I have a unique sexual appetite when I show up to my dates in a matching sweater set and sensible nude flats? "I've never gotten what I want in bed, not only because I don't ask for it, but because the men who I choose to date... have resigned themselves to the predictable married life."

"There's nothing wrong with predictable. You *should* have predictable."

"Oh." Startled, I press a hand to my chest. "Are you still here?"

A dangerous light flashes in his eyes. "Yeah." Spoken through his teeth. "I'm still here."

"Shouldn't you go evaluate the possible murder weapon? I assume you'll bring it to the Barnstable police once you've cataloged—"

"We're not finished with the other conversation."

"No, I think we are. You've given me a lot of food for thought."

"You misinterpreted the food." He jabs the air with a long, blunt index finger. "I gave you apples and you took oranges."

I stop walking and face him, doing my utmost not to notice the way his long hair blows around him in the wind, making him resemble a Scottish highlander on his way back from battle or something. "How did I misinterpret? You're telling me I'm too wholesome to attract men who will...be aggressive with me—"

"Taylor." He pinches the bridge of his nose, a vein ticking in his temple. "Aggressive is the wrong goddamn word. I would kill a man for being aggressive with you." He says something else under his breath that I can't hear, but it sounds like, *I'd kill him no matter what.* Or *I need to work on my putt.* I can't be sure.

"I've been going about dating all wrong. I'm giving off the cherished wife vibe and none of the sex kitten vibe. It's all stuffed down under the surface. Like you said, men need things spelled out in thick red Sharpie. Meanwhile I've been using a pencil. Of course I'm drawing in all the Boring Bobs." Mentally, I'm already making tweaks to my dating profile. I'm really on to something here. Reluctantly grateful for his input, I smile up at the bounty hunter. "Forget the hookup panties, I need a whole hookup outfit."

Myles stares at the spot I vacated long after I keep walking, hands partially raised like he's trying to reason with a ghost. Why is his face so red?

I'm halfway up the stairs leading from the beach up to the rental house when Myles catches up with me. "I'm not sure I like what I've unleashed here," he grunts, falling into step beside me, though his legs are so long, he has to take two stairs at a time. "This is why I usually keep my mouth shut."

"Do you?" I bite my lip to keep from laughing. "I hadn't noticed that trait."

"It's your fault," he gripes, looking over at me. "Stealing guest books. Finding evidence. Forcing me to show up and see you."

"Oh my *God*. Apologies for the terrible hardship."

"Yeah, well, it is a hardship when you always look so fucking beautiful and I'm trying to keep my hands to myself." On the sidewalk in front of the house, he blocks me from walking any further. I'm not sure I could have, anyway, because his words have turned my legs to rubber. "Forget what I said on the beach. Don't change. Not your clothes or your vibe. There will be a guy eventually who isn't a complete moron and he'll..."

"Pick up on my big sex kitten energy?"

Myles swallows. Loudly.

His huge hands slide up my hips and my breath catches, nipples tingling into points. It's a waste of time to pretend I'm not attracted to him. I've been ignoring that fact for the last five minutes, distracting myself with new dating profile color schemes and now, when I'm looking him in the eye, I know why I needed that distraction. It hurts to be kept at arm's length from him. I don't know why. Don't know how it's possible when I just met him yesterday. But I had an instant awareness of him that I've never experienced with a man. Like there is a tiny but powerful magnet in my tummy and Myles is holding the counterpart.

"You pick up on my big sex kitten energy, Myles. Don't you?"

"Yes," he mutters gruffly, stepping forward to bury his nose in my hair. Inhaling. "God, yes, Taylor. You know I do. But I can't—"

"I won't expect anything else from you."

His head comes up fast. He searches my eyes warily. "What do you mean?"

"I mean..."

What *do* I mean?

It's all coming together now, as I look into this man's face. This man who was a stranger this morning but now, by some crazy twist of fate and momentary bravery, is the only other person in this world who knows my secret. He might be mean and unavailable and slightly dangerous, but my secret feels safe with Myles. He talks about my plight in such practical terms—no judgments. On top of that, I'm *very* attracted to him, I'm on vacation and there is a pretty good chance I'll never see him again after I leave the Cape.

Do I want to go back to my boring dating pool of beige prospects and settle?

Or do I want to go home to Connecticut and reach for more with the confidence I can only gain from experience?

Ignoring the ominous pang in my chest at the thought of not seeing Myles again, I curl my hands in the front of his T-shirt and savor the answering rumble in his chest. "Help me learn exactly what I want. And how to ask for it."

He tugs me close by the material of my skirt and our laps meet, both of us biting our lips and exhaling unsteadily over the contact. The unmistakable proof that he wants me. "You're the kind of woman who comes with strings, Taylor."

"M-maybe." I force myself to mean the next part. Really mean it. No matter what happens, I have to remember this man is not for me. Not for anyone. He's made that clear and I won't make the mistake of thinking I can change his mind. "I might come with strings, but I won't attach any of them to *you*."

A trench forms between his brows.

He opens his mouth to speak, closes it.

Then heat floods into his eyes, a dam visibly breaking inside of him, and I'm being thrown over his shoulder and carried into the house.

CHAPTER 8

Myles

*W*hat am I doing?

Something bad. Something very unwise.

Put her down. She's not for you.

Tell that to my fucking stomach. Or my chest. Both of which locked up tighter than the US Treasury when I saw her standing on the beach. First there was relief to see her safe. Then there was this bone-deep satisfaction that I haven't even begun to unpack. All I know is I liked her waiting for me. I liked us arriving at the same destination and breathing the same air. Even when she's pissed at me, which has been most of our acquaintance, it doesn't occur to me to walk away. Or take off. It's almost natural to stick. Or follow her siren song of an ass all the way home. Jesus, what has gotten into me?

She's wife material.

She's someone's future wife.

That should be the reason I go back to my motel room and drink whiskey until the peppy apple scent of her dulls in my blood. Instead, the fact that she's someone's future wife is the reason I'm kicking open the rear screen door, with my cock already at full mast. I'm jealous. God, no wonder people do stupid shit when they're feeling this way. It's like my insides are all gummed up and functioning improperly. I'm sweating, muscles tense. And all I can think about is ruining her for anyone else.

Apparently jealousy goes hand in hand with selfishness.

That gives me pause.

Selfishness. Now that's a sin I'm familiar with.

I don't want to be that way to Taylor.

I *can't*. I...like her. I like her sense of humor and the way she swings wildly from one extreme emotion to the next, as if she's feeling too much of everything. She's all bright splashes of color on the gray canvas I've been staring at while half awake. She's mischievous and doesn't let me get away with being rude. Why don't I *hate* that? Shouldn't I?

Bottom line, this is messy. This attraction between us is so fucking messy, I would be downright irresponsible—a bastard—for giving in. I'm the experienced one. When she says she won't tie any of her strings to me, I shouldn't take her word for it, nor should I want to commit cold-blooded murder to the man who earns those strings. Yet I know if the nameless, faceless son of a bitch was in front of me right now, I'd be doing a life sentence in no time.

No.

Pull back. I'm just in the moment, right?

I'm touching her. I'm hot as hell to swap orgasms.

I've never needed on this insane of a scale before, so my emotions are probably heightened. As soon as we work this out of our system, I'll have my head back on straight.

I just have to make doubly sure she's on the same page, so I don't lead her on.

"Taylor," I say, dragging her off my shoulder, her tits sliding over my shoulder and pressing up against my pecs. *Damn.* As soon as we're eye level, I keep her there, which means her feet are dangling nearly a foot off the floor and I try really hard not to dwell on how protective that makes me feel. My hold tightens. Roughly. "Hey. You understand this is physical. Nothing more. Right?"

"Right." She nods, those vivid green eyes trained on my mouth. "I promise. You're a tool of self-discovery for me. That's all."

"Right." Why am I suddenly made of stone? "Okay."

My throat feels uncomfortable. Maybe I just need clarification.

"So when you say tool—"

"Should I take off my clothes?" Earnestly, she searches my face. "Or are you going to?"

Fine. Fuck it. I'm a tool of self-discovery. Sold. "Me. I'm taking them off."

I don't even know where we're going. Only that I'm suddenly carrying her through the living room to the back of the house to get away from the multitude of windows that look out onto the street. We enter one of the bedrooms— one that doesn't look to be occupied—and I kick the door shut behind us, settling Taylor on her feet.

My palms sweat as I look her over, taking in our height difference and her trusting expression. Her hard nipples, windblown hair and flushed cheeks. I'm a split-second from backing her onto the bed, hiking up her skirt and just ringing myself dry between her legs. But a quickie is not what we're doing here, is it? She asked me for something.

Help me learn exactly what I want. And how to ask for it.

There is a purpose here. If I forget about it...

That's too much proof that she's getting to me.

She's not, I reassure myself, while removing my weapon. Engaging the safety and setting it on the dresser. "Here's the thing, Taylor," I say, my voice sounding like a buzzsaw. "You won't know what you like until you've had it. You might not even like it..."

Her lashes momentarily shield her eyes, like she's shy. Fuck me for being so turned on by that. "Rough?" she asks.

The saliva in my mouth dries up. "Yeah. Rough." I take a step in her direction, my pulse going from a gallop to a sprint. "I'll show you a little. You tell me if and when I go too far."

"Do we like...designate a safe word?"

"We don't need a safe word. You just say stop." The urge to comfort her wins before I have the chance to arrange a battle. Tugging her close by the front of her tank top, I keep pulling until my lips meet her forehead and I kiss her there. "I know what stop means, sweetheart."

She nods. Trusting me.

My heart knocks faster.

This is getting too personal already. That's not what she asked from me and I don't have it to give anyway. With a lot more rigor than intended, I unzip her skirt and shove it down past her hips. The soft denim has barely pooled around her ankles when I grip two tight handfuls of her ass and yank her up onto her toes. The gasp she lets out against my throat burns me alive. Once again, I am this close to pinning her beneath me on the bed and fucking the tension out of us both, fast and furious, but somehow, even with my dick harder than iron, I restrain myself.

"Still think you want to be manhandled?"

Halfway through my question, she's already nodding eagerly.

Sweetly.

Sweetly? I wouldn't know sweet if it bit me in the ass.

Teeth gritted, I spin her around to face the full-length mirror standing in the corner of the room. I watch her eyes connect with us. The study in contrasts we make together. Her in a tank top and panties. Pretty. Wide-eyed. And then me behind her. A jaded motherfucker with three days' worth of beard growth damn near twice her size. This is what she asked for, though. Isn't it? She's still on her toes, her sexy backside flush to my lap right now, gently grinding left to right, for a reason. She's been hungering for something and not being fed. How is it possible to be relieved by that and find it unacceptable at the same time?

I pinch the hem of her tank top between my fingers, taking a few seconds to graze her belly with my thumb, because goddamn, she is so soft. Her ass stills in my lap at the action, her eyelids fluttering. She likes it. As much as she wants a taste of hard and fast, she likes being touched gently, too, and knowing I shouldn't, I file that away for later. *Later?* Yup. Can't help it. Can't help cataloging the acceleration of the pulse at the bottom of her neck when I peel the tank top over her head, leaving her in cream-colored panties and a matching...

"What is this?" I ask, running my index finger back and forth under the thin shoulder strap, looking down over the top of her at those two full, ripe tits, cupped in lace. How they plump when I tug on the strap. Fuck. I can barely keep from growling. "It's not a bra, but it's not fit for public, either."

"Oh, um. Yes," she murmurs, chest rising and falling. "It's a bralette."

Never heard of one. "Cute."

Her eyes flash to mine in the mirror. "I don't want to be cute."

"Guess we better take it off then."

I watch her toes curl into the rug. Nervous but excited. "Good."

Instead of working it up and over her head, I surprise her by drawing the straps down her arms, then slowly dragging the dainty lace garment down her ribcage, belly, hips. And then I stop, settling my mouth against her ear. "You pull it the rest of the way. All the way to your ankles."

She's breathing harder now.

She knows something is coming—and she's right.

I'm not operating some kind of game here, though. I'm moving on distinct reflexes that come directly from this woman. How she moves, how she breathes, what it means when she swallows harder than usual. It's like I tune into her channel and some untapped source inside of me knows how fast to move, how slow, when she's ready for more. I'm too mesmerized by the sight of her sexy, tan-lined body in the mirror to worry again about the fact that these blind reflexes have never existed in me before. That they're specific to her.

Taylor chews her lip a moment, then takes hold of the bralette, shimmying it down over her hips in a way that makes her naked tits jiggle. Rounded and full and topped with pouting nipples. I groan at the intense rush of pressure between my legs, tearing my attention from the reflection of her breasts in order to look down, watch her bend over right there in front of me in a thin pair of panties, pulling the bralette down her knees, over the curve of her calves, until the lace touches the ground.

But I don't let her stand up.

I slide my fingers into her hair and keep her bent over, pulling her head back. Just her head. Slowly fisting her hair tighter and tighter until she whimpers.

"Jesus. Look at you." My free hand twists in the back panel of her underwear. Twists and twists until she cries out because the material is so tight over her pussy. Separating her lips and ass cheeks, applying pressure to everything in between. "Would anyone call you cute now?"

Still being held in that bent over position, she studies her reflection through glazed eyes. "No," she hiccups. "No."

"No. Me either." I lean back slightly, tugging her twisted panties to one side, groaning at what I reveal. "Well, let me clarify. I can see your tight asshole and nothing could stop that from being cute, but the rest of you?" I press my lap to the taut curve of her ass, letting her feel the painful effect she's having on my cock. "Now *you're* a girl who likes to fuck dirty."

A shudder wracks her body and I have the most compelling urge to gather her against my chest, warm her up. Tell her how beautiful she is. But I'm not going to pretend I'm not enjoying this. What we're currently doing. Taylor watching herself in the mirror. Witnessing the surprise come over her, the change in how she sees herself. She's nearly naked, bent over in front of an unscrupulous man, tits on display, mouth swollen, pupils eclipsing her irises.

Lust. She's in it.

My God, so am I.

I've never been harder in my life.

Or at least that's what I think. Until she seeks out my eyes in the mirror.

And says, "Rougher."

So much blood travels south so fast, I almost double

over on top of her. I'm aching to pull down her panties and pump home from behind, just like this. She's wet. I don't need to feel her pussy to know it. The evidence is part of my consciousness. It's in my veins. She's practically trembling in front of me, her ass working up and down in my lap. Hips tilted up. I know what the hell she's asking me for.

I twist her fisted panties one more time, lace biting into sensitive flesh until she cries my name, her thighs starting to tremble. "You want me to slap the cute out of this ass?"

"Yes."

My hand is already moving, but not to spank her. Not yet.

No, I reach between her legs and massage her pussy roughly, leaning down to mutter praise against her spine. Drawing her so close to me I can't tell where she ends and I begin. I'm losing control here. I'm no longer thinking objectively. Sensation is leading me completely, along with a driving hunger for her satisfaction. The best she'll ever have. As soon as she begins to grind her sex into my palm, I let go, remove my hand from between her thighs and rain a smack down on the supple curve of her right buttock.

I don't know what I'm expecting. Gratification, yeah. A feeling of authority, sure.

I get those things.

But just like that morning, a savage sense of responsibility takes over, demanding I soothe her immediately afterward. Like it's my job. My right. I cup the place where my palm connected and rub it, my mouth kissing up her spine and burying in her hair. "Good. That's a good girl."

Even while I'm kissing her neck, licking over sensitive spots and whispering words in her ear, I raise my palm again and bring it down even harder—and she whimpers, "Yes, yes, yes," so I do it again. I repeat the pattern three more times. Spank, soothe, spank, soothe until her knees are so weak, I'm holding her up. "Rougher," she whispers.

And I'm done. I'm fucking done.

I might be dominating her, but she's owning me.

I let Taylor go down on her knees and I straighten, grappling with the zipper of my jeans. My composure is in the incinerator. All I hear is her asking me for rough. *Rougher.* All I can think about is getting my cock in her gorgeous mouth and she wants that, too, or she wouldn't be helping me lower the zipper over my painful swell of flesh. She wouldn't be exhaling on my belly, kissing me there with tongue, totally unrestrained, tilting her face up to meet my groaning advance, allowing me to sink my cock into her mouth without waiting or teasing or playing games. Yes. *God yes.*

Just urgent. Just rough.

"Blame the size of it on every goddamn thing you do. Never been bigger or harder in my life. A little twitch of that ass and I'm stiff. *Fuck.* Just like that. I'm hard even when you're pissed at me, baby."

In the spirit of giving her what she needs—Christ, when did I ever want anything else?—I take two fistfuls of her hair, wrapping the silky strands around my wrists and I sink deep, deep, deep, grinding in and out of her sweet, giving mouth, hips rutting up and back like an animal and she loves it. God help me, she takes me deeper than I'd ever expect her to offer and then some, dipping her tongue into my slits and ridges and using her hands to fist fuck me. I've died and gone to heaven. No, higher. I'm in an undiscovered promised land.

"That's good, Taylor. That's so fucking good. Lick what you did. Suck what you did." On some indescribable level, I know I'm not going to feel complete unless this ends inside of her. I want her mouth on mine. Want my body anchoring her. I need her skin, her scent, her heat. "You and that dick-tease mouth get on the bed," I rasp, drawing myself out from between her lips with a pop, urging her to her feet, turning, backing us toward the bed. "On your back, Taylor. Panties off. I swear to God, I'm going to fuck you sideways."

"I would like that very much," she says breathily, falling onto her back and struggling to get the underwear down. There's a mouthwatering flash of wet flesh—

Glass shatters behind me.

I don't think. I throw myself on top of Taylor, covering her completely with my body, arms wrapped around her head. Sharp stings of glass land on my back one by one, burning pricks that definitely draw blood. Out of the corner of my eye, I see a large red and white buoy tumble to a stop on the ground near the side of the bed—and rage blooms inside me to an unholy degree.

Taylor could have been hit by that buoy.

"What...what was that?" she whispers, the fear in her voice making my stomach drop.

"I've got you. You're safe."

Stay objective. Easier said than done. I'm almost dizzy with rage. I wait several beats to make sure nothing else is coming. Then I slide Taylor off the bed and rush her to the bedroom door, blocking her from the window with my body the entire way. "Go to the bathroom and lock the door."

She hesitates, going up on tiptoes to stare at the broken window over my shoulder. "Oh my gosh. Even the vandalism is nautical-themed."

She's making *jokes* at a time like this? All I can see is her unconscious and bleeding on the bedroom floor. I let my guard down. I let it down. *"Go. Now."*

As soon as she disappears into the bathroom and I hear

the lock click, I fasten my jeans as quickly as possible and jog to the front of the house, gun in hand. There is a set of taillights at the very bottom of the hill turning on to the main road, but it's too dark to get a description of the vehicle, let alone a license plate number.

"*Goddammit!*" I roar through my teeth, ripping out my cell phone to call the police.

A voice answers in my ear a moment later, but I have to hang up, because I'm not ready to respond. I'm thinking of the woman inside. How utterly lost I've been in her for the last half an hour. Lost enough that I stopped paying attention, my effectiveness compromised. And because of that, she could have been *hurt*. One day around Taylor and I'm not just breaking my rule about letting my emotions get involved while I work a case, I'm shattering it.

And now that there is obviously a real threat toward her, I *can't* let it happen again.

CHAPTER 9

Taylor

*L*ast night was a doozy.

In oh so many ways.

What happened with Myles...

Well, I'm not sure what happened with Myles.

I must be very extremely naïve because when he carried me into the house, I thought we were going to make out. Roughhouse. Maybe, at the very most, do some heavy petting. I don't blame women for having sex on the first date. Actually I think it's a wonderful time saver, finding out up front if you've got a dud. In the past, I've needed several dates before I'm even comfortable being *alone* with the man, let alone allowing him to breach the inner sanctum.

It's only happened a few times in my life. I'm a real tough sell.

Not for Myles, apparently. As soon as he put his hands

on me, it was a race to the finish line. I couldn't get close enough. Couldn't experience enough. Pulse hammering, mouth dry, legs trembling, panties sodden. I mean, who *was* what?

I like her.

Stepping out of the glass-enclosed shower stall, I dry off slowly while looking in the mirror, turning my head left and right to observe the faint whisker marks on my neck. A hot shiver passes through me, zapping straight down to my toes and leaving them tingling. I'm still keyed up. I never came down, not the entire night, despite the police arriving to take our statements and deal with a hyper-pissed-off Myles. As soon as he let me out of the bathroom last night, he stood behind me with crossed arms and a scowl while I talked to the police. And then he led me upstairs, deposited me unceremoniously in the bedroom...and never came back.

I take my bikini top off the peg and tie it on. The nylon chafes my sensitive nipples and I let out a bumpy exhale. My eyes drift shut automatically and scenes begin to play out in my mind, the way they've done all night. The way he looked at my breasts. Hungrily. His fist winding the back of my panties, tightening the lace between my legs until one little yank could have given me an orgasm. The smooth, heavy slide of him into my mouth and the way he towered over me, hips thrusting in crude grinds. Flexing his authority while being totally at my mercy. I've never felt so incredible. So bold.

I lean forward and brace my forearms on the bathroom vanity. I'm still slightly damp from the shower and I press my thighs together now. Hard. Watch my breath fog the mirror. I think of him behind me, hulking and irritable. He takes his shirt off and throws it on the floor, grips my hips and jerks them backward into his lap.

Good girl, he says. And I barely trap a moan. Why do I like that so much? I should hate it. I shouldn't want to be put on my knees and have liberties taken with my mouth when this man has been such an unholy jerk toward me, but I'm so drawn to him, it hurts. The sting of his palm on my bottom woke me up, made me gasp for air, for mental purchase. I was painfully awake...and while I want more, I'm worried. I told him I wouldn't let my strings attach themselves to him and I meant it.

I meant it.

But I didn't expect how I would respond to him. So it's probably for the best that he didn't come back last night and finish what we started. It's for the best if I take a step back.

There's no law against fantasizing, though.

Permission makes me loose limbed. Makes my breathing pick up as I bend forward over the sink and press my mouth to the crook of my elbow, two fingers slowly delving between the shower-softened folds of my sex. A sound shudders out of me when I find my clit, teasing the edges. Surrounded as I am by steam from my shower, the bathroom is intimate. I'm alone. I'm allowed. To rake my teeth down the sensitive inner flesh of my arm and push down on my button of flesh, rubbing it more roughly than I normally would, trying to chase the high from last night, even though I know, I somehow *know* he's the only one who can give it to me.

I can find a little relief, though. I can—

"Taylor!" My brother's voice is muffled, coming from beyond the bathroom and bedroom. Out in the hallway. "Breakfast is on the table. I made waffles. Figured we could use that homemade boysenberry syrup we bought at the farmer's market yesterday morning."

My forehead hits the mirror. "Damn," I whisper, sides

heaving, no idea if I'm still slick from the shower or layered in sweat. I can't believe I didn't pack my vibrator. It just seemed like a weird thing to do when going on vacation with my brother. I'm way out of practice with manual masturbation. For all I know this will take all morning. They'll send a search party and find me in here trying to convince my fingers to vibrate.

"Are you okay in there?" Jude calls.

"Yes," I croak, clearing my throat, pushing off the sink. Jude walked through the front door last night while I was being questioned by the police and turned as white as swan feathers. The last thing I want to do is worry him more. "Be right down."

I fan my flushed neck on the way into the bedroom, pulling on bathing suit bottoms and a loose pair of black cotton pants. One good thing came from my sleepless night, at least. In the interest of getting some distance from the bounty hunter and regaining control of this vacation, I booked a Groupon for a snorkeling lesson for today. All the way on the other side of the Cape.

Yes. Distance.

Perspective.

Both good things.

Which must be why I'm standing at the window and looking down at where Myles slept last night. On the porch of the house with a gun tucked into his waistband. He's still there now, looking at something on his phone. A notebook rests on his thigh.

On your back, Taylor. Panties off. I swear to God, I'm going to fuck you sideways.

My sex squeezes at the memory of what we almost did. It would have been wild. *I* would have been wild, welcoming his strength, begging him to use it on me. And he would have. I can't help but be grateful toward Myles. For once, a man not treating me like I'm good for introducing to mom and nothing more. I was a sexual being last night. A woman.

Unfortunately, I didn't just feel physically close to the bounty hunter. So much more went into giving him my trust. More than I realized. And when he didn't come back last night, he left me exposed. A kite in the wind. I didn't realize he'd have that kind of effect on me and I don't think I should let it happen again. Not when he's spelled out very clearly that he spits in the eye of love and tradition and everything I'm looking for.

As if he can feel my eyes wandering over the thick breadth of his shoulders, Myles tilts his head back and our gazes clash in the window. His expression heats, his mouth pressing together in a grim line. When the fluttering in my stomach begins to spread lower, I step back hastily, reaching for the hairbrush on my bed and raking it quickly through my hair. I dab on some moisturizer with SPF and apply some crushed apple lip balm before leaving the bedroom. When I get downstairs, my brother is sitting at the kitchen table in front of his plate of untouched waffles.

"You should have started without me."

"Hey." He ignores that, passing me the boysenberry syrup as soon as I sit down. "How are you feeling?"

We both turn to look at the first floor guest room. Glass has been swept into a corner and thick, construction grade plastic taped over the window. "Fine. Do you think I should call Lisa and explain what happened with the window? I hate to bother her about something so stressful when she's grieving her brother."

Jude chews on the tines of his fork. "Myles probably

already called Lisa. You mentioned he's only doing this job as a favor to her boyfriend, but he still has to keep her apprised of happenings. And a buoy through the window was most definitely a happening."

"Yeah," I sigh. "You're probably right."

We're silent while spreading butter on our waffles and dousing them in syrup. "Speaking of the private investigator..." Jude squints an eye in my direction, lowers his voice. "When you told the police you and Myles were 'just talking' in the bedroom during the buoy incident, you were doing that rapid blinking thing you do when you're lying." His lips twist to hide a smile, fork digging into a bite of waffle. "I'm not prying. Just...you know. I'm surprised by your choice of vacation hookup. Not in a *bad* way. Just in a surprised way."

My face is the color of a stop sign. "I mean, there *was* talking while we were in the bedroom. That wasn't a total lie."

Jude looks at me while he chews, amused and saying nothing.

"I, um..." I fumble with my silverware. "Well—"

"You don't have to tell me, T."

"I want to. It's just that you're usually the one telling me about *your* love life. It's not usually this way around."

He smiles around a bite. "You're too kind to call my meaningless hookups a love life, T."

"Have you spoken to Dante lately?" I ask before I can think better of it.

Jude stops chewing, quickly looks down at his plate. When he finally swallows, it's like he's ingesting a fish hook. Why on earth did I say that? How stupid of me to bring up his best friend in the same breath as his love life. Now it seems like I am lumping in one with the other and that is definitely not the case. Probably. I don't know. "No. He's film-ing, I think?" He laughs, but I can tell it's forced. "Last week he was in Singapore. This week he's in New York. I don't know. I can't keep track of him anymore. I stopped trying."

Just let it drop.

I'm having a lot of trouble doing that lately. "He used to call on Sundays. He doesn't do that anymore?"

Jude hesitates. "He does. I'm just...usually in the middle of something. Or he fucks up the time zones and I'm asleep." He rolls a shoulder. "We'll touch base eventually."

I nod. "Good. Tell him I said hi."

"I will." Jude tips his head toward the porch where Myles is now pacing back and forth, speaking in a low voice into his phone. "He camped out there all night. Guarding you."

"Guarding *us*," I clarify, licking syrup off the tip of my pinkie. "And I think he's just lying in wait so he can catch the perp if they return to the scene of the crime."

"Are you sure about that?" I'm glad to see the character-istic amusement back on Jude's face. Just not about this. "Dude seems kind of smitten."

A skeptical laugh bursts out of me. "What is your defini-tion of smitten? Because last night, I'm pretty sure he called me a spring bridezilla waiting to happen."

Jude chokes and I jump to my feet, prepared to perform the Heimlich maneuver.

Eyes watery, he waves me off. "I'm fine. Oh my God, he didn't."

"He did."

"And you still...*talked*...to him? Before the buoy hit?"

"Yes." I've only just picked up my fork, but I set it back down with a *thunk*. "Oh my god, I hooked up with him after he called me a future bridezilla. What is *wrong* with me?"

Jude blows out a breath. "Maybe you're attracted to his honesty."

"Maybe. Or maybe I'll jam this fork into his rectum—"

Someone clears their throat from the front entrance.

Jude's and my heads whip around to find Myles leaning against the doorjamb, notebook at his side. Watching me. Wary, as usual. "Morning," he drawls, pushing off the frame and sauntering into the kitchen. "Going to steal some coffee. Figure you won't mind, since I spent the night protecting your asses."

"No one asked you to do that," I say brightly. "We can look after ourselves."

He grunts, back muscles shifting beneath his T-shirt as he fills a mug.

I'm not at all interested in the way those ancient jeans hug his butt.

Couldn't care *less*.

Jude is looking between me and Myles, growing more and more uncomfortable by the minute. My brother hates sustained silences. Both of us do, really, because my parents enforced a no talking at dinner rule after particularly harried workdays. They were tired. They'd placed us neatly in our boxes and nothing I said could change their impression of me. If I rode my bike with no hands for a whole five seconds or volunteered to say the Pledge of Allegiance on the loudspeaker at school, I was still play-it-safe Taylor to them. Somewhere along the line, I stopped trying to change their mind. *And* my own.

All those years ago, Jude and I would sit in silence at our dining room table, side by side, bursting with news from school and friendships, we were forced to swallow it down until we could debrief later, alone in the patch of hallway between our rooms. Now as adults, we tend to chatter to fill any conversational voids, especially at meals. *Not this time,* I try to communicate with a shake of my head at Jude, but he's turning red with the need to say something, anything. "Throw yourself on a waffle, if you want," Jude says, sounding like a burst balloon. "The griddle is still on."

The bounty hunter grins at me over his stupidly huge shoulder. "Don't mind if I do."

Jude mouths an apology to me. His phone lights up on the table, momentarily distracting him. With a swallow, he quickly shoves the device into the pocket of his board shorts. The action is not lost on me, but I can hardly question it right now. Not with an ogre in our midst. "What's on the agenda for the day, big guy?" Jude asks the bounty hunter. "Car chase? Chalk outline tutorial?"

I shake my head at my brother in disappointment.

"I don't share leads with suspects," states the infuriating man.

"Really?" I exclaim. "We're *still* suspects even after someone threw a buoy through our window?"

"Jude doesn't have an alibi during the time of the buoy tossing. Could have been him trying to throw me off your trail."

Based on the bounty hunter's casual tone of voice—and the fact that his back is facing me despite an assortment of knives resting on the table—he doesn't *really* suspect us. But the fact that he won't mark us off the list or freely share information angers me all the same.

"I should have called the police last night when I found the gun, instead of you. Officer Wright is much better at communicating."

"Wright runs his mouth. He shouldn't have told you jack

shit to begin with." I was wrong. Myles is not in a casual mood at all. When he turns around, his knuckles are so white around the mug of coffee, I brace for it to shatter. "These are the consequences of him sharing classified information with you. Now someone is out there pissed off that you're digging. Pissed off enough to do something that could lead to you getting *hurt*. Do you understand that?"

I twist around in my seat. "Use your indoor voice, please. There is no need to shout at me."

"I'm not shouting."

"You might as well be shouting!"

He looks at me like I've just grown a horn in the dead center of my forehead. "What are your plans for the day? I don't want you going anywhere without me."

"Unless you want to go snorkeling, that's going to be pretty difficult."

"Snorkeling." He pauses in the middle of dumping batter onto the griddle. "Someone sent you a clear threat last night and you're going snorkeling?"

"Jude is *amazing* at anything water related," I say, patting his arm. "There's no reason we have to let a broken window ruin his vacation."

"*Our* vacation," my brother corrects me.

"Yes, that's what I meant."

When it grows silent in the kitchen, I turn to find Myles frowning at me. He looks like he wants to say something, but he coughs into a fist and turns to monitor his waffle. "You're one of these people who plans a lot of activities on vacation, instead of lying on the beach and taking it easy like everyone else, aren't you?"

"I can lie around and relax at home. A vacation is a chance for *doing*." I add more boysenberry syrup to my plate for dipping. "What do you do for fun on vacation?

Make fun of babies? Push old ladies down steep hills in shopping carts?"

Jude snorts into his coffee, clearly entertained.

Myles doesn't give us the satisfaction of a rejoinder, though. No, he drops his plate on the table and sits down, taking a long sip of coffee. "Cancel the snorkeling, all right?"

"No way."

"I need to meet with the police today. They've agreed to share a copy of the ballistics report. The coroner is coming back today or tomorrow with a TOD. I don't have time to babysit you while you look at starfish."

"TOD is time of death," I whisper across the table to my brother.

Jude sets down his mug, affronted. "All right, look," he says, looking at Myles. "You're obviously a lot more qualified to act as a bodyguard, but I'll be with her when we go snorkeling. I wouldn't let something happen to my sister."

"You're right, I am a lot more qualified," Myles says without missing a beat.

All traces of Jude's affable nature are gone. "I can handle myself."

Myles raises a dubious eyebrow at Jude, coolly sipping his coffee.

That does it. I'm going to stab him.

Double Homicide on the Cape. It's going straight to the top of the podcast charts.

"You seem doubtful. Why?" Jude leans back in his chair. "Because I'm gay?"

The bounty hunter calmly reaches for the syrup. "Nope. My brother is gay and he'd scare the balls off an ox."

Jude tilts his head at me.

As if to say, *didn't see that coming.*

Join the club. I haven't foreseen *any* of the curves this

man has thrown me. In fact, I'm only now remembering how he opened up to me on the beach last night about his divorce and the kidnapping case. He shared with me. And my gut says that wasn't easy for him. Or typical. He's not very easy to stuff into a labeled box, this man. *Dang it.*

"You said..." I resume eating, because I need something to do with my hands. "Didn't you say your brother is a detective in Boston?"

A curt nod from the bounty hunter. "On his way to a promotion last I heard."

"You don't speak to him very often?" Jude asks.

"Never. And before you ask, it's not because he's gay." He shoves a bite into his mouth, talking around it like we're eating in a barn "We don't talk because he's a prick." He jabs the air between us with a fork. "Where are you going snorkeling? I'll call and postpone it for you."

The smile I send him is pure saccharine. "Join us if you must, but we are going snorkeling. I already paid for the Groupon"

"Hey." Jude holds up his phone, the screen of which is covered in messages. "Do you mind if I invite the burger guys from yesterday?"

A snicker sneaks out of me. "Is that how you labeled them in your phone?"

Jude grins. "Yup. There's an asterisk and a note here, too." He taps the phone to his lips. "The blond one liked grilled onions and sauerkraut on his burger. Steering clear."

"Wise move." I stand up and begin to gather the dishes. "Their names were Jessie, Quinton and Ryan. And invite them of course, the more the merrier."

Jude hesitates, splitting a look between me and Myles. "Ryan is the straight one who just got his MBA in finance, right?"

I have to think about it. My mind was pretty stuck on the case last night. And on a certain grouchy bounty hunter, but I won't be admitting *that* part to anyone. "Yes, I think so."

My brother hums. "He was asking about you, T. After you left. He was disappointed when you didn't come back."

Myles's knife scrapes his plate, long and loud.

We stare at him awaiting an explanation.

The seconds tick by.

"Keep your distance from Burger Guys," Myles draws out, finally. "They're suspects, too."

Me and Jude throw up our hands. "Oh, come on. That doesn't make any sense," I say. "What possible motive could they have?"

"Might not be clear until it's too late." The bounty hunter jerks his chin at Jude. "You met them on the beach?"

"Yeah..." Jude responds warily.

"Did they introduce themselves to you? Or the other way around?"

"They approached me." Jude polishes an invisible apple on his shirt. "They usually do."

"The guilty party will often find a way to insert themselves into the investigation." Myles scoots his chair back with a loud scrape and brings his plate to the sink, frowning at us over his shoulder. "For all I know, you're all in cahoots."

It finally dawns on me. He's messing with us.

"This is your playful side, isn't it? You look like a bear with his paw caught in a beehive, but you're actually joking around."

Myles totally ignores my hypothesizing on his way to the front door. "I'm going downtown to remind the police I'm not going away. I'll be back in half an hour." He slides on a pair of Ray-Bans but they do nothing to hide his sour expression. "I guess we're going snorkeling."

"Thank you in advance for scaring off all the fish!"

The door rattles on the hinges in the wake of his departure.

"Oh my God." Jude falls back in his chair, face wreathed in amusement. "The sexual tension between you two has escalated. I didn't think that was possible."

"There is no..." My shoulders slump. I pretend to cry. "Fine. I know."

"Maybe it's the perfect vacation fling," he points out with his fork. "You don't even like each other. There's no chance of anyone getting attached."

A motorcycle engine cranks to life outside, accelerates, roars off down the block.

And then it's gone altogether.

"Yeah." I force a smile. "It's perfect."

I'm standing at the sink a few minutes later scrubbing down the breakfast dishes, when there's a knock at the door. I trade a surprised look with Jude, who is still sitting at the table scrolling through his phone. "I'll get it," he says.

I draw a butcher knife out of the wooden block on the counter. "I'll come with you."

Jude muffles a laugh with his hand. "You could never in a million years use that for anything but chopping onions."

"I could nick someone," I whisper back. "Long enough to stun them and run."

He ruffles my hair, tugs me into his side and we approach the door together. When we reach the entrance, he leans in and looks through the peephole, rocking back on his heels with a lot less tension in his frame. "It's a woman. Young. I don't recognize her."

I take a turn looking through the hole. "Hmm. Can we help you?" I call through the door while making a stabbing motion with the knife. Jude's shoulders shake with silent mirth.

"Yes! Hi!" the woman answers brightly. "I have a quick question about the recent murder that took place across the street. Could you help me out?"

"What is your question?"

She hesitates. "I don't really feel comfortable doing this through the door."

I shrug at my brother. He shrugs back. "Two of us. One of her," he whispers. "Plus you're packing."

"Right." I turn the lock. "Okay, we're coming out."

As soon as the door opens, a man steps into view.

With a camera on his shoulder.

The woman produces a microphone from behind her back and holds it in front of my face. "Is it true that you are the one who discovered the body?"

I blink at my reflection in the camera lens. "Um..."

With a curse, Jude herds me back into the house and slams the door. But not before the reporter can fire off a second question. "Our sources tell us someone threw a buoy through your window last night. Is it true you're being targeted?"

Jude turns the lock.

We slowly back away from the door.

"Targeted," I snort. "That's a little extreme, isn't it?"

"*So* extreme," Jude confirms. Then, "Right, T?"

I haven't really taken the time to process the repercussions of the buoy being chucked through the window, but having it laid out in such stark terms has my stomach bubbling.

"Let's fail to mention this to the bounty hunter. Just in case he's not thrilled about us appearing on a camera that was definitely rolling," I suggest, setting the knife down on the closest surface. "It's probably not a big deal. It's not like we answered her."

My brother's laugh turns into a gulp. "Right."

"Maybe we should go before he comes back."

"You read my mind."

CHAPTER 10

Myles

*N*eedless to say, I'm not in a great mood when I pull into the parking lot of Something is Fishy Snorkel 'n' Fun. Taylor's car is here, along with two other ones I don't recognize. I already hate whoever is driving them.

They left without me.

I returned from downtown and her car was gone. It took me under ten seconds to jimmy the lock on the back door and it was a *real* delight to find a random butcher knife just sitting out in the open, nobody around to ask for an explanation. My heartburn is acting up like a son of a bitch. I'm convinced my antacids have been replaced with placebo. I should be investigating Oscar Stanley's murder and instead, I'm chasing a second grade teacher all over Cape fucking Cod. Because the possibility of her in potential danger has me in a headlock.

And because she's a suspect, too, I'm forced to remind myself.

I'm definitely not stomping across the beach in steel-toed boots because the idea of her in a bathing suit in front of other men gives me a splitting headache.

That has nothing to do with it.

I prove myself a liar almost immediately. Taylor comes into view down in the cove—in bikini bottoms and a rash guard—smiling and nodding at the instructor like an A-plus student. Beside the instructor there are four other men present. Jude is here, thankfully. I don't mind her brother. He seems decent. But there is some dude, I'm guessing it's MBA Ryan, who looks a lot more interested in Taylor's body than he is in the body of water behind him, and the burn shoots into my throat like a geyser.

How many men show interest in her per day? Ten? Twenty? It's getting ridiculous.

I'm shoveling a handful of antacids into my mouth when Taylor catches sight of me.

"Oh," she says weakly. "You found us."

I look dead at Ryan while crushing the white tablets between my teeth.

"H-*how* exactly did you find us?" Taylor asks.

"I looked for the snorkeling place with the stupidest name," I inform her. "You *would* pick a place called Something is Fishy."

Gasping, she shoots a look at the instructor. "He's only joking."

"It's fine. My daughter named it when she was eleven." There is a mesh bag full of equipment resting in the sand at the man's feet and he gestures to it now. "Will you be... uh...joining us? I'm not sure I have large enough flippers..."

I kick off my boots. Leave my socks in the sand. "I'll manage."

The instructor starts to pass out the equipment. Goggle-snorkel combos and flippers. Life jackets. I take everything he hands me, but I can already tell nothing is going to fit, so I don't put any of it on. Taylor frowns at me the whole time. Good. *Fine.*

"All right, we're going to split up in groups of two," says the instructor.

"Taylor..." Ryan begins.

She turns in his direction.

Over the top of Taylor's head, I promise him a slow death with my eyes.

"Fuck off," I mouth, very precisely.

"I'm going to pair up with Quinton," he blurts, feigning interest in one of his life jacket buckles. "B-but I'll catch you on a flippity flop, yeah?"

The others waddle off down the beach in their gear, listening to the older man explain how to keep their goggles from fogging up. Instead of following them, Taylor crosses her arms and cocks a bikini-clad hip, making my fingers itch to tug on the strings.

"Did you hear that?" I drop all of the equipment, except for the goggles and snorkel. "He'll catch you on the flippity flop."

"Oh shut up."

The look she's giving me is pure venom. I want to kiss her so bad, my stomach is in knots. *Don't you dare.* Some annoying sense of self-preservation warns me that I can't get used to having my hands and mouth on her. I can't make it a habit or it'll be impossible to break. I've resolved to back off from this woman or risk becoming too distracted.

If I put myself in a position to make another life or death

mistake, what was the point of leaving Boston in the first place? Didn't I turn my badge in and leave so I wouldn't have the power to misread evidence and ruin another case? Another set of lives?

Clearly interpreting my silence as irritation—with her—Taylor turns on a heel in the sand and sashays toward the far side of the cove. "Could you just stay on the beach, please? I'd actually like to enjoy myself."

Of course, I follow her, fascinated by the way her bikini bottoms are creeping up the sweet split of her ass, revealing more and more cheek as she goes. "You heard him, half pint," I say gruffly. "It's a buddy system."

"Obviously we will never be buddies." Her steps slow a little. "Not unless you want to share with the class anything you learned at the police station."

"Nope. You want to tell me why there was a knife at the front door of your house?"

"Nope."

I grind my teeth. Not only because we're at odds and I find I really don't...enjoy that. Being combative with people is normal for me. It's how my family communicated. In blunt facts and fights and insults. Honestly, I could give a rat's ass if people think I'm a disagreeable bastard. And it's embarrassing to admit, even to myself, but I kind of wish Taylor would smile at me more. She did it a yesterday, didn't she? What needs to happen on my part in order for there to be more smiles?

There's nothing dangerous or irresponsible about smiling.

It's safer than sleeping together. Right?

Last night on the beach, when I told her about some of the uglier parts of my past, she did a whole lot more than smile at me. I have to make sure we don't get that far again

—for her safety and the good of the case—but the longer I go with her angry at me, the more restless I become. Why can't I just be indifferent to her like I am with everyone else?

I don't have the answers. I just know I don't like her walking away from me angry.

Disappointed.

That trust she gave me last night...I can't help wanting another hit.

I have to give up ground in order to receive some, don't I?

Shit.

"Listen, Taylor..." I take hold of her elbow and draw her to a stop, trying not to obsess over how smooth she is. Everywhere. Although, might as well admit it. I've lost the battle over obsessing about her body at this point, as evidenced by the fact that I've been carrying her red, lacy little hookup panties around in my back pocket since Thursday. "Time of death came in early. Oscar had been deceased for twenty-four hours when you found him. Your alibis checked out. So..."

Her face brightens and my heartburn evaporates. "We're not suspects anymore?"

"No."

"Oh." She breathes a laugh. "You hated telling me that, didn't you?"

"Yes." Wow. That response was way too quick to be believable. I plant my hands on my hips, but drop my hands almost immediately. "No. I didn't hate it."

She's squinting up at me into the sun. No shades.

Without thinking, I take mine off and put them on her.

They're so big on her, they slide right down to the tip of her nose and she goes momentarily cross-eyed watching them slip. Why does it feel like there is someone doing gymnastics in my chest? "Well." I jerk my head at the cove. "Go look at some fucking fish."

She bursts out laughing and the glasses fall off completely.

I catch them before they hit the sand.

"What's so funny?"

"Well." She struts off toward the rock formation and here I am again, keeping pace with her. "I was thinking if you were one of my students, I'd ask you to draw me a picture of your feelings. And they would probably look like the cover of a death metal album."

The word "feelings" in itself makes me jumpy, so I push the conversation in another direction. Because at least she's talking to me now. Not quite smiling yet, but there's time.

No there isn't. You're supposed to be investigating a murder.

"What are you like?" I ask, more curious than I have the right to be. "As a teacher."

"Well..." We enter an opening in the rock formation, stopping in front of a shallow tide pool. Overhead, there is a rocky overhang that blocks the sun and she peers up at me in the absence of light, as if deciding if she can talk to me. Trust me. I make a mental note about the timeline of our acquaintance. I was mean, also known as my usual self, until last night and once I let up, she softened. Trusted me. Mean again this morning, lost that trust. Maybe I should just stop being mean. That seems like the only route here if I want her to...

What?

Like me?

What good is liking me going to do her? Or me, for that matter?

"I'm a crier," she says finally and my worries take a backseat. For now. "I cry all the time. I'm famous for being found weeping in the staff supply closet."

I don't like that at all. "Why?"

"The kids. They say the most honest, beautiful things. They're too young to be guarded and it's especially notice-able with the boys. You know? Men sort of learn early to keep their feelings to themselves, but my second graders haven't been taught that yet." When I notice the moisture in her eyes, so much pressure squashes down on my chest that I physically take a step back, but she doesn't seem to notice. "On the last day of school, one of them said, 'Thank you for being my school mommy, Ms. Bassey' and I almost required oxygen."

"Are you going to require it now?"

"No." She swipes at her eyes as if crying out in the open is the most natural thing in the world. "Why? This is noth-ing. Level one tears, at best."

"Jesus Christ."

"Do they make you uncomfortable?" She toes off her sandals and wades into the water, her curious attention drifting over to me. "You don't have to answer that. You look like you're being suffocated by a giant squid. My parents didn't love the crying, either."

With a grunt, I strip off my shirt and toss it down onto the shore. After flipping on the safety of my gun and leaving it close, I quickly follow her into the water. There are a lot of slippery rocks out there. I should probably stay near her, just in case she stumbles across one of them. "Your parents were hard-asses like mine?"

"Not hard-asses. Just really courageous. Their job requires them to be levelheaded and unselfish at all times. To focus on the greater good. No time for breaking down or giving in to messy emotions. It's a waste of time. You probably agree with that, don't...?"

Her question trails off when she glances back at me.

Abruptly, she stops wading, color filtering into her cheeks.

I raise an eyebrow, ready to prompt her into finishing the question. Then I realize why she's distracted. I could have sworn I took my shirt off last night when we were burning the world down, but apparently not. Her shell-shocked expression says it's definitely the first time she's seeing me bare from the waist up. Those eyelids of hers are filling with more and more sand by the minute. Damn, she likes what she sees. Against my better judgment, I make a mental note of that, too. Taylor doesn't mind thick. Doesn't mind the chest hair or the tattoos.

Or the various knife scars.

Nah, she likes it all a lot. How in the *sweet hell* am I going to keep my hands off this woman? "You were saying, Taylor?"

"Was I saying something?"

Her husky tone of voice puts more than a little life in my cock. "You were asking me if I agree with your parents. That crying is a waste of time."

"I would rather you didn't answer. You'll ruin..." She waves her hand in the general direction of my torso. "This. That."

Damn, she came right out and said she likes my body. I'm as surprised as I am turned on. The fact that I'm thrown off by her unabashed response is probably why I ask my next stupid question. "Better than an MBA?"

She purses her lips, clearly opposed to giving me the satisfaction. "Better?" Turning and continuing into the water, she flips her hair back. "I don't know about that. *Different,* maybe."

I'm grinding my jaw as I follow, my mouth going dry over the water lapping up and over her knees, skimming up the backs of her thighs. Thighs I would give my life savings to have wrapped around my face, if I thought for a second I could have a fling with Taylor and still maintain a level head while I'm in Cape Cod. Where my concentration is concerned, unfortunately, I'm already on thin ice. "Yeah. I do agree with your parents. But that doesn't mean *everyone* has to live...suppressed. Levelheaded all the time. The world would be a pretty cold place without the criers."

I draw even with her and she looks up at me slowly. Cautiously. "You think so?"

"Yeah." I clear the weirdness from my throat, liking the hope in her eyes a little too much. Especially when it's directed at me. "Now people who sing Kelly Clarkson in the shower? We can probably take or leave them."

A smile blooms across her mouth and she laughs, the light, tinkling sounds traveling around the cave. When she visibly reels her pleasure back in, I almost grab her shoulders and shake it back out of her. Gently, of course.

"What are you thinking about?"

That marks the first time in my life I've ever asked anyone that question.

"I was remembering the way Jude used to encourage me to cry when he could tell I needed a good jag. Thank God for my brother."

All right, he's more than decent. I might have to be nice to him, too. Fuck my life.

"And then I started wondering why don't you talk to *your* brother?"

Discomfort snakes into my middle. "I told you. He's a

prick."

"But couldn't you be pricks together?"

She smiles at me to let me know she's joking and I come very close to smiling back, despite the uncomfortable topic. "He doesn't exactly agree with my career path. He wants me to come back to Boston and open the private investigation firm, like we planned." I rake an irritated set of fingers through my hair. "Like nothing ever happened, you know?"

"You mean with Christopher's kidnapping?" she asks quietly.

"Yes," I half-shout, before softening my voice for her. She remembered his name? "Yes."

"What does your brother think about what happened?"

"Kevin? He..." Saying any of this out loud is like having my organs removed with pliers. "Right after it happened, he said there is one in every detective's career that hits harder and this was mine. And it's worse because a child is involved. He doesn't think the right solution was obvious, but that's a hard pill to swallow when I can look back and see it clearly."

Christ. This is the last thing I wanted to talk about today. Or any day.

But maybe it's a good thing, because it reminds me I'm not here to play boyfriend to a sexually frustrated second grade teacher from Connecticut who wants kids and a husband and the whole nine yards. "I'm only investigating Oscar's murder because I owed a friend a favor, but I don't belong doing this. Official investigations. It's a one-time deal."

"And you're afraid of messing it up."

I start to deny it, but hell, she's right. "Yeah. Fine. Who wouldn't be?"

"I don't know," she murmurs, studying me closely. Too

closely. "Maybe someone who isn't punishing themselves so hard."

My throat constricts. "You don't know anything about it, Taylor."

Despite my forbidding tone, she isn't done pursuing this. Am I relieved or angry about it? I have no idea. Only that I'm not budging and neither is she. "I know you were invested in the case because of a childhood friend you lost. Not for selfish reasons. Or negligence—not you. You're right, I don't know all of the details, but I know you must have had good intentions."

"Good intentions aren't enough in a life or death situation. Like this one." The need to distract from the wounds inside of me, wounds becoming more and more visible by the moment, wins. "What happened last night shouldn't happen again, all right? I'm responsible for letting it get that far and I'm sorry. But I just want to solve this case and get back to hunting bounties. There's no room for a diversion."

"Okay." She's flippant, but there's something up her sleeve. I can tell. And by the way, I already want to take back everything I just said, even though I can't. Even though putting a stop to this budding...whatever is the right thing for both of us. "Just do me a favor, Myles. If you're not interested in distractions with me, don't tell my other prospects to fuck off."

Damn. Caught. "How..."

"I saw your reflection in Ryan's sunglasses. *Idiot.*"

Hearing her say another guy's name out loud twists up my nerve endings like a fork twirling spaghetti. "Oh, I'm sorry." I lean down until our noses are almost touching. "You *want* flippity flop guy?"

"Better than a panty thief." She shakes her head. "Why did you steal them anyway? Red isn't really your color."

I'll burn them before you wear them for anyone else. That is the totally out of bounds chaos going on in my head. And no way can I let it come out of my mouth. "I'm saving you from putting them on for a guy like that—and being disappointed."

She presses her nose—her cute, perfect little nose—right up against mine. "Who I wear them for is none of your business."

I'm rapidly forgetting my firm resolution to keep a safe distance. To treat her less like a desirable woman and more like a part of the investigation. My brain is firing off warning signals, trying to remind me what happens when I stop being objective. I'm feeling too many things at once when it comes to her and I don't know how to subdue something this urgent.

What makes it worse is she *likes* the rougher side of me. Asked for it by name last night. She's all but inviting it out of me with her glazed eyes right this very second. They're glued to my mouth, her fingertips tracing the cuts of my abs.

"That so?" I press my lips tighter to hers. Flush. So we're trading breaths in a rush. "Get that mouth away from me before I fuck it again."

Her intake of breath is reedy. It's followed by a trembling moan. And I'm screwed.

I'm so beyond screwed.

And I'm almost angry about how thoroughly she sways me. Tempts me. I gather the front straps of her life jacket in my hands and yank the woman up onto her toes, her gasp bathing my lips and I just look at her. Look into her eyes and try and figure out what the fuck is so different about her. Which turns out to be a big mistake. Huge. Because she doesn't even blink. She lets me look and doesn't flinch away from the intimacy, the way I've always done. To avoid a situation where my guard will have to come down. No, she shows me she's not afraid of it and dares me to come join her, even as her pulse races in her neck. That's only one of the things that makes her different—her vulnerable courage —and like I said, I'm screwed.

Because her mouth is ripe and slick and pouty. And I know what kind of pleasure it gives when she's turned on. I'm erect, balls heavy, sweat rolling down my spine. I couldn't stop my mouth from raking side to side across her sweeter one if I had the willpower of ten thousand men. With a groan from deep in the recesses of my chest, I stop trying to fight the need that is simply too great. Still looking her in the eye, I unbuckle her life jacket and throw it down into the water. The rash guard is pulled off and thrown aside, leaving her tits out, covered by nylon triangles. God, she's sexy. I want her. Need her. Without the impediments between us, she just sort of melts into me, my hands delving into her bikini bottoms, clutching her buns and throwing her up against me.

We dive into a kiss as she lands, her thighs hugging my waist, and the relief of having her as close as I need her staggers me back a step. And my driving hunger demands that I untie my board shorts and finish what we started last night. Just give her the business right here in knee-deep water, fast and furious and necessary. But then she mewls against my mouth, our tongues stroke together and we sink into a real kiss, the kind we've been dancing around without following through and my knees...my fucking knees turn to jelly.

What is happening here?

I don't know. I'm too busy stealing as much of her taste as I can get. I'm greedy. I'm desperate. Twisting her lips with mine, right then left, my tongue occupying her mouth over and over again, with possession, with familiarity, growling when her heels dig into my ass and she climbs higher on my body, nails scoring my scalp, my back. It's a kiss more personal, more intimate than sex, at least any kind I've ever had and I physically cannot stop. She's so sweet. So addicting and...she's a match for something inside of me, as scary as that is to admit. But I don't have time to come to terms with it right now. Now when her taste is apples and ocean air and vanilla. And her pussy rides up and down against the aching ridge in my shorts, unconscious, hungry movements that I urge on with my tight handfuls of her ass.

"I've got a rubber in my wallet," I rasp when we break away, sucking down lungfuls of air. "We using it, sweetheart? Am I using it to give you a pounding?"

"Yes. Yes." She kisses my jaw, my mouth, nails digging into my shoulders. "Then maybe I can go back to making smart decisions."

Those words, spoken on a sawing inhale an exhale, twist a screwdriver between my ribs, even though I completely understand where she's coming from and I can't be mad at her. Couldn't fathom being angry with her right now, even if she sucker punched me. Not when she's clinging to me, giving me trust I'm not sure I've earned. I'm powerless to do anything but worship her. God, I just want to *worship* her.

Reluctantly taking one hand from her backside, I shove a hand into my pocket, bring my open wallet to my mouth and remove the condom with my teeth. Without taking my eyes off her beautiful green ones, I toss my wallet onto the shore and tear open the wrapper, pushing the ring of latex down the front of my shorts, gritting a curse when I encounter my stiffness. Jesus, I'm hard as nails. I'm going to come fast, so I'll need to give her clit a lot of attention to bring her over the edge with me. No way I'm leaving this woman behind.

"You're going to be so big inside me, aren't you? Big and mean," she whispers against my mouth. Then she dips down and scrapes my neck with her teeth, licking the sting away and colors—fucking *colors* are exploding behind my eyes. "You're going to keep me safe and make it hurt a little at the same time, aren't you?"

There's no word for the sound I make. It's hoarse and hungry and shocked and could only come from a man at the point of no return. She's killing me. I didn't know I liked to be...praised. Maybe I don't. Maybe I just like it from her. Maybe I'm already hooked on it. Yeah, I am. "Safe," I mutter thickly, walking her into the shadows, ripping at the strings of my shorts. "You're so safe with me, sweetheart, baby, going to cram you so full and kiss it when I'm done—"

"Help!"

At first, I swear to God, that's my dick talking. He *is* in dire need of some help. I'm throbbing, already letting beads of precome out into the condom, this beautiful woman has her back arched, waiting for me to fill her up, finally fill her up and give her the ride of her life.

But it's not my dick shouting for help.

It's someone else. Someone outside the cave.

No.

This is a nightmare. I'm asleep in bed having a goddamn nightmare.

"Help!" calls the voice again.

And then, *"Taylor!"*

Her eyes shoot wide, legs dropping down from my waist, her feet splashing into the water. "Oh my God, that's my brother. He sounds hurt." She flaps her hands, looking down at her aroused body. After a moment's hesitation, she stoops down and splashes herself with cold water, which—for my money—doesn't help matters whatsoever. Because now she's flushed and the bathing suit is clinging to everything, including her hard nipples. And yet, she tries to charge out of the cave like that.

I catch her around the waist by the crook of my elbow, hauling her to a stop mid-air.

Still speechless with the worst case of blue balls mankind has ever seen, I carry her over to the rash guard and hand it to her wordlessly. "Thanks," she murmurs, puling it over her head and splashing to shore, running out into the sunshine. It takes me a breathing exercise and remembering a particularly grisly crime scene to make my erection subside, but it finally loses the worst of its vigor and I follow Taylor out of the cave while pulling on my shirt and securing my gun back in place.

Everyone is standing around Jude on the beach, watching Taylor fuss over him.

Jesus. His foot has blown up to the size of a cantaloupe.

"Jellyfish got him," the instructor informs me when I make my way over to the group. "No worries. One of the fellas already pissed on it."

"That would be me," Ryan informs Taylor, before glancing back at me, turning pale and taking a giant step away from her.

"Looked like a sea nettle. Unless he's allergic to the venom, it'll just hurt for a couple of days," says the instructor. "He should be fine."

"Physically, anyway," Jude says, dazed. "I've been peed on, though, so...mentally? This calls for vodka."

"Let's get you back to the house." Taylor offers her shoulder for Jude to lean on. "We'll put you on the couch with an icepack and—"

They take a step and Jude winces, hissing a breath.

"Does it hurt to walk?" Taylor looks like she's about to

burst into tears.

Instead of standing here and acknowledging that her tears make my chest feel like a shipwreck, I shove my feet in my boots without bothering with socks or laces. Sighing, I stride forward. "I've got him. Go get the backseat of your car ready."

"You've got him? How—"

I scoop her brother up against my chest and head up the beach. "Taylor," I call back over my shoulder. "Backseat. Get it ready."

"Yes. Coming." She jogs past me and Jude, rubbing my arm and giving me a grateful look as she passes. I grunt at her back, cataloging every detail about her in a sweep.

She didn't put her sandals back on.

The parking lot asphalt is going to burn her feet, dammit.

I hurry to catch up in case she needs to be carried, too.

"This rescue would be a lot more romantic if you weren't mooning over my sister," Jude says, laughing while in obvious pain. "But it's pretty decent of you regardless."

"I'm just trying to save time. It would have taken you a week to hobble up to the parking lot and I'm on the clock."

"Whatever you say." I frown down at him, but his mouth only twitches. "You looked a little piqued coming out of the cave, bounty hunter."

"Shut up."

He laughs.

We reach the car a minute later and I set Jude on his feet, carefully, where he can lean against the side of the vehicle. As predicted, Taylor is hopping back and forth, trying to keep from burning off the soles of her feet. I wrap an arm around her waist and pull her up against me. "Stand on my boots."

"Oh," she whispers, her hands flattening on my chest, toes perching on mine through the thick leather. "Thank you."

I nod once, walking us around to the driver's side of the car, step by step, my forearm braced against the small of her back. I'm sure we look completely ridiculous and yeah, I could definitely just carry her, but there's something about this position I like. Maybe because she's looking me in the eye. Or because the twin movements of our legs feels like teamwork. Whatever the reason, it's dangerous, but that fact isn't going to penetrate my thick skull until she drives away and I can snap out of this trance she puts me in.

"I'm going to make tacos tonight," she says, looking at my chin shyly. "You have to fuel yourself for the investigation, right? You...I-I mean, if you'd like to come, it would be the least I could do after you carried my brother to the car like some kind of action hero."

"I was walking this direction anyway."

She smirks at me.

Don't kiss her. Don't even think about it. But Jesus, those lips are begging for me. "I'll be patrolling outside the house, in case the buoy thrower comes back. That constitutes doing my job. But I can't come to dinner, Taylor."

I say it with the kind of finality that she knows my staying away is about more than tacos. It's bigger picture. Spending time together. Every minute I'm around her, we get in deeper despite my best intentions. Despite the warnings I keep giving myself. This has to stop. Because I'm pretty sure if we'd gone any further in that cave, I'd be promising her the moon. I'd be promising her things I can't —and never have delivered on. I have no reason to believe I could suddenly be good at relationships. My last one was rocky from the start, not because of an abundance of fighting, but because I cared more about my career. Now? I've got a shit load of baggage and no permanent address, for crying out loud.

"Okay." She chews her bottom lip for a beat, then goes up on her toes and kisses me on the cheek. "Bye, Myles."

My chest rumbles.

And then she steps down off my boots and climbs into the driver's side. The instructor hands her forgotten sandals through the passenger side and Jude passes her the car keys from the backseat. With one more glance at me through the window, she pulls out and leaves.

I'm no longer touching her. And I damn well like touching her, which might be why I reach into my back pocket to stroke the lace of her red panties. Just to have *some* sort of contact—

They're gone.

I start, checking the other pocket. Not there, either.

Taylor stole back her hookup panties. Snuck them right out of my pocket. How did she know they were there in the first place? And what does it mean that she took them back?

Who I wear them for is none of your business.

"Son of a bitch," I mutter, popping an antacid into my mouth.

With a stomach full of broken glass, I return to the motel, determined to go over my case notes and plan my next moves. Not think about shit like red lace panties and women who cry over children being nice to each other.

Do your job and go home.

You'll forget her eventually.

Like in a hundred years or so.

Maybe.

Not even a little bit.

Fuck.

CHAPTER 11

Taylor

From the corner of my eye, I watch Myles's motorcycle drive past the house for the second time in an hour. The sky is beginning to darken, the smell of Saturday barbeques is in the air. Some cloud cover has drifted in, as it is wont to do on the Massachusetts coastline. There is a chance of rain, as usual, but it isn't stopping vacationers from enjoying the ocean, their flower-laden wrap-around porches and big, frosty pitchers of margaritas or cans of beer. The sound of laughing children and conversing adults drifts up from the beach on the snatches of music, breezing in through the open windows of the rental house.

I'm in the kitchen chopping up radishes. Onions are pickling in a bowl beside the sink.

Myles doesn't know what he's missing. I make insane tacos.

What is the big deal about coming to dinner, anyway? It's just food.

My knife pauses in the act of cutting a radish sliver.

What happened last night shouldn't happen again, all right? I'm responsible for letting it get that far and I'm sorry. But I just want to solve this case and get back to hunting bounties. There's no room for a diversion.

I'm distracting him. That's why he won't come eat my delicious taco.

Tacos. Plural.

I've had some time to reflect since we came back from the disastrous snorkeling outing. I took a really long bath and walked on the beach while Jude read a Sedaris book in the backyard hammock. And I'm beginning to develop a suspicion. When I told Myles this relationship was temporary and I wouldn't tangle him up in strings, he clearly didn't believe me.

Why would he?

I invited him to dinner. I told him about my childhood. I *cried* in front of him.

For godsakes, Taylor. The least I can do is *act* like hookup material. Of course he keeps retreating. He's being...decent. Isn't he? He's trying to do the right thing by keeping me at arm's length. Not only for the good of his investigation, but because he obviously doesn't believe I can have a totally guilt-free, uncomplicated fling.

And maybe, just maybe...he's right.

I don't know what happened this morning, but when he carried Jude to the car, I might have felt a weird flop in my chest. A very noticeable one. That flop sent reverberations all the way down to my toes and I...well. I did what any red-blooded woman would do when she experiences a very distinct chest flop.

I came straight home and Googled him.

Detective resigns after kidnapping case misfire.

When I saw the headline, I almost closed the browser tab. What kept me scrolling was the picture of Myles. Clean-shaven with dark, close-cropped hair, coming down the steps of a government building in a suit. All of his distinct lines were there. The brawn of his shoulders and the brittle irritation of his jaw. But he looked so different. Younger, less road weary.

I already knew the beginning of the story. Myles was working the Christopher Bunton case. But the three-year-old article helped fill in the blanks. He focused the investigation on the wrong suspect. A neighbor with a record of assault. A man with no alibi. A loner. But it had turned out to be the stepfather, a man heavily involved in the investigation and respected in the community who also wanted more freedom. Less of a financial strain on his bank account. He'd conspired with his sister to take Christopher across state lines and sell him to a couple he'd found on the internet who were willing to pay for an under-the-table adoption. By the time the investigation shifted, Christopher had been living in his new home for a month. In bad conditions. Not being fed properly. Sharing a room with four other children. Sent out every day to beg on the street and bring home what he earned.

Traumatized Boy Returned to His Mother.

That was the second article that mentioned Detective Myles Sumner.

He'd failed to mention he'd solved the case. Brought the boy home.

Of course he'd completely left that part out.

Myles is mean and rough—actually, more like serrated —around the edges and spectacularly crass. But thanks to him continuously proving he's more than just his bad temper and surly attitude, I am utterly intrigued by him and my attraction to him is sprouting teeth. Sharp ones that dig in a little more every time he rumbles past on his bike and I feel the vibrations on my inner thighs, my belly twisting long and low. I've been left hanging twice now, reaching a sexual high and not seeing it through to completion and I'm not going to lie, it's beginning to get to me.

Bright and early tomorrow morning, I'm going to the local sex toy shop.

Needs must.

I must.

There is no way I can make it another five days without an orgasm after being driven so thoroughly to the edge. I'm going to buy the newest model they've got with all of the bells and whistles and then I'm going to take it with me on the longest clawfooted bath time in history. Tomorrow morning, this vacation truly begins.

Myles rides past on his bike again.

I stab a radish with the tip of my butcher knife.

Something is different this time, though. He stops and parks outside of the house. I hear a woman's voice mingle with his guttural tone. Is he talking to someone? Setting down the knife, I leave the kitchen and cross the living room to look out the front window.

Lisa Stanley. Oscar's sister is outside. She's halfway up the steps to our porch, but she appears to have stopped to speak with Myles.

"I just thought I would swing by to check on the house. And the Basseys, of course," she says brightly. "The broken window is being replaced tomorrow and I wanted to make sure they'll be here to let the men in."

Myles's grunt reaches me through the door. My mouth tugs at one end.

I'm starting to enjoy his caveman sound effects.

The silence ticks by.

"Anyway," Lisa sings awkwardly. "I'm sure you're busy with the investigation we hired you for..."

"I'll be coming in with you. I have some questions to ask you, anyway."

The bounty hunter's tone leaves no room for discussion. Is he...suspicious of Lisa? Before that question is fully formed, I'm shaking my head. Of *course* he's suspicious of her. Everyone is a suspect to Myles. Except us now, thankfully.

Not wanting to be discovered hovering behind the door, I open it and give Lisa a sad smile. I can't imagine what this week has been like for her. "Hi Lisa. How are you?"

She's obviously relieved to see me after Myles's abrupt greeting. "I'm hanging in there, darling. How are you?"

I'm slightly caught off guard when Oscar's sister embraces me. With my chin unexpectedly perched on her shoulder, I watch Myles jolt forward on the stairs, his fingers flexing at his sides, like he wants to reach for me. Or us? What is up with him?

"Hey Myles," I murmur.

He dips his chin at me, his gaze intense but guarded. "Taylor."

I tug out of Lisa's arms and gesture to the house. Through the screen door, I can hear Jude hobbling in from the backyard. "We're about to have tacos if you want to join us. I just have to brown the meat."

"Oh no, I won't keep you," Lisa says, rubbing at the back of her neck. Probably because Myles is drilling a hole in it with his eyes. Oscar's sister glances back at him with noticeable nerves. "Will you be here tomorrow between one and three? I just need you to let in the window guys for a few hours."

"Of course. I'll make sure one of us is here."

Jude darkens the doorway to my right and holds out two uncapped beers to our visitors. "Thank God you're both here," says my brother. "Someone has to help us drink all this beer."

Chuckling, Lisa only hesitates a second before wrapping her hand around one of the bottles. "I'll just have a few sips. Lord knows I earned it. Today has been the day from hell. The second one this week!"

I gesture for Lisa to come inside and she glides past me, linking her arm with the one Jude offers. He explains his injury to our temporary landlord on their way over to the kitchen where Jude offers her one of the stools placed in a row along the island, then takes one across from her. Myles watches them over the top of my head, a muscle ticking in his jaw.

"What is up with you?" I whisper.

"Just stay close to me."

He doesn't give me a choice. He's hot on my heels all the way back to the kitchen, positioning himself with a hip against the counter adjacent to the stove. His attention seems to be everywhere at once. On Lisa, on the meat I'm cooking. He tips my elbow up a little when I'm adding the chili powder and I smack his hand away—and the action causes an immediate pause in Lisa and Jude's conversation.

"You two certainly seem to be well acquainted," Lisa remarks, turning my face crimson.

"That buoy was a clear threat. She could have been hurt." He is staring at Lisa with such intense speculation, it's a wonder she hasn't burst into flames. "I plan to find out who did it. In the meantime, the Barnstable PD can't spare a patrol car to watch their Connecticut asses, so it's just going to be me. For now."

"You requested protection for us?" I ask, my spatula suspended in animation.

"I asked for protection *in addition* to me. I wouldn't trust you to someone else." He takes a long pull of his beer. "You're going to burn that meat, half pint."

So I am.

I fumble with the burner knob, twisting it into the off position. "What do you care if I incinerate it? You said you wouldn't have dinner with us."

"That was before I smelled what's going on here." He jerks his chin at the kitchen island where I've set up the taco bar. "You pickling those onions?"

"That's right."

This time, his grunt has the clear ring of approval.

I'm shaking my head at him and smiling at the same time. I'm losing my mind. "Excuse me," I say, shooing him back a few steps so I can get a bowl out of the cabinet he's blocking. Before everyone got here, I was climbing up onto the counters to retrieve various serving dishes, since they are all on the top shelf. Now I stand there, frowning at the big bowl on the top ledge, waffling over doing the same thing with an audience. Especially the landlord.

"What do you need?" Myles asks, setting down his beer.

I point at the bowl on the highest shelf. His lips jump, but thankfully he manages to hold in whatever joke he wants to make about my vertical challenges. He steps into my personal space before I have a chance to move out of the way, his hand sliding along the small of my back to my hip, settling there. Squeezing. Twisting a bolt in my abdomen that seems to be connected directly to my sex. All while he easily plucks the serving bowl off the upper shelf.

Apparently I'll be going vibrator shopping tonight, instead of tomorrow morning.

The speculative silence from Lisa and Jude is deafening.

"Um. Lisa." I wet my parched lips. "Why has it been the day from hell?"

She groans loudly. After a moment of digging through her purse, she pulls out a neon green flyer and smacks it down on the island. "Would you look at this...this crusade to ruin the livelihoods of honest, business-savvy people? It's Mayor Robinson again. Coming after folks like my brother for renting homes. Homes they *own*. This whole rigamarole about the peepholes is only adding fuel to her fire."

Myles and I trade a look. He shakes his head very slightly and it's obvious what he's telling me. Don't say anything about the press conference in front of Oscar's house. I have to assume that means he doesn't want me mentioning anything else about this morning, either, including the letter we found in the floorboard.

Jude picks up the flyer, gaze traveling across the page. "She wants to put a ban on vacation rentals in Cape Cod?"

It's a good thing I haven't gotten around to telling Jude. I haven't told him a lot about developments in the case because a. I don't want him to worry that I'm too involved. And b. because I want him to focus on relaxing. Leave the murder to me.

"Yes, she does." Lisa already has most of her beer drained. "To be fair, she is getting a lot of heat from the year-round residents to make changes. They don't like the constant turnover of out-of-towners. A few loud parties are ruining it for the rest of us."

"Don't forget a murder," Myles interjects, bottle poised in front of his lips.

"That is hardly dinner conversation," I whisper at him, accompanied by an elbow nudge. To Lisa, I say, "Do you think the mayor will succeed?"

"I don't know. She's holding a big rally in town tomorrow. It's building steam." Lisa sighs and slumps in her stool a little, but when I set down the bowl of meat and plate of taco shells, gesturing for everyone to dig in, she begins piling her plate with the rest of us. "You know..." starts Oscar's sister. "I've been thinking." She glances toward the back bedroom. "What if that buoy was meant as a warning for me?"

"What would the suspect be warning you about?" Myles gives me a pointed look. "It's not like *you're* meddling in the investigation. You're not involved."

"My boyfriend hired you," Lisa points out.

Myles adds enough hot sauce to his taco to kill a goat. "Yes. But if we're operating under the belief that whoever threw the buoy through the window also killed your brother, they are almost definitely aware you don't live here, Ms. Stanley. They're close enough to the investigation to know the Basseys relocated to this rental property."

Perhaps that fact should have occurred to me before, but it hasn't. Not until now.

"You think we're being watched." When did I move closer to the bounty hunter? I don't know, but his ample body heat keeps me from losing my appetite completely. "Are we definitely ruling out the random buoy theory?"

"That was never a theory," Myles answers, chomping into his taco. He chews for a few seconds while I try desperately not to name his throat muscles. Connor, Wilson, Puck...Jameson. "This is a good fucking taco."

The race is on to stem the flow of pride that races through me. I don't manage it. At all. "Thank you. I know." I take a normal, human-sized bite of my taco. "Aren't you glad you decided not to be stubborn?"

He tosses the other half of the taco into his mouth. The *whole other half*. "Yeah," he says around the bite. "Could have added a little more chili powder, though."

"You had to ruin it." I kick him in the shin.

He pokes me in the side, eyes twinkling, his attention drifting down to my butt.

He drains his beer.

My hips press unconsciously to the island, goosebumps rising on my neck. Down my arms. Dear Jesus, how late does this sex shop stay open? I swear if I get there and the doors are locked, I'm going to cut a hole in the ceiling and rappel in like James Bond.

"What makes you think the buoy was meant for you, Lisa?" I ask.

She shrugs jerkily. "Just a weird feeling I've been having. Like...I don't know. An eerie presence is following me around." Her laughter is forced. "I'm sure the weird feeling has been brought on by the terrible way my brother died."

I reach across the island and squeeze her forearm. "You're traumatized. Of course."

Jude hands Lisa a napkin to wipe her eyes, patting her back with a comforting hand.

I lean sideways a little too dramatically, trying to see some actual tears.

Come on, woman, give me one.

Myles tosses a picture of the potential murder weapon down right in the middle of the taco bar. "Do you recognize this gun?"

"Myles," I gasp.

He weighs my outrage, then visibly decides to proceed anyway, the jerk. "Lisa?"

With a heavy swallow, she picks up the photograph. "I don't recognize it." She lets it drift back down to the island. "Paul keeps a Beretta locked up in a safe. That's the only weapon I have access to."

"I didn't ask if you had access to it."

She pauses in the act of reaching for a second taco shell, drawing her hand back slowly. Me and Jude are staring at each other like stone statues, eyebrows up near our hairlines. It reminds me of how we would freeze during rare arguments between our parents, not knowing how to intervene or if we should leave the room. "I'm going to head home. Oscar's estate lawyer is dropping off a bunch of documents bright and early in the morning and he claims they're important," Lisa says finally, smile tight, sliding off the stool. "Don't forget to let in the window guys tomorrow afternoon."

"We're on it," Jude says, saluting her.

Myles growls until she's out the door.

I start to follow in her footsteps, intending to engage the lock behind her, but Myles hooks a finger in the back waistband of my skirt and tugs me backward, performing the task himself.

"Lisa is your main suspect, isn't she?" I whisper when he returns. "Oh my gosh, that was like something straight off the ID channel. I didn't see it coming. I mean, of course it's always the people closest to the victim, but—"

"Take a deep breath, half pint."

Jude slides me his beer and I take several gulps.

"You caught her off guard with the picture on purpose, didn't you?" This comes from Jude.

Myles shrugs. Goes back to doctoring a second—possibly third taco.

"Come on, bounty hunter. Give us something." I give him a flirtatious shoulder shimmy, but he only looks exasperated by it. "Don't I get brownie points for finding the murder weapon?"

"Ballistics haven't come back yet." He frowns at me while devouring the taco. Is he caving on sharing information with us? He looks like he's caving. I give another shoulder shimmy, just in case, and he sighs. "Spoke to Oscar Stanley's lawyer today. Lisa Stanley is the beneficiary of her brother's estate. All of these rentals become hers now."

My brother and I slap the island in unison. "Follow the money trail," Jude says. "Don't I always say follow the money trail?"

"Yes. You do." I nod at Myles. "He does. Any time we watch *Dateline* together. My brother has a very analytical brain. It's incredible."

"Great," Myles says dryly. "Look, it's not a wrap. She's just a person of interest. To me, anyway. The cops still have a hard-on for the father."

"I've seen that porn."

"Jude!" I snort. Then I click an imaginary pen and get down to business. "So. Currently our suspects are Judd Forrester, Lisa Stanley and Sal next door?"

The bounty hunter's eyebrows draw together. "I never said Sal was a suspect."

"Don't you watch *Fear Thy Neighbor*? Sal *hates* renters. Oscar owned four properties on this block alone. Couldn't the revolving doors on all sides of his house drive Sal to a murder of passion?"

"There are a few holes in that theory." He ticks them off on

his long fingers. Do *not* name his fingers. Joe, Hubert, Rambo...
"One, this wasn't a crime of passion. Whoever murdered Oscar
Stanley waited until the whole town was occupied with Fourth
of July celebrations. Not to mention utilizing the fireworks to
mask the sound of gunfire. All of that speaks to premeditation.
Two, Sal nearly shit his pants when I told him to leave you
alone or risk having that broom handle shoved up his ass. And
three, he was at a barbeque in Provincetown on the night of
the murder. Confirmed by several witnesses."

"Wow." I'm so turned on I can barely breathe. "You've
done a lot of work."

He gives me a meaningful look. "That's why I'm here."

I'm back to wanting to kick him. "So right now, the
suspects are Lisa and Forrester?"

"For now. Forrester has an unregistered Glock—like the
one you found on the beach, Taylor. Barnstable PD brought
him back in for questioning and he claims it isn't his. I still
don't like him for the murder, but obviously we can't rule
him out."

Jude hobbles to the fridge for another beer. "Okay,
moving on to the second person of interest. Why would Lisa
want the murder investigated if *she* pulled the trigger?"

"The perp likes to insert themselves into the investigation," I murmur, recalling what Myles told me yesterday,
echoing the criminal trait I've heard many times before on
Etched in Bone. They always return to the crime scene.

Something else occurs to me and I gasp.

"If the murderer ends up being Lisa, you'll have to break
the news to your friend, Paul."

"Yeah." He clears his throat hard, sets down his half-
eaten taco. "I'm heading out now. Lock the door behind me.
Keep the windows closed and secure. I'm going into town to
check in with the police, then I'll be back."

This is it. My chance to sneak out to the sex shop. I'm going to walk straight in there and ask for the vibrator with the earthquake setting.

"Sounds good," I respond with a grin.

His eyes narrow suspiciously at my bright tone and I busy myself with cleaning up.

Myles looks like he wants to say something, but he turns and leaves, closing the door with a firm click behind him.

Jude steps into my line of vision. "All right. What are you up to?"

There are some things a girl can't even tell her non-judgmental best friend/brother. As in, I'm so hard up for an orgasm that I'm sneaking out while there is a murderer on the loose. "Nothing." I hide my face behind a cabinet, pretending to search for something. "That was me trying not to point out to Myles that he's finally sharing clues. I was trying to be casual."

"Right." Jude opens his mouth to say more, but his phone vibrates in his pocket. He pulls it out and looks at the screen, shoving it right back into hiding. "If you're sneaking out behind Mad Myles's back, I'm coming with you, though. Just to be safe."

"I'm going to buy a vibrator," I blurt.

"Cool." He limps over to the counter and scoops up his keys, waggling his eyebrows at me when the roar of the motorcycle engine recedes into the darkness. "I'll grab a drink at the closest bar while you browse."

CHAPTER 12

Myles

I knew Taylor had something up her sleeve.

Not in my wildest imagination did I think it was this.

Across the street from the Sweet Nothings—the most discreet sex toy shop I've ever seen in my life—I sit on my bike in the shadows, watching as she casually strolls past the entrance, waiting until she's alone on the sidewalk, passersby having ducked into the tavern next door. Then she backs up one step at a time, throwing herself into the shop in a blur.

Just like that, she's in a sex toy boutique. *You've got to be joking.*

Am I pissed? Hell yeah, I'm pissed.

The fact that she would put herself at risk by coming out at night without me means my skin is roughly the temperature of the sun. At least she brought Jude with her. Initially, that gave me *some* form of relief. But after they parked in the municipal parking lot, they parted ways on the other side of the road. Jude vanished into the tavern and I can see through the window that some fella has already bought him a drink. He's distracted. Who is with Taylor now? *No one*, that's who. And far stranger things have happened than a woman being assaulted or abducted in public. Goddammit.

I get off my bike and start to pace.

It takes me about fifteen seconds to admit that Taylor's recklessness is only partially to blame for my fevered skin. My sweaty palms and jumpiness.

She wants—needs—an orgasm so bad, she's risking her neck for it.

And I'm to blame.

That isn't arrogance talking, although, sue me if it is. I've brought her to the brink of climaxing twice without delivering. Thanks to a rogue buoy. Thanks to Jude getting stung by a jellyfish. Sure. But that doesn't make the facts sit any better. Not at all. She's horny, I'm the cause, and she's about to get the relief she needs from somewhere else.

That's not just a bitter pill to swallow, the damn thing is stuck in my throat.

Yeah.

Yeah, I don't think I'm capable of letting this happen. I'm just not. I'm sure this makes me an intrusive bastard, but I can't fucking stand the idea of her sailing over the edge with some piece of silicone when I'm the one who drove her there. Created the need in the first place. Until now, I was using the fact that we haven't had sex to console myself, as agonizing as it has been to maintain that boundary—one that I've almost crossed twice now. As long as we don't have sex, I'm focused. As long as I'm not sleeping with her, I can maintain my professionalism and objectivity. Right?

Yeah.

Only...Taylor's pleasure coming from anywhere but me makes me want to kick a hole through the plate glass window advertising lingerie, massagers and aromatherapy in gold script. What is she picking out in there? Will I be able to stand by while she drives home with her purchase and uses it to get herself off?

Nope.

No way in hell.

"Son of a bitch," I mutter, preparing to stride across the side street.

Before I get the chance, she exits the shop, a small purple bag clutched to her chest. Instinct has me scanning the immediate area for any kind of threat. By the time I'm done, she's already walking at a fast clip toward the lot where she parked. Alone. At night. In a strange town. Holding a bag from a sex toy shop. What the hell is in that bag?

Telling myself it's none of my business doesn't help. Nothing short of giving her the orgasm myself is going to help—that's the truth. And with that very ill-advised, very tempting thought circling my mind, I follow her into the parking lot. Just to make sure she's safe. That's what I tell myself. I'm just going to make sure she gets to the car without incident, but when she turns around and spots me, eyes widening, quickly attempting to hide the bag behind her back, this dangerous combination of affection and lust propels me forward, closer, closer until we're toe to toe. Until her back is pressed up against the side of the car.

"Hey Taylor," I say, planting my hands on the roof of her car.

"H-hey." Oh Jesus, she's so excited about whatever she

just bought, her pupils are the size of hockey pucks. "What are you...are y-you following me?"

"I'm protecting you."

"Oh, right." She wets her lips and my blood rushes south, stiffening my dick right up. "H-how long would you say you've been protecting me? Ten minutes? Two?"

"Long enough to know it's not sunscreen in that bag."

"Maybe it's tampons," she says quickly. "Very private. For my eyes only."

"I'm not falling for that."

"You're not?"

"No."

"Oh." She is still trying to keep the bag stuffed behind her back. "Well, I was just going to leave this in the car and go get Jude. I don't want to walk into the bar with...whatever it is."

I bring our mouths closer and her breathing accelerates. "What is it?"

"None of your business, Myles."

My lips brush sideways across hers, making her eyelids droop. "Your unsatisfied pussy is my business and we both know it, Taylor. We've been edging each other for days."

She shudders. "Can you please stop talking to me like that?"

"Why? You like it too much?"

"Yes," she whispers.

"Give me the bag."

"What are you going to do with it?"

"It depends what's inside."

"Just some lavender oil."

"And?"

She squeezes her eyes shut. "Something called a G-spot Thumper."

"Really." I drop my right hand and I bring it up between her thighs, gripping her pussy tight beneath her skirt. Yeah. No fucking way something called a G-spot Thumper is taking the honor of making her come away from me. "What about your clit?"

"It does that, too," she whispers in a rush, her free hand curling in the front of my T-shirt. "There's a nubby thing."

"Good. Give me the bag, sweetheart."

She wedges it in between us, eyes unfocused.

After one more slow rub of her flesh through her dampening panties, I take the bag. Toss the tiny bottle of oil onto the roof of the car. "We won't need that."

"But—"

I rip the vibrator package open with my teeth.

"Oh boy. Look at you. Um…" A dizzy headshake. "The salesgirl said it might be partially charged, but she wasn't sure…" I press the button and it fires to life. "Oh," she rasps, mesmerized by the vibrating purple toy. "There it goes."

I work her skirt up to her waist, leaving it loosely bunched there. God almighty, those thighs. That ripe-looking mound in between them. *Mine. For right now.* "I shouldn't be doing this, Taylor."

"I know," she says breathlessly. "I'm distracting you from the investigation."

"An investigation that you're a part of, whether we like it or not."

"Uh-huh."

Stop talking. Now. You say too much to this woman. "But that way you kiss me? Like you're curious and overwhelmed at the same time? The perfect rhythm of your hips when you rubbed on my cock this morning, begging to get banged. And Christ, the way you sucked me off…" I spit on the vibrator and shove it into her sunshine yellow underwear, grinding the vibration right where she needs it, listening to her stuttered moan, memorizing the shock of pleasure that transforms her expression. "I already know you'd be the best fuck I'd ever had by a million miles and that's making it very hard to stay out of these panties, Taylor, you understand me?"

"Yes yes yes."

"I'm going to handle this mean little throb, because it's all for me, isn't it?" She nods unevenly, and gratification like I've never known spreads inside me like spilled paint on a canvas. Responsibility, possessiveness. Shit I never expected to feel in my lifetime. "We're going to take care of this ache and get back to work, you hear me?"

"Loud and clear," she says in a rush.

"You tell me when you're ready to have it inside of you."

"*Now.* I'm...I'm..."

I drag a finger through her slit, coming out of it soaked. "A wet little thing. Aren't you?"

She's already starting to shake. Jesus. Jesus, she's trembling. Lips parted. Eyes glassy, thighs restless, back arched. It's taking every iota of willpower not to give her this cock up against the side of the car, but there is an unseen collar around my neck, put there in the name of self-preservation. If I have sex with this woman, if I indulge us without rules or boundaries, there will be no turning back. Somehow I know that with total certainty. I won't be able to stay away when this is all over. Hell, I can barely keep away now. And if something happened to her...if I got distracted and missed something like last time...

I kiss her, hard, refusing to think about it. Kiss her so long and with so much hunger that we're both sucking in oxygen by the time we come up for air.

"Myles," she whimpers against my mouth—and I know

exactly what she's asking for. So I look her in the eye and pump the curved, spit-slicked end of the vibrator into her pussy, slowly, slowly, until my knuckles meet her damp lips and she's sobbing. "Please, please," she chants. "*Please.*"

Goddamn. It's happening again. Just like in that cave, just like in that bedroom before the buoy crashed in, I'm losing myself. I'm sinking into her so completely, nothing else matters. There's no parking lot, no street, no crime to solve. If that isn't a warning signal, I don't know what is, but I can't keep my mouth from raking over her soft one, capturing her whimpers and twining our tongues together in a way that says, *yeah, that's right, I'll fuck you so nasty, you'll never be the same.* Can't stop myself from pressing that vibrating nub to her clit and loving the way she jerks between me and the car, her thighs hot and restless around my hand.

And we're in this other place right now, this place with no pretenses, so I open my mouth and everything I've been keeping trapped in my head comes pouring out.

"You're so beautiful, sweetheart." Keeping her clit stimulated, I work the thick curve in and out of her wet entrance. Nice and slow and deep, deep, deep, pressing when I can't go any further. Grinding. Listening to her gasp and beg for more. "Your eyes. Your smile. Yeah, you've got me dying over those, then you throw in that ass. *God.* I'd kill to hit this from the back. Hell if you don't move in a way that says you're ripe and tight where it counts."

"Oh my God, stop. Stop. No, don't stop. Don't stop." Her mouth is on mine, hungry, tongue kinky, hand gripping my shoulders as if she'd like to climb me and never come down. Not sure I would let her, either. "Pretend," she cries into our next kiss. "Pretend it's you."

Just when I think she's done blowing my mind.

Later, later maybe I'll stare into space and marvel over this second grade teacher asking me to play-fuck her with a vibrator, but right now? Ah Jesus, all I can do is comply. I position the toy in front of my bulging zipper, flatten her upper half against the car and I fuck her with the vibrating silicone. As if it's attached to me. I'm painfully aware that it's not, but her enjoyment eclipses my agony. Her ass is squeaking ever-so-slightly up and down the car door, my hips thrusting between her semi-spread legs, vibrator sinking in and out, and she's biting on that bottom lip, tits puffing up and down, because here it comes, any second now she's going to get swallowed by an orgasm and I get to watch. Me. I have that privilege.

"Every time you use this thing, remember that my cock is bigger," I growl against her ear. "And I'm somewhere out there, thinking of you while I stroke it."

God help me. I'm not even inside of her, but I swear I feel her clench on the heels of those words. Her fingertips tear at the front of my shirt and she pants, whines my name, rolls her hips and works out the orgasm, her pleasure slipping down the vibrator and pooling in my palm. Coating my fingers. She rides the thrusting silicone, her thighs pulsing around my working hand, her tits swelling in the neckline of her dress and I just marvel. I damn well marvel.

"Masterpiece," I rasp, kissing her, muffling her cries. "You little fucking masterpiece."

"*Too much!*" she screams into my mouth after a few more seconds and I carefully tug the smooth curve from inside of her, slamming it down on the roof of the car and kissing her like my life depends on it, fingers tunneling into her hair. My cock is swollen and pounding in my jeans. She's wet. She's kissing me back, still horny. I could have her right here, right now. Next time she comes, I'd feel that cinch of her pussy around me and it would be heaven. I can finally get rid of this pain in my balls that I haven't been able to bring myself to handle alone because everything inside has her fucking name on it—

There is a loud slam behind me.

My life flashes in front of my eyes.

Mentally, I bolt out of the fog and assess the threat, gun pulled from the small of my back. Weapon pointed at the ground, I back Taylor between me and the car, looking for the source of the noise. And I realize with a sweep of relief that it's the door of the tavern. A group of rowdy young people are stumbling out of the bar, knocking the door into the side of the building in their exuberance. My adrenaline takes a nosedive and I'm suddenly covered in cold sweat. She's saying something to me, but I can't hear her over the ringing in my ears. Anything could have happened while I was kissing her with my back turned. *Anything.* Am I out of my mind to put her at risk like that? I'm not fit to be a detective. I'm not cut out for this. If I manage to solve this case and leave without anyone getting hurt, it'll be a miracle.

"Get in the car," I say to her, my voice like gravel. "Call your brother and tell him you're waiting. Both of you need to get home."

"Myles—"

"Please, Taylor. Just do it."

She looks like she wants to argue, but climbs into the driver's side, instead. Makes the call to Jude. A minute later, her brother comes out of the bar humming and I stride past him without saying a word, even when he calls my name.

I need to get my head back on straight. Now.

She's been satisfied. No more slip-ups now.

Not even when the slip-up tastes like redemption.

CHAPTER 13

Taylor

I hold up a handful of sand and let it sift through my fingers, the little grains carried off on the Sunday morning Massachusetts wind. The cool, misty air is exactly what I need on my skin after waking up from a dream about Myles this morning. If I was a good swimmer like Jude, I would fling myself into the Atlantic in an attempt to finally cool down, but I'm much better off watching my brother take a dip from the shoreline.

Turning on my butt in the sand, I look back at Myles standing at the top of the staircase leading down to the beach. A phone is pressed to his ear and he's speaking into it with that husky drawl, his eyes covered by Ray-Bans. His dark hair is blowing in the wind. From my vantage point down below on the beach, he's back to looking like an ancient highland warrior who time traveled and found himself clad in jeans and a hoodie.

When he spies me watching him, he pauses mid-sentence, jaw tightening. But he resumes his pacing conversation a moment later. Letting him see my exaggerated eye roll, I angle myself toward the ocean again in time to find Jude limping—only slightly now—out of the surf, slicking the hair back from his face and grinning. My smile blooms automatically.

"When did he get here?" Jude asks, holding his hand out for a towel.

I toss him the bundle of blue terrycloth embroidered with an anchor. "He's been here on and off all night. That's him. On and off. Hot and cold."

"What happened between you two in the parking lot last night?"

Even in the cool breeze, I'm suddenly swamped in heat, bombarded by images. The moving memories that caused me to toss and turn all night, only to finally fall asleep, wake up and find the sheets sweaty. Myles ripping open the packaging of my Thumper. Spitting on it. How his upper lip curled in a snarl every time he thrust the toy inside of me. His possessive kisses. The way he moaned when *I* peaked. Am I just supposed to carry on with my normal life after that frenzied public encounter? I don't see how that's possible. My clothes feel different, nerve endings on high alert, buzzing all the way to my hair follicles. I've been fired into a heightened state of awareness, then dropped from the mountain peak.

"In the parking lot?" It isn't the first time Jude has asked me. It's obvious that *something* happened. I took three wrong turns on the way home. I've been responding in one-word sentences, but now that I've processed—mostly—what happened, I need someone to confide in. "First there was some kissing." No need to go into detail. I'm not even sure I could say what happened without sweating through my yoga pants, anyway. "Then we broke up even though we were never dating in the first place. We've been ending our non-existent relationship since we met, actually. It's kind of our thing."

"Huh." Jude turns briefly and gives Myles a wry salute. "He just doesn't want to try the long-distance thing, or..."

I snort. "Oh, we are nowhere near dealing with practicalities like driving distance, whether or not our political views align or if he'll let me put up my Christmas tree in November. He claims I'm a distraction from the case. He..." It feels weird, talking about Myles's past out loud with someone else, but I remind myself this is Jude. "Before he turned to a life of nomadic bounty hunting, he sort of mishandled a kidnapping case in Boston. This is the first time he's investigated a crime since it happened and..."

"He doesn't want to mess it up."

"Yes." I pull my knees up to my chest, wrapping my sweatshirt-covered arms around them tightly. "He's punishing himself. And I have no choice but to let him. It's not like we're boyfriend and girlfriend or something. We've never even been in the same place at the same time without an argument breaking out."

"And yet he spent the night camped outside your window. And he's pacing at the top of the staircase wanting precious Taylor back inside where it's safe."

"Yes. Knowing Myles, he probably hasn't eliminated the ocean as a suspect."

Jude chuckles. Scoots closer to me in the sand and puts an arm across my shoulders. "Every once in a while, a guy comes along that throws you off balance, but you'll find your footing again."

"Has that happened to you?"

He scoffs, turns his face toward the far end of the beach. "Nope. I was just generalizing."

I hum in my throat. "Are you sure about that?" I ask, gently poking him in the ribcage. "I've always tried not to interfere in your relationships. I've never really had to, because you don't settle into them long enough to warrant a conversation. But..." His muscles are already tensing. He knows where this is going. "Do you want to talk about Dante?"

"God no." Water droplets fly in every direction when he shakes his head. "No. I definitely don't want to talk about Dante."

"Has he been calling you since we arrived?"

"Before we arrived. During. After. He won't give up."

"Give up on what? I thought you two were just friends?"

"We are," Jude rushes to say, slicing a hand through the wind. "Friends. Nothing more. He's straight, Taylor."

"I know..."

When they were younger, that seemed to be a concrete truth.

As they grew up, got further into high school...the fact that Jude's best friend dated girls exclusively didn't seem like such a given. How could Dante date when he was always with Jude?

"Dude plays Goliath in the Phantom Five franchise. Last I heard, he was moving in with Ophelia Tan—his gorgeous co-star. There is no mistaking his preferences and I wouldn't want to question them anyway. Dante is Dante. I would never want to change him. I just wish he would go live his incredible life and stop trying to...keep this going."

I can't hide my confusion. "Keep your friendship going?"

"It's complicated, T." He smiles to soften the steel in his tone. "Just trust me when I say it's complicated."

"Okay." I nod, lay my head on his shoulder. "I'll leave it alone."

His cheek rests on the top of my head. "Thank you." He's quiet for several moments. "I like uncomplicated a lot better, anyway. You?"

Wiggling my bare toes in the sand, I consider the question. "I don't know. I've been on dates with a lot of uncomplicated guys. They all have their tax portfolios and a best friend named Mark. They golf. They have a favorite dry cleaner. That's what I wanted. *Want*. But..."

"The bounty hunter is messing with your head?"

"He's like eating a spicy breakfast burrito after years of having oatmeal for breakfast."

He wraps his arm around me tighter. "Dammit, right?"

"Yup. Dammit."

"The worst part is...I like him. I *like* him. At first I thought he was flat out mean, but now I just find him honest. And when I think back to the dates I've been on with potential husband material, none of those conversations seem remotely authentic. I like being around Myles because I know exactly what I'm getting. He doesn't lie. Ever. And so when he says something meaningful or kind or complimentary, it's like...Christmas morning. That sounds so stupid—"

Someone clears their throat behind us.

My heart flies into my mouth, denial like a red-hot poker between my ribs.

Intuition is already telling me who just made that chugging sound.

And I'm right. It's Myles.

The bounty hunter towers behind us, boots sunk partially into the sand. Scowling.

That scowl is all for me, but his eyes? Those are soft. Surprised. Vulnerable.

"Hey, man," Jude says, finally breaking the awkward silence. Myles heard me. He obviously heard everything I said. Do I just adopt a new identity and join a commune now or what? How is this kind of thing usually handled? "Busy morning?"

Myles jerks out of his trance. Sort of. He's still looking at me. "What?"

"I said..." Jude isn't even bothering to suppress his smile. "Have you had a busy morning stalking my sister?"

"Protecting," he bites off.

"Right." Jude splits a look between the two of us. "Me and Taylor were just about to head up to the house and make some breakfast burritos."

"Funny," I mutter, finally gathering the wherewithal to stand up, dusting the sand off my butt. I face Myles reluctantly and it takes me a few beats to realize what's different about him. He doesn't know what to do with his hands. Usually they are confidently crossed or gesturing or making notes in his phone. But they just seem kind of lost in space right now. My embarrassment over being caught mooning over him—out loud—dissipates slightly. "Do you want to have breakfast burritos with us?"

He shakes his head. "No."

I blink at his abrupt tone. Nod. Start walking toward the stairwell.

"I have a meeting at the police station later this morning. Ballistics report is finally in," Myles explains, following me. "I need to get my ducks in a row first."

"I understand," I say, passing him a smile.

"I can't tell if you mean that."

"Our version of a breakfast burrito is basically everything that was in the taco last night, except the tortilla is soft and we add eggs," Jude says. "Taylor never lets leftovers go to waste."

"You can't tell if I mean what?" I ask Myles, the three of us stopping at the base of the stairs.

The bounty hunter plants both hands on his hips, searches the sand, as if trying to find an explanation. "It seems like you're not okay with me skipping burritos."

I'm completely confused. "So what?"

Now he's getting irritated. "So I just want to commence my day without you mad at me, Taylor. Is that so much to ask?"

"Since when do you care if I'm mad at you?"

"Hell if I know!" he roars.

"Usually we add avocado to the burritos, but we didn't find a ripe one at the market, so..." Jude scratches his eyebrow. "No avocado today."

Myles is back to having no idea what to do with his hands. I know what I would like him to do with them, but I'm really beginning to think letting this man touch me was self-destructive from the start because now it's all I can think about.

"What are you thinking about now?" Myles steps closer, narrowing his eyes and searching my face. "I can tell it's not good."

"My thoughts are private, Myles. Go get your ducks in a row."

"Fine. I'll come for the fucking burritos."

I throw up my hands. "Oh my *God*."

"We *tried* adding refried beans once, but that's a lot to handle first thing in the morning," Jude says, patting his stomach. Several beats pass. "Hey, can you two stop blocking the stairs so I can get the hell out of here?"

I step to the right. "Sorry."

Jude takes off hobbling as fast as possible on his injured foot.

"What is with you this morning?" I ask Myles.

He rakes a hand down his face, drawing my attention to the dark circles beneath his eyes, the weariness bracketing his mouth. "Everything was fine until I heard what you said about me."

My cheeks heat. I already strongly suspected he'd over-heard my confessions to Jude, but having it confirmed turns my face into a furnace. "I don't understand. It was difficult hearing that you have some positive qualities?"

"I don't know what it was."

"See? Honest. I like that about you. So *what*? Take me to court."

He looks like he's chewing an invisible stick. "Well I like that you're stubborn and compassionate. And brave, even though you don't see it."

Those words are a warm hug. A tight one that grows more and more snug until I have a hard time breathing. "Thank you."

With a succinct nod, he paces away from me to stare out at the ocean. It's incredible, really, what has been unlocked inside of me since the start of this trip. First, I realized I'm a lot stronger and more resilient than I ever knew. And now? Right this very moment? This blunt, infu-riating human is confirming it. What I've secretly hoped is true about myself all along—and I'm becoming more deter-mined than ever to embrace those more unshakeable parts of me.

What do I want?

Do I want to give up on this case I've become invested in? No.

Do I want to walk away from my acquaintance with this man leaving things undone?

No. If it was up to me, we would go back to his motel room this very second. There is a wealth of physical urges inside of me that I strongly suspect can only be tapped by Myles. Yes, I'm afraid of going home never having experienced them. But at the same time, I don't want to be a distraction to him. This man houses a lot of pain. He lashes out to hide it. And maybe I'm too soft in nature, but I can't stop wanting to help. As much as I want to prove to myself that I'm brave and viable, I also want Myles to realize he had one bad case back in Boston. That doesn't mean he has to walk away from his whole life. A career that he's obviously meant for.

Bottom line, he's holding me at a distance for a reason. I have to respect that.

But he's right. I'm stubborn.

I've wanted to help solve Oscar Stanley's murder since the beginning. To solve the puzzle and in the process, prove I'm more than just play it safe Taylor. Now I have the added wish to be of some assistance to Myles.

Whether he likes it or not.

Whether he *knows* it or not.

"Are you coming for burritos?"

"Yes," he growls, turning from the ocean and storming past me.

I smile at his back and follow. "I was thinking..."

"Jesus, here we go."

"Nothing bad. I just need some new reading material. And since you're so determined to babysit me, I was hoping to tag along into town with you this morning?" He stops abruptly when we reach the street, steadying me when I stumble. Eyeing me suspiciously.

I'm the very picture of guileless. Outwardly, at least.

"I just want to browse the library."

He's not buying it. "You're sure that's all you have planned?"

"I mean..." Needing to distract him, I smooth a palm up the center of his pecs and he gives an audible swallow, watching my hand as it moves upward, then back down in the direction of his belt buckle. "If you want to revisit the parking lot, I won't object."

"Taylor," he rasps, grasping my wrist, holding it away while he gets his breathing back under control. "Don't do this to me, sweetheart."

I pull my hand away, pretending his rejection doesn't make my throat hurt. Not when I grasp his purpose and sympathize with it. "Will you let me tag along or not?"

"Of course I will."

"Good." I force a smile onto my face, even as his rebuff continues to sting. It's rejection my brain understands, but my heart doesn't want to accept. "Let's eat."

He stands still in the middle of the road for another few seconds, a vein ticking in his temple, until he eventually follows.

CHAPTER 14

Myles

*W*hat am I going to do about this woman?

Taylor leans down to refill my coffee mug and it takes every ounce of my willpower not to take the pot out of her hand, set it down and pull her into my lap. In fact, I'm pretty goddamn positive it would feel like the most natural thing in the world. And the more I begin to admit things like this to myself, the more determined I am to keep my hands off of her.

When we first met, I decided she was the relationship type, the settling down kind.

Not for me.

She was *not* for me.

Then she throws me the rough sex curveball and I think, maybe...maybe I could give in and show her how it's done.

She proceeded to show *me* how it's done, instead.

Rougher. More.

Pretend it's you.

She's ruining me with her mouth and her trust and her apple-scented skin. I can't sleep or think straight, let alone focus on this case. And now...now that I overheard what she said about me on the beach, I'm exposed. I'm worrying about her feelings like it's my fucking job. I want to be the man she thinks I am. Maybe I always have been and I hadn't met the right woman for me yet. Maybe I've just been running so long I can't see myself clearly anymore. But when she smiles at me...I do. Or I start *trying* to see him.

I don't want to try, though. I've gone down the path of attempting to be good and noble and heroic and it turned out I was meant to be the villain. Being the villain has been easier than facing the past—and I never should have taken this case, either, because deep down, there *is* hope germinating. Hope that I can move forward from what happened. Taylor is watering that hope, giving it sunlight. But moving past what happened to that kid...no. No, I won't be absolved. I won't excuse my actions by letting go.

If I'm not careful, I'm going to have a repeat performance, too. With Taylor. I need to stay focused, protect her, figure out who killed Oscar Stanley and move on. End of story.

Unfortunately, my resolve is on seriously shaky legs.

Taylor returns to the coffee maker with the half-empty pot and I lean back to watch her walk. Because sweet Jesus, who sold her those tight pants? She might as well be naked. I can see the outline of her thong through the gray nylon. I have to grit my teeth against the urge to follow her into the kitchen and yank those buns up into my lap. Where they belong.

"You ready to go?" she asks, looking through her purse.

Totally unaware that she's making me hard and doing strange things inside my chest at the same time.

"Yeah." I shove away from the table and stand. "Just the library, right, Taylor?"

She blinks at me innocently. "Yes. Just the library."

Bullshit.

But we're going to see how this plays out. If I don't take her into town, she'll simply go on her own. There's no way I'll get any work done if I'm worrying about her safety. "You good to take my bike?" I ask on my way to the door. When she doesn't answer, I turn back around with my hand on the knob. "Half pint."

"I'm thinking about it."

I cross my arms and lean back against the entrance. "What has you worried?"

"Crashing." She is wringing her purse in her hands. "There is no hard outer shell on a motorcycle, Myles. Or airbags."

"I'm aware of that, Taylor."

"But I *am* trying to be braver." She comes toward me like a woman walking a plank, seconds from plunging into alligator-infested waters. "I suppose that means chancing death once in a while, right?"

Taylor talking about her own potential death is going to bring my breakfast back up. "You are never in danger if I'm with you," I say, caught off guard by my own confidence. Where is that coming from? Her? Because of what she said on the beach when she didn't know I was listening?

Now she blinks at me. "I know I'm safe with you. It's other people on the road I'm worried about." My pulse beats faster as she crosses the room toward me. "I trust you."

"Hmm." I can't look at her. Not with warmth spreading from my throat down to my stomach. "I guess I like that."

"Me trusting you?"

I grunt. Nod, in case the grunt didn't make my answer clear.

And she slips her hand into mine.

It feels so good, I almost pull away. Hand holding is not part of the job.

None of this is part of the job.

Yet here I am, leading her to my bike by the hand like a doting boyfriend. Putting my helmet on her head gently and helping her onto the rear of the seat. She looks so fragile on the extra-large piece of machinery that sweat starts to bead on my hairline. I swear to God if another car comes within ten feet of us, I'm going to go fucking ballistic. Why did I suggest we take the bike? Is it too late to drive the car?

"I'm starting to get excited now," she says, smiling at me through the helmet. "Should I just hold on to my purse?"

"No." I take it out of her hands and stow it in one of the saddlebags. "You'll be holding on to me."

"Roger that."

When I straddle the bike and her arms circle my waist, face pressing into the back of my shoulder, so many things happen to my body at once. My muscles tense with purpose. Protectiveness crams into my midsection. My tongue turns thick in my mouth, skin clammy in some places, hot in others. To say nothing of my swollen cock, which has been in perpetual misery for so many consecutive days that I'm beginning to get used to the pain. Mostly, though, it's the organ firing in my chest. Pumping like crazy. Somehow I know I'll never have another woman on the back of my bike besides Taylor. She's the last.

No matter what happens.

With that uncomfortable thought hanging in the air, I squeeze the clutch lever and start the bike, slowly pulling onto the road, exhaling jaggedly at the way her thighs tighten on either side of my hips, arms cinching around me like a belt. I go slow. Slower than the speed limit. Every pothole and road sign is a potential threat.

"Faster," she calls over the wind, squeezing me. Even though gunning the engine makes me feel like I'm going to be sick, I do it anyway, because I'm proud of her. For being brave. Facing her fear. Trusting me to do it with her. And hell, I'd be lying if I said I didn't like the way she clings to me, her warm pussy against the small of my back. Her sexy, thong-clad butt is perched on the rumbling engine of my bike and that makes me hungry. Makes me think of hot, sweaty sex. Makes me think of us in bed, instead, while she screams *faster* in my ear. Why won't I just beat off and get rid of some of this pressure between my legs? Just this morning, I returned to my motel room to shower and change. Could have worked out some frustration with my hand, but I couldn't do it, despite my dick being harder than a two-by-four. My body knows nothing is going to come close to the real thing. Taylor.

God, I want to fuck her so bad. Might as well admit that I can't...I can't do it because my heart is involved. Or I would have spent the night in her bed by now. In and out. No entanglements. No sickening fear of missing something in the case and getting her hurt.

Or worse.

My hands are starting to turn to jelly on the handlebars, so I swallow the dark direction of my thoughts and focus on getting her to town safely. When we reach downtown Falmouth, it's packed.

"Oh, I forgot," she calls into the dying wind. "The rally."

I nod, slowly navigating us into one of the municipal parking lots. There isn't a spot in sight, so I park illegally between a car and a gate, earning me a smirk from Taylor when I draw off her helmet. "So." My voice sounds like cut glass. "What did you think?"

"I loved it," she breathes, putting her arms around my neck. "Thank you for convincing me. And not making fun of me when I balked."

"No one makes fun of you ever again," I blurt.

It's such a stupid thing to promise. I have no way of making that guarantee. But what else am I supposed to say when she's beaming at me like I'm her hero? Are vows just going to come flying out of my mouth now? Next I'll be promising her a house and babies and a trip to Disneyworld. Matching shirts don't sound quite as heinous as before.

Jesus. Listen to yourself.

I haul her off the bike and keep her up against me, on her tiptoes, her face flushed with exhilaration from the ride. And there isn't a damn thing in this world that could stop me from kissing her. I surprise myself by locking our mouths together carefully, gently, winding her hair around one of my fists and slowly introducing my tongue, stroking it against hers, savoring her flavor. Her apple scent. Rumbling when she whimpers, maintaining the slow pace. Devouring her gradually from above. This kiss is different than the ones before. I'm...what *am* I doing? Adoring her? That's what it feels like, this deliberate wind of tongues, the succulent, nibbles of her lips, my lips, in between the longer, deeper bouts of kissing. We're making out like we have all the time in the world and fuck, fuck I like that too much. All the time in the world.

With a curse, I force myself to break the kiss.

Taylor leans into me dizzily, tightening a screw in the center of my ribcage. What the hell am I going to do with her? I distract myself by retrieving her purse and handing it over.

"I'll go with you to the library," I say abruptly, brushing my knuckles against the back of her hand, hoping she'll want me to hold it again. When she places her smaller hand in mine, I let out a breath I didn't know I was keeping prisoner. "Then you can sit in the police station during my meeting."

"I won't be able to browse with you looking over my shoulder. Besides, it's broad daylight," she says, shaking her head. "Go to your meeting. I'll meet you afterward." She grins at me. "We can get ice cream."

I snort. "Do I look like the kind of guy who goes on ice cream dates, half pint?"

"No," she sighs. "I guess you don't."

We walk in silence for a few seconds. "What flavor are you getting?"

Her fingers squeeze mine. I'm fucked.

"Friends and residents of Falmouth and Barnstable County," the mayor says into the microphone, her voice echoing down the town's main shopping street. "I hear your complaints—and rest assured, I am here to help."

Taylor and I slow to a stop outside of the police precinct, taking in the scene in front of us. The mayor is standing in the back of a truck, holding a microphone attached to a makeshift sound system. There are magnetic signs clinging to the doors of the truck reading, "Re-elect Rhonda Robinson." Spread out in front of her appear to be hundreds of locals holding posters and wearing shirts that say, "Renters:

Go Home." They chant those words over the mayor's speech, despite her bespectacled assistant, Kurt, making calming gestures at the crowd.

Is it my imagination or is Kurt looking at Taylor instead of the swelling audience?

Nope, he just did it again.

He pushes his glasses up his nose, fumbles his clipboard and leans sideways to get a better look at her through the teeming mass of bodies.

I lift our joined hands to my mouth and kiss her knuckles.

The assistant quickly drops his gaze to the clipboard.

But despite the satisfaction currently swarming my belly...that is the kind of man Taylor is going to end up with, isn't it? A clean-cut man her age with a noble profession. I can see that guy with kids, teaching them about the value of community service and bringing them to child yoga classes and nature walks or whatever the fuck.

"Oh look," Taylor calls to me over the noise, and damn, I'm grateful for the distraction. How long can I distract myself from where this is leading, though? To a bumpy landing. An end. There's no other option, right? "There's Sal."

I follow her line of vision and land on Taylor's temporary neighbor, nestled in the audience with his matching T-shirt. As if sensing our attention, he glances over and does a double take. There's a snarl on his face, as if he's mid-chant, but when I bare my teeth at him, he melts into the mass of bodies and disappears.

"If you personally have a grievance regarding a vacation rental in the vicinity of your property or you feel the owner is displaying negligence, such as renting to visitors who haven't been thoroughly vetted or failing to enforce our community rules," continues the mayor, "please email or call my office. My assistant, Kurt, is standing by to make a record of your issue and advise you on getting it resolved, while my office works on limiting vacation rentals in our area and keeping this neighborhood what it has always been. A peaceful place to live."

"You campaigned on this promise four years ago!" someone shouts in the crowd.

"My kids can't even play outside with all the drunk driving!"

"How is anyone supposed to sleep with the constant partying?"

"I can hear the renter beside me singing in the shower! She screeches like a barn cat!"

Taylor gasps. Sputters up at me.

The chuckle builds deep inside of me, too big to contain. And there I am, laughing in the middle of the sidewalk when I'm supposed to be investigating a murder. Can't help it, either. It feels fucking great to laugh. I can't even remember the last time I did with anyone but her.

Taylor wrinkles her nose at me, but there's pleased humor in her green eyes. Eyes I can't seem to look away from. When she lifts onto her toes to speak in my ear, I automatically lean down to meet her halfway. "You've already broken your promise to never let anyone make fun of me ever again. Next you'll be calling me Shaquille."

I drop a kiss onto her pouted lips. "How about I buy you an extra scoop of ice cream, instead?"

She avoids my next kiss. "Is that the best you can do?" A playful shove at my chest. "Go to your meeting. I'll meet you at the ice cream place in an hour."

I point to the sidewalk between my boots. "Come back here and kiss me."

Those teeth sink into her bottom lip and she shakes her head no.

Tease.

She's teasing me. Making me want more. Making it impossible to not take...everything.

God help me, It's working.

CHAPTER 15

Taylor

"*Y*ou are such a *badass*," I whisper to myself, a noticeable spring in my step. Not only did I ride a Harley this morning, I avoided suspicion from the most suspicious man I've ever met. He thinks I've come to the library to check out the latest bestseller—and actually, I might, just to kill two birds with one stone—but what Myles doesn't know is that the county clerk's office is attached to the library and it's my true destination.

There is a significant part of me that just wants to check out a few books and go meet Myles for ice cream. Engage in none of this deception. But earlier on the beach, I decided to help solve this case, any way I can. For me. For Myles. If there is something I can do to stop him from punishing himself over the past and maybe, just maybe, consider becoming a professional investigator again, I want to do it. I have to try and make a difference.

And seven years of listening to *Etched in Bone*, I know one thing. There is always an overlooked clue. In the initial stages of an investigation, the bigger components like time-lines and opportunity and physical evidence are the primary concern, but it's when the detectives circle back to the beginning and look deeper into the killer's personal connections? When they pick apart the paper trail? That's when the murders get solved.

Myles mentioned that Lisa Stanley stands to inherit the properties owned by her brother. That definitely gives her motive to kill him. Money is oftentimes a prime motivator.

But here's the thing.

It's not cheap to buy property in Cape Cod. Especially on the ocean.

And Oscar Stanley was a retired postman.

Something about that doesn't add up. It's possible he had family money, like an inheritance or perhaps an injury settlement that helped him purchase these in-demand properties one by one, but those are details that should be explored. This is where I can be useful. This is where I can prove to myself that I'm not the kind of woman who sits back and lets everyone else take risks while I blend in with the background.

Shoulders set with determination, I move through the stacks all the way to the back of the library and push through the glass door separating it from the county clerk. "Hello," I say brightly to the woman behind the desk. "I'm looking for property records."

She nods, picks up a pencil. "Address?"

"There are multiple addresses."

"Of course there are," she sighs.

Twenty minutes later, I have my printouts. Using my hip

to open the glass door, I walk back into the library and find a quiet table in the biography section, spreading Oscar Stanley's property records out in front of me. I check my phone to make sure Jude hasn't called or texted—and he hasn't. Neither has Myles. Good. The menfolk are occupied.

I'm free to snoop.

I drop my phone onto the table and go through the first record, which belongs to the property where Oscar was murdered. Nothing is odd about it that I can see. His name is the only one listed as an owner. It's when I move on to the next record that my spine begins to tingle. Under owner name, there is Oscar Stanley.

But his name isn't the only one listed. *Evergreen Corp.*

It's on the next record, as well. And the next three.

Oscar Stanley didn't own these properties alone.

He had a business partner.

And everyone knows that business partners are the most likely to commit murders, second only to spouses. I have to tell Myles—

I'm halfway through my thought when something heavy slams into the side of my head.

Pain detonates in my temple and everything goes black.

"*Taylor!*"

Consciousness slowly returns, but I immediately wish I was still out cold.

My head is throbbing and I can smell blood. That's bad enough.

But there is also a bounty hunter shouting an inch from my face.

I crack open an eyelid and he whispers a prayer at the ceiling, then gets back to shouting. "Are you okay? Where else are you hurt? Tell me you're okay."

"I'm okay. Stop yelling," I command in a strangled whisper.

"Stop *yelling*? You're laying here *bleeding* and you want me to stop yelling?" His hands race over my body and back up to my head, the brownish moss color of his eyes eclipsed by dilated pupils, sweat trickling down the sides of his face. Is he shaking? "What the fuck happened?"

"I don't know." When I realize there is a crowd of people around us, a lot of them on the phone to what sounds like 911, I struggle to sit up. "I was sitting here. Someone hit me. With a book, I think. It felt like leather."

"There was a book on the ground. Over here on the floor," calls the county clerk receptionist who helped me earlier. How long ago? How long have I been passed out on the floor of the library? "There's some blood on it. Probably hers."

"Christ," Myles grits out, appearing seasick.

Someone assaulted me.

A nervous sound escapes my lips and I'm promptly pulled into Myles's arms. The warm safety of his body makes me forget about our audience and I simply wrap myself around him, legs around his waist, arms circling his neck, desperately needing the heat. I'm cold, teeth chattering. It feels like I've been pulled out of an icy pond.

"Myles."

"I've got you, Taylor. I'm right here." He's taking deep breaths, as if trying to calm himself down, but I can tell it's not working. "Are there cameras in here? I want to know who did this. *Now.*"

"No cameras, sir. I'm sorry." A male voice. There's a

pause wherein all I can hear is my heart racing along with Myles's. "There's an ambulance on the way."

"I don't want the ambulance. I just want to go home."

"You could have a..." He swallows thickly, his Adam's apple moving against the uninjured side of my head. "It could be a concussion. Jesus. I left the meeting as soon as I saw the ballistics report. The gun you found on the beach was not the murder weapon, Taylor. It's still out there. And I could feel something was off. I should never have left you alone—"

I process the news about the ballistics report, a weight sinking down to my knees. "This is not your fault. I'm in a public library in the middle of the day," I say into his shoulder. "I should have been safe."

"But you weren't, Taylor. You weren't."

My intuition is whispering that this is a bad turn of events. Not only because this is the second time I've been the target of violence, but in trying to help Myles, I might have inadvertently made everything worse.

"I'm okay."

"I need a paramedic to tell me that, all right? Stay awake, all right? Eyes open." Several seconds tick by and I slowly notice his muscles tensing beneath me. "Is that your paperwork on the table?"

Oh dear. This is not the time. "I suddenly feel woozy."

Myles stands with me in his arms and strides into one of the stacks, away from the listening ears surrounding us. If I'm not mistaken, he's also moving us in a subtle rocking motion. But he's still breathing fast, the warm bursts pelting the side of my head. "Believe me, I just want you lying down in a bed somewhere with ice on your head, but I need information now, Taylor. Someone *hurt* you."

"Right. I know. Okay." I swallow. "It never made sense to

me that Oscar Stanley, a retired postman, could afford so many vacation homes. Obviously he might have received an inheritance or otherwise, but a partner made more sense. So I came to check the property records and I was right. I'm...drawing a blank right now on the name of the corporation because I'm still slightly dizzy—"

He makes a miserable sound, his arms tightening around me.

"But on every property besides the one where he was murdered, there was another name listed on the deed. Not his sister. Some corporation."

For a moment, he looks pensive, then we're walking back toward the table where the paperwork is still sitting. "So far, I only checked the property records on the first house," he says, looking down at the documents.

"You would have circled back. Investigators always circle back."

"But you decided to do it for me and almost get yourself killed before that could happen." His throat works. "Before I could find what I missed."

"Yes. I'm a teacher. We have a thirst for knowledge...and also being right. Myles, I don't like your grim tone of voice."

Nor do I like how he has gone stone cold against me. He settles me on the edge of the table and gathers the paperwork up into a stack, folding it once lengthways and shoving it into the back pocket of his jeans. I'm trying to catch his eye so I can determine what's wrong, but a paramedic breezes into my line of vision, along with a police officer I recognize.

"Officer Wright," I exclaim, unable to stave off a smile. The sudden movement of my mouth causes my head to throb and I wince. Myles curses and starts to pace.

"I wish we were reuniting under better circumstances," begins Wright.

"Me too. How have you been?"

"I've been better, actually." He jerks a thumb toward the street. "Thank God that rally ended a while ago. The locals are rowdier than they look—"

"Enough with the small talk," Myles shouts from a few yards away, expression thunderous. "Someone check her fucking head."

Wright whistles under his breath, pulling out a pen and notepad.

"I have been summoned," mutters the paramedic. He examines my wound, makes a few notes. Shines a small flashlight into my eyes and asks me a series of questions before clicking it off. "Not a concussion. Just a nasty cut. I'll bandage it up and you can head home."

Wright snort laughs. "*Head* home." He looks at Myles. "It's funny because she has a head wound."

"How is that funny?" Myles growls. Continuing to stare down at the officer, Myles drops into the chair I occupied earlier, drawing me down off the table into his lap. I can feel that more blood has escaped from the wound in the last few minutes and he regards the broken skin with a pale face. "Fix it."

"Are you angry with me?" I whisper in his ear.

"We'll talk about this later."

Wright hunkers down in front of me with his notepad. "All right, first question." A grin spreads the corners of his mouth. "Are you two a thing? This seems like it might be a thing."

If Myles unclenched his teeth right now, I'm pretty sure fire would spew forth.

"We're not a thing," I answer for us.

Myles starts, turning his frown on me. "Well hold on. That's not completely accurate."

"Yes, it is," I say to Wright. "Not a thing. Write that down."

"What do you call hand holding?" Myles asks me.

Wright pretends to make a note, murmuring, "So there has been hand holding..."

"I don't know what you consider 'thing' material, Myles." I'm as perplexed as the bounty hunter appears to be. After all, I'm only stating the truth. "But you don't just get to...to accidentally slip and fall into a relationship. Conversations must be had. Questions have to be asked."

"Like what?" Myles and Wright say at the same time.

On top of having a head wound, my face is starting to flame. These two men are looking at me like I'm crazy. Do I have the process all wrong? I've never encountered this level of skepticism about it. Although that might be because I've never detailed my beliefs out loud. "Well. One party asks the other party to be...permanent. And monogamous."

"Like a marriage proposal?" Wright wants to know. Oh God, he's taking notes.

"N-no. Not quite. More like..."

"Asking someone to go steady?" Myles finishes for me, amusement dancing across his features. I suppose I should be grateful he's no longer scowling, but I'm not.

My mouth snaps shut and I can no longer look them in the eye. Wow. Have I unconsciously been carrying around these beliefs since high school? When my first boyfriend asked me to be his girlfriend, I assumed that was how it would work forever. An establishing of boundaries. A clearly stated intention.

Shouldn't it be?

Yes. It should.

I shrug. "I don't know what it's called. But he hasn't given me the words a person needs to feel secure and comfortable. We're not a thing."

Myles's amusement goes out like a light.

"Okay, let's get this wound cleaned," says the paramedic, kneeling down beside Wright, who begins asking me questions that *actually* pertain to my assault.

"Did you notice anybody when you walked into the library?"

"No one but the people behind the counter." I point them out where they are still hovering nearby.

"Did you have any odd encounters before you entered the library?"

"Only with Myles. Our encounters are always odd." The joke is barely out of my mouth when something wonderful occurs to me and I gasp, turning in the bounty hunter's lap to face him. He's looking down at me, appearing as though he's trying to chew through a piece of metal. "*You're* a suspect this time."

"Not technically," Wright interjects. "He was in a meeting with us."

I raise an eyebrow at Myles. "I'll need to work up the timeline to be sure."

At first, I don't think he's going to respond. He's just going to continue glaring, that muscle popping in his cheek. But then he leans forward and speaks into my ear, low enough that I'm the only one who can hear him. "I'd take a bullet between the eyes before I raised a hand to you, Taylor. The fact that you have to spend a second in pain makes me want to die. Are those the kind of words you're talking about? Because they're the only ones I've got."

Oh my. It's very hard to concentrate on giving my statement after that, but I get through the final series of questions. My cut is salved and bandaged. No sooner have I thanked Wright and the paramedics before Myles hefts me up against his chest and carries me out of the library's rear entrance.

"I texted Jude to come pick us up, but he didn't respond."

"He has been ignoring his phone because of Dante."

"Who?" Myles asks absently.

"Never mind. You know, I don't need to be carried. I'm fine to walk."

No response.

A black sedan is waiting behind the library and Myles carries me there, sitting us both in the backseat. The driver gives us a curious glance in the rearview, but leaves the parking lot and pulls into traffic without asking questions.

That's when my adrenaline crashes like scaffolding from ten stories high.

Cold permeates me and I begin to shiver, despite the heat Myles is radiating against me. The last half an hour replays like a dream. Was I really discussing relationships with a police officer or is my brain playing tricks on me? The *thwack* of heavy leather connecting with the side of my head replays over and over again until it's hard for me to breathe and the shivers are only getting worse.

"Taylor, you're shaking."

"I know."

His voice is very calm, but there is a layer of anxiousness just below the surface. "You told the EMT you weren't nauseous. Did something change?"

"No, I'm just realizing what happened. Or how much worse it could have been."

"Welcome to my world."

"Now that there's no...buzz. Or activity. Or questions to answer..." I rub my bare arm and Myles immediately takes over that duty. "I'm fine. I'm just really, really cold."

He nods, a knot moving up and down in his throat. "Almost home. I'll fix it."

I can fix it myself. That's what I want to say. That's what I *always* say, in one form or another. But I don't want to be in charge right now. I just want this man, who I trust, to get me somewhere warm where I can process everything that happened. "I don't really think you're a suspect, Myles."

"Of course you don't, sweetheart." He kisses my bandage carefully. "I never thought you were one, either."

I like him like this—gentle and reassuring—as much as I like him honest and blunt and gruff. There's more to him than meets the eye. Layers upon layers. Didn't I somehow already know that? "We never got our ice cream," I say into his throat. "I was dying to know which flavor you would pick."

"Cookie dough."

"*Really?*"

"Married to it. Never get anything else."

"I'm flabbergasted. It's so frivolous."

"Peach-flavored beer is frivolous, half pint. Cookie dough ice cream is unmatched."

"Spoken like someone who hasn't tried butterscotch."

"And never will. That's a grandma flavor."

Midway through my gasp, I realize he's trying to distract me from what happened—and it's working. He's soft on the inside. Did part of me sense that from the beginning? Yeah. Yeah, I think so. Now he's carrying on a conversation about ice cream even though the vein in his right temple looks like it's going to tick out of his head. "I'm okay, you know."

He swallows a sound. "Goddammit, Taylor."

I can't stop myself from leaning up and kissing his chin. He closes his eyes at the contact, dipping his mouth to mine, our breaths tripping over one another's. "Please," he urges gruffly against my lips. "Stop."

"Stop what?"

"I don't know. Everything. No matter what you're doing, it gets to me. When you're pissed or laughing or hurt or not even *with* me, I get torn up over it."

"That's them. Those are the words," I whisper, shaken, chest twisting.

He's shaking his head. "Taylor, I'm leaving after I solve this case. As soon as I find out who did this to you, I'm going to lock them up and throw away the key. Then it's back to bounty hunting. You in Connecticut. Me on the road. I'm not going to be your boyfriend. You're not going to fix me. I'm not going to settle down. All right? If that's what you're thinking could happen..." His jaw flexes. "I've done everything I can to give you the opposite impression."

"I know, Myles. I..."

"What?"

"I haven't gotten that far. As in, the future. A future where you're my boyfriend. I haven't imagined what would come next if we were together. It hasn't even entered my mind."

Now he looks angrier than ever. This man is so *confusing*.

"I just want to be with you *now*," I murmur, sitting up straighter in his lap, ghosting my mouth over the rapidly beating pulse at the bottom of his neck, my hand smoothing up the front of his shirt. "I need to be with you. Just for now."

I work my lower body in a slow circle on his lap, but he

grabs my hips before I can complete the revolution. "You're *hurt.*"

Mouth pressed to his ear, I whisper, "Being hurt only makes me need you more."

The car pulls to a stop outside the rental house.

Myles blows out an unsteady breath. "Shit."

CHAPTER 16

Myles

*O*ur shoes have been left at the front door and I'm carrying Taylor through the house. I'm half hoping Jude is home to provide a distraction, half hoping he's not.

Okay, fine. A lot more than half of me is hoping we're alone. Maybe even all of me. But I should *not* be bringing this woman up the stairs to her bedroom. Christ, she was just attacked. My fucking blood is hot, it's cold, I don't know what it is. All I know is when I saw her lying unconscious on the floor, my world tipped sideways. I've never felt that combination of ice-cold fear and violent rage before and I never want to again. This is why I am a bounty hunter. I don't get attached to anyone.

I can remain emotionless. Robotic. Efficient.

It's too late for that now. With Taylor.

I'm a *storm* of feelings over her. So many that I can barely pick them out of the blurring whirlwind and try to define them. I'm protective of her, proud of her, lustful to the point of pain, adoring and confused. Because I know, I damn well know that if I fuck her, I'm going to grow even more attached and leaving is going to gut me, yet here I am, putting one foot in front of the other. Holding her against my chest like she's fragile, maybe to try and fool myself into forgetting she wants to be treated—*manhandled*—like she's far from breakable.

My stones are aching. My head is crowded. My chest is a fucking crime scene after she was assaulted on my watch. Mine. All because I missed a detail. Again. I missed something. But she's kissing my neck and I've got a cock that could punch a hole in a window and damn...she's growing more adept at teasing that spot under my ear by the second, her teeth closing around my lobe and tugging. Licking. Kissing.

She told me in the Uber that she hasn't considered a future for us.

As much as that messed with my head, it's very convenient for me to believe her promise right now. That she hasn't considered us long-term. It takes away the guilt over hitting and quitting a girl who should be carried to the wedding altar on the wings of a dove. Brought home to mom. Given whatever she wants until she's deliriously happy.

I'd never be able to do that. I don't know how.

I can't even protect her.

That thought has me stomping extra hard into her bedroom, kicking open the bathroom door and striding to the shower. Settling Taylor onto her feet and twisting the knob into the on position.

"What are you doing?"

"Getting you warm."

Maybe...maybe I can resist this. Maybe I can deposit her into the shower and wait outside, last another day without giving in to my raging hunger for this woman. Sex has never been anything but a diversion for me. An itch to be scratched. But it would be a commitment with Taylor, no matter what she says. Even if she really means what she says about this being temporary. A need for now. *My* heart and head would make the commitment. *Mine.* As in, I'd be committing her to memory for the rest of my life. Could I just go on about my business alone once I know she exists? I don't know. I have no fucking clue.

"You're still cold, right?" I ask, gesturing to the shower.

She nods.

The bathroom is already beginning to fill up with steam.

She's two feet away from me with her bandaged head, asking me for comfort with her incredible green eyes. I'm hanging by a thread and it frays even more. And more when she looks down at the outline of my erection, wets her lips... and strips off her tank top.

Oh yeah.

Fuck. Those *tits.*

That tank top must have had one of those built-in bra things, because she sure as shit isn't wearing one now. Just those tight pants—

And they go next. Slowly. She hooks her thumbs in the waistband and bends forward, sliding the material down her hips, over the smooth globes of her ass. *Leave the bathroom*, I order myself, when her thong is on fully display. But I'm glued to the spot. What man wouldn't be with this fucking princess giving him a striptease, steam from the shower making her tits and belly and shoulders and cheeks dewy? Making her glow? Especially when the princess wears her underwear just this side of tight and when she straightens, kicking away her pants, there is nothing left to the imagination.

"That pussy might as well be out. I can see every little inch of it."

She steps into the shower, letting herself get covered in warm water, and watching the thong get plastered to her sex, I start to pant, my hand tightening on the edge of the glass shower door. "If you want it out, make it that way," she murmurs, her voice blending in with the pelting water, making this all sound like a dream. Yeah, a dream. Reality drifts further and further away as she soaps her body. Her chest and thighs and her panties. She soaps up that sweet mound right through the purple material and I lose it. My reservations hit the deck and I reach into the shower, wrap an arm around her waist, ripping her out of the stall with a growl.

I carry her dripping across the bathroom floor and slap that tight ass down on the vanity, already unzipping my jeans. And she's killing me, absolutely slaying me in her current state of dripping wet, suds sliding down her nipples and belly, lips parted and whimpering. I shouldn't have let my lust triple and quadruple and turn infinite like this. Now she's got a head bandage and I'm too hard to do anything but bang her into next weekend.

"Taylor," I grunt, shuddering with relief when I finally get my cock free from behind my confining zipper. My body is screaming at me to rip off her soaked thong, enter her in a hard pump and don't stop until I come. But this fucking adoration, this...way she has my chest in a vise, has me tilting her chin up and looking her in the eye. "Tell me you're not too hurt for this. Tell me you're not just shaken up and needing comfort."

"I do. I need comfort. Just from you." She trails a finger

down my stomach and up the underside of my cock, causing me to grit a curse. "But I've wanted this, too. And I wanted it before today. It's not the aftermath talking, Myles."

"If I took advantage of you, I'd never forgive myself—"

"You wouldn't." She kisses me once, twice, lingering pecks. "You couldn't."

"Tell me you trust me," I beg against her mouth while my hands yank her to the edge of the vanity. Quick. Her soaked sex colliding with my cock, pushing it up against my stomach.

"I trust you," she says, unevenly, searching my eyes.

And warning bells are going off. This isn't just sex. We've barely started and my chest feels like it's going to crack wide open, but there's no turning back. Not when her nipples are aroused and she's opening her thighs for me, letting me raid her mouth with my tongue. I'm so horny, I could probably grind on her panties a few times and come, but that's not good enough. Nothing is good enough for my girl, so I end the kiss and go down on my knees, loving the way she moans when she realizes my intention, her fingers pulling at my shirt to get it off.

As soon as my head is through the neck hole and I'm shirtless, I hook a finger in the crotch of her thong and yank it left, kissing the split of her pussy. Kissing it with just my lips, then familiarizing it with my tongue, parting her pliant lips and searching for that nub. *There.* So sweet. So swollen, even before I start teasing it. Letting the flat of my tongue ripple against her, then stroking, nice and easy, rougher when she sobs my name. Her hips are beginning to struggle on the vanity, her thighs alternately opening wide and hugging my face.

"Myles."

I hum into my next lick. Incapable of answering when

she tastes this sweet.

"Don't treat me like I'm fragile, just because of what happened t-today. Okay?" She struggles to breathe in between every few words. "Not you. Please. I especially need to feel...feel strong now."

Give her what she wants. Give her what she's asking for.

What she's been asking for since the beginning.

It's not just her plea, it's my Taylor-sense encouraging me to be rough, to fulfill that craving she confided in me—and God knows I'm not a gentle giant. Definitely not right now, when I want her so bad, I can barely see straight or think clearly. *Mine.*

Test the waters. See where her bar has been set.

"That's a pretty little cunt, isn't it?" I say in between drags of my tongue, watching her face. Reading her. Gauging her mood. Finding out where she's at. And when she rolls her hips sharply into my next lave of her clit, her fingers tangling in my hair, I know. I know how Taylor wants to be fucked. Fast and nasty and hard. That's what we've been dancing around for days. And it's good for me, it's good, because I don't have a goddamn clue how to make love.

This is as close as I'm ever going to get.

I lean sideways a little and slap the wet flesh between her thighs. Not hard. Just enough to get her attention and roll those beautiful eyes back in her head. "Myles."

"What?" I smack it again, noticing she's wetter this time. Damn. Perfect, perfect woman. "You like when I spank you in front?"

"Yes," she whines through her teeth.

I can tell if she's sweating or just covered in dew from the shower steam, but every inch of her is glistening, including her sex, and it's the hottest shit I've seen in my thirty-four years. This girl-next-door schoolteacher glowing with moisture, her legs spread for my mouth. The smack of my hand. I'm not even inside her yet and I'll never recover. Never.

My hands travel up her thighs, through the slickness on her heaving ribcage and close around her breasts, squeezing, before I go to work on her nipples. They've gotten hard every time we've been on the verge of fucking—hell, they pucker up even when we're *eye* fucking. Extra sensitive. As soon as I brush my thumbs over those peaks, her trembles get more intense and I go faster with my tongue. Faster and faster, up and down on her clit until she's got one hand yanking at my hair, the other clutching the edge of the vanity. She screams behind clenched teeth and quakes through her first orgasm, and God help me, I lick it up. I bask in that sweetness and let her see I'm eager for it, proud of it, and she shakes all the harder for my animal grunts and lapping tongue.

But there's a frantic pulse inside of me, urging me to my feet. Crowding into the V of her thighs with cock in hand. My jeans are around my ankles and I'm a mess. A moaning, dripping mess and there's nothing in the world that can save me but her. Looking into her dazed eyes, I see nothing but encouragement. I want to be sure, though. "You need to stop, sweetheart, we'll stop. You hear me? On a fucking dime. Whether it kills me or not."

"I don't want to stop." She scoots another inch toward the edge of the sink and tugs on my hips, digs her nails into them. "I don't want you to hold back, either."

My sides start to heave, harsh breaths from my nose causing the steam to swirl in between us. Fingers fumbling for the condom in my pocket. *Rip. Roll.*

Jesus, I'm a bull waiting for the gate to open.

"Should we turn the water off?" she says, her focus zeroed in on my mouth.

"No." I crowd in close, pressing her face into my shoulder, positioning myself at her warm, wet entrance with my other hand. When I've got just the head tucked inside paradise, I circle my hands around back of her and take two handfuls of ass. "If anyone comes home, the shower is going to muffle the sound of me bottoming out in this pussy."

I drive forward, not slow, not fast, somewhere in between, and I don't stop until I'm buried and I actually shout. While she sobs into my shoulder, I shout at the swiftness of my balls jacking up, throbbing against my undercarriage. And it's no wonder, because she's a dream. Like I knew she'd be, but a million times better. Slick and snug and pulsing. Despite the very real threat of coming too early, I can't stop my hips from grinding her into the counter, trying to gain more ground inside of her. Needing all of her to be mine. *Mine.*

"You still want it rough, now that you feel what I'm working with?"

Her breath escapes in a rush against my shoulder. "Y-yes, please. Yes."

"You're too sweet between the legs to say please, Taylor. You just ask for Daddy and I'll do the rest." Yeah. And doesn't that word make her clench like a motherfucker?

Thought so.

I bite down on the slope of her neck and begin thrusting. Fast. Hard. I have to bar a forearm around the back of her hips to keep her from slipping and hitting the mirror, but hell, she's incredible. She lets her neck loosen and fall back so I'm looking right at her shaking tits while I pound in deep. The steam has made her shiny all over, plastered her hair to her neck and cheeks. God. God. I can't get deep enough inside of this woman. The way she rolls her lower body into every surge of my hips is breaking me. Making me more frantic, turning my self-control to dust. Our flesh is smacking together, wet and eager, and I'm nearly using all the force I've got on her. Nearly.

If I keep this pace up, I'm going to come. It's inevitable. We're caught in a rhythm that's only supposed to happen at the very end, at the top of the peak. Mentally, emotionally, I'm not ready yet, though. I need more of her. I haven't absorbed enough of Taylor. So I slow down slightly, but continue to push my cock deep, deep, my right hand coming around front so I can play with her clit. She whimpers my name, both of us looking down to watch my thumb strum that beautiful nub. Faster and faster, her chest rising and falling with exertion, the fingers of her right hand spearing through my chest hair, twisting until I groan.

"Go on. Scrape me up, baby," I growl on top of her mouth. "*Fuck me up.*"

She rakes her nails down my shoulders and I lose my grip on the slower pace, once again railing her on the sink, my thumb working overtime on that swollen button until finally, finally, she's shuddering, crying out into our wet, messy kiss, her pussy convulsing around me. So tight that my ears start to ring and my hands move on their own, crushing her against me, my hips pressing her thighs wider, wider, so I can feel every little tremor. Oh my God. My God. This woman is a fucking drug. No, she's the high. And I'm not done. I won't be done.

"More," I rasp, lifting her off the sink, no idea of my destination. Only that we need to stay in this bathroom. This private world of ours where tomorrow never comes. I carry her, mouth to mouth, across the marble floor. I might never let her feet touch the floor again, this fucking princess. I'm swallowing vows that are dying to be made. My cock is so stiff, I'm half delirious. It's unacceptable that I haven't given her all of me yet. All of me. She asked for it, didn't she? Yeah.

I slide her down the front of my body, turning her to face the glass shower stall.

"Keep it dripping. I'm going back in."

I'm not sure if she knows exactly what's coming or if she just flattens her palms against the glass for balance, but it's exactly what needs to happen. We're so in sync, I briefly wonder if I'm dreaming. But no. No, she backs that ass up into my lap and I grind between her cheeks and almost blow over the perfect friction. It's *so good*. There's nothing more real than her. Than us.

Heart pounding wildly, breathing erratic, I yank Taylor up onto her tiptoes and slam into her from behind. I don't muffle her scream in time. I don't even bother. Nothing matters but her sodden cunt and the way she's clawing at the glass, working her hips in jerking little circles, giving me a standing lap dance that has me groaning at the ceiling. "You trying to make me nut, sweetheart?"

"*Yes*," she gasps, those fragile muscles at the base of her spine flexing with the motion of her lower body, steam dappling her spine. Glorious. Beautiful. Perfection.

"Could have filled this condom ten times by now, Taylor, I just don't want to stop." I wrap her hair around my fist and pull back, raking my teeth hard up the side of her neck, closing my teeth around her ear, and Jesus, it makes her pulse wildly around my cock. Loving it. Loving the roughness. So I give it to her, no holds barred. I stoop forward, keeping her elevated on her tiptoes, cheek pressed to the glass of the shower stall, and fuck her hard enough to make her teeth clack together. "Do you want me to stop?"

"*Faster.*"

Son of a bitch. My vision splits into two. She's wrecking

me. There's a part of me that almost hates myself for using *any* ounce of aggression on a woman, but the evidence that she needs it, craves it, is everywhere. Soaking the hair between my legs, tightening up around me like she's going to have another orgasm and I speed her toward it. Both of us. I let that final barrier against my strength drop and she's off the ground now, she's bent at a ninety-degree angle, ass in my lap and I'm grunting with every thrust.

"Ruined me for jerking off before I even had you. Didn't you, Taylor? Knew you'd be extra slick around this cock. Knew you'd love me breaking you off."

This has to be too much, too aggressive, too revealing, but I can't stop and then...I have no idea how we get here, but she's on hands and knees on the bathroom floor, hair trapped in my fist, my hips smacking off her ass. I'm out of my mind. It's too much. It has to be too much for her, right? If my heart feels like it's going to explode out of my chest?

But then we meet eyes in the glass of the shower stall. It's fogged up, so I can barely make out her features, but I can see her mouth open in an O. I can see she's present, being fulfilled. Her eyes open and I can't tell if she's looking at me, but Jesus, just the possibility that she might be watching me when I'm this vulnerable, this stripped bare, on the verge of ejaculating harder than I ever have in my fucking life, is enough to fire me off the map. Completely off the grid. My balls empty with so much force that I forget my own name.

"Work it tight, baby. Baby. Perfect for me. Jesus *Christ*. Don't you ever get hurt on me again. Don't you *ever*." I'm moaning words into her wet neck that don't even make sense, but she's hit a third peak, she's coming with me, and there is nothing in this world that makes better sense than Taylor squeezing around me, gasping, calling my name while her knees squeak up and back on the marble floor because I'm still pumping away. Can't stop. Can't stop even though I'm almost on empty. "*Taylor.*"

I don't recognize my own ragged voice, but she seems to know what I'm saying. What I'm asking. And she turns, climbing into my lap. Clinging to me with her arms around my neck, her still trembling legs around my hips. I'm too stunned by the intensity of what just happened to do anything but fall back onto my ass with her safely in my arms, trying desperately to organize my thoughts or at least breathe correctly, but it's pointless. All I can do is sit there in a daze. This second grade teacher just rocked my fucking world.

Minutes pass before our breathing goes back to normal.

I'm incapable of figuring out what happens next. What I would like to do is keep her in bed for a month. Or maybe a whole calendar of months. But should I sleep with her again? Wouldn't that be leading her on? We decided this would just be about sex and if I can just pretend there isn't a landslide of unfamiliar feelings happening inside of me, maybe I can stick to that—

"Yeah." Her arms drop from around my neck and she sits back, yawning, more drowsy and gorgeous than anyone has the right to be. "Yup, that's definitely how I like it." She kisses me on the cheek. A peck. On the cheek. "Thanks for helping me confirm."

She's off my lap before I know what's happening, turning off the shower and disappearing into the bedroom. Thanks for helping me *confirm*? What exactly is going on here? I don't know, but I'm damn well going to find out.

I push to my feet and haul my jeans back up, cursing when I stumble slightly to the right. Jesus, she really did a number on me. Everywhere. Even my chest hurts. "Taylor," I bark, joining her in the bedroom. Finding her already in some dress that looks like a long T-shirt. "Thanks for helping me confirm? What the hell is that supposed to mean?"

She wrinkles her nose at my question, as if the answer should be obvious. God, she's very, very pretty, glowing after her three orgasms. "I mean exactly what I said. Thank you for not treating me like the future head of the bake sale committee. You trusted me to know what I wanted and you gave it to me. I appreciate that. But we agreed to no strings." There's no deception in her eyes. No guile. She's not playing a head game with me. She really means it. We almost altered time and space in that bathroom and she's content to walk away. And now here I am, the first man alive wishing a woman *was* playing a head game with him. What is wrong with me? This is exactly what I wanted. To experience her without anyone getting attached or hurt. When I say nothing, she prompts me with a raised eyebrow. "Remember?"

"*Yes, I remember,*" I shout, but it comes out funny. What's wrong with my throat?

She keeps going. "I'll be more confident in asking for what I need now."

"It's not going to be..." I stop myself before I can say the rest. *It's not going to be like this with anyone else.* Saying that out loud makes me a bastard. I'm not offering her a relationship. How dare I ruin her optimism when it comes to having one with somebody else? How dare I want to track down everyone who might hold her hand in the future and lock them in the lion cage at the zoo? And watch them be devoured while they scream for help?

I don't have that right.

I have no rights to her.

Feeling utterly numb, I watch her sail past me.

"Excuse me," she murmurs. "I need to find Jude."

CHAPTER 17

Taylor

*O*ne foot in front of the other. Down the stairs.

I can do this. I can have a fling and not get emotionally involved.

Yes I can.

I'm not going to acknowledge the pressure building behind my eyes or wrestling outward from my ribcage. It's ridiculous. I went into that bathroom with realistic expectations, didn't I? Myles was very clear that he didn't want serious. The very idea of a private school teacher from Connecticut dating a bounty hunter is totally *absurd*. I told myself when we got the lust out of our systems, I could walk away with some perspective on my sexual preferences. And whoa. I got a lot more perspective than I bargained for. A lot.

Comparing what I just did with Myles to the awkward, no-frills sex in my past, I have to laugh. I laugh right there on the staircase leading down into the living area. Did I have a feeling sex with Myles would blow my other experiences out of the water? Yes. Unfortunately, I didn't anticipate this absolute conviction that I'll never in a thousand years be able to replicate what it felt like to be with the bounty hunter. Never.

There is nothing I can do about the situation, though. He's going to solve the case and go back to his job. I'm going to return to Connecticut. Just like he said. So I need to be a big girl about this. No strings. That was the expectation and nothing has changed. I have no reason to expect anything more from Myles and I won't. We slept together. People sleep together all the time. I'm not going to make a mountain out of a molehill.

Even if he is definitely a mountain.

A big, powerful force of nature.

I almost trip on the bottom step and there's a hissed breath behind me.

Myles is following me down the stairs, his T-shirt slung over one brawny shoulder. Of course he's trailing after me. He has to leave through the front door, doesn't he? I give him a polite smile over my shoulder, but he only frowns back. "Taylor—"

The front door of the house opens and Jude walks in. Takes off his sunglasses and tosses them onto the entry table. When he sees me he stops dead in his tracks.

With a sigh, Myles skirts past me, finally pulling on his shirt. "I need to make a phone call," he mutters, a deep crease between his eyebrows as he looks down at me. "About what you found in the property records."

I nod. "Okay."

"I'll be right outside."

"Okay."

He very obviously wants to shake me and I have no clue

what I've done wrong. With a sharp curse, he starts toward the front door. Jude steps into his path, however, putting a hand on Myles's chest to keep him from going any further. "You're not going anywhere until you tell me why my sister has a bandage on her head."

In the midst of my jumbled thoughts over Myles, I failed to see how this scene might look from Jude's perspective. I'm coming down the stairs with Myles stomping after me, his surly nature on full display. There is a bandage on my head and I probably look like I've just crawled on hands and knees through a monsoon. I'm not sure I've ever seen my brother—or anyone—go white as a sheet, but I have to clear up whatever he's thinking right away.

"Jude—"

"If you hit my sister," he says to Myles. "I will murder you."

Oh dear. I jog forward to get between them. "No. Jude, he didn't—"

"I didn't hit Taylor." Myles holds up his palms and looks Jude in the eye. Totally calm. Not downplaying my brother's concern or getting defensive like I'm scared he will. "I would never hit Taylor. You're a good brother for making sure."

Jude exhales quickly, his chest dropping a few inches. It's like he's coming out of a trance. But Myles waits and his words are acknowledged with a nod before he drops his hands. "What happened?" Jude asks, coming closer and examining the bandage.

"I can't hear the recap again," Myles rumbles, taking out his phone and striding toward the front of the house. "I'll be outside."

Jude stares after him. "I should probably go apologize."

"No," I say, watching the bounty hunter duck beneath

the doorframe. "I don't think he requires one. Isn't that lovely?"

"Yeah, it is," Jude agrees after a second. "If anything, I think he was proud of me."

"Isn't that lovely?"

"You already said that, T."

"Did I?" A notch forms in my throat while watching Myles pace on the porch, phone pressed to his ear. "Must be this head injury."

I detail the attack to my brother with as little emotion as possible. There is no sense in upsetting him. Yet somehow he still seems to be on the verge of tossing his cookies by the time I'm finished. "I'm fine, really. It could have been worse."

"I shouldn't have let you get wrapped up in this," Jude says, gathering his hair in a fist and holding it there on the top of his head. "You're always looking out for me and this was my chance to return the favor and where was I? Sleeping on the beach."

"That's good! It's your vacation."

"It's *our* vacation, Tay—"

A car screeches to a stop outside of the house. Followed by several more cars braking, engines cutting out. A lot of talking and shouting ensues. As though a portal has opened and a crowd has been shaken out from another dimension.

One deep voice stands out from the others.

"Oh no." Jude's eyes slide shut. "Oh God, he actually came."

"What?" I split a look between the front door and my brother. "Who?"

"Dante."

"Dante is *here?*"

"Yup."

Arms linked, we slowly edge toward the front window,

but most of my view is blocked by one very muscular back belonging to Myles. "What the fuck is all this?" he's shouting.

"Myles," Jude says, tapping the bounty hunter's back through the window screen. "It's okay. He's not a threat." My brother's voice rises to a shout. "He's just stubborn!"

"You're the one refusing to see me for no good reason," calls back Dante—and I can't help it—warmth spreads in my chest like melted chocolate. "I'm coming in there."

"I beg to differ," Myles drawls, though there is a steel edge to his tone. "Taylor?"

"Yes?"

"Why is the kid from the Phantom Five movie on your porch?"

I massage his tense shoulders through the screen, but they remain as hard as concrete. "We know him. He grew up with Jude. They're best friends."

"Are we?" comes Dante's disembodied voice. "Pretty sure my best friend isn't supposed to avoid me. To the point where I have to see him on the news to find out he's vacationing where a murderer is at large."

"On the news?" Myles repeats, throwing us a dark look over his shoulder. "What is he talking about?"

Dante clears his throat. "Can we do this inside? I was followed by a few paps."

"Let him in, Myles," I say. "He's safe."

"There are a lot of people out here, Taylor," Myles answers. "Get away from the window."

Jude and I take several giant steps backward, leaving us between the living room and the kitchen. "Done."

The front door opens and there is Dante. But he's not the slightly awkward, quietly handsome kid I remember. No, he's a taller, thicker, stronger version with soulful brown eyes, midnight hair and a five o'clock shadow on his square, movie star jaw. I should have expected the transformation. After all, I've seen both Phantom Five movies in theaters. I've watched him jump off a skyscraper and land on the wing of an airplane, fight a twenty-foot robot and...make love. My face heats a little when I remember *that* scene from the second movie. The one where he has hate sex with the beautiful villain played by one of my favorite actresses. I bite my tongue before I can ask Dante what she's like in real life. Because it's not my moment. Not my reunion. It most definitely belongs to Dante and my brother and it's *not* what I'm expecting.

I expect Dante to call Jude a flake. I expect Jude to give some witty retort and toss his hair and all of it to culminate in a back-slapping hug. Instead, Dante stops just inside the door and scowls at Jude.

"Holy shit, you're alive," Dante deadpans. "Good to know."

Jude rolls his eyes. "Jesus, Dante. Save some drama for the movies."

"We could have easily done this over the phone."

My brother unlinks our arms and hobbles toward the fridge. "Could you please settle down and have a beer—"

"Why are you limping?" Dante's golden brown skin loses some color. He turns to Myles who has just entered the house behind him. "How did Jude get hurt? Aren't you supposed to be their bodyguard?"

Myles kicks the door shut to a flurry of camera flashes. "The hell I am." He spears me with a warning look. "When were you two on the news?"

To someone who is just meeting the bounty hunter for the first time, his personality might come across as forceful. Or aggressive. But not to me. I recognize the line of worry between his eyebrows and the way he can't seem to get a swallow down. We've made this man's job infinitely harder and he's rolled with the punches. He could have left us vulnerable. Sure, he shouts and curses and he doesn't have a tactful bone in his body, but he's...a wonderful sort of asshole. Isn't he? He's *my* asshole.

Oh God. I'm in trouble.

"I'm starting to wonder if this guy is the reason you're limping," Dante mutters, crossing his arms over his superhero chest.

And I don't know what happens inside of me in that moment. I just sort of lose it.

Is that the second time in five minutes that someone has accused Myles of inflicting bodily harm on us? Yes. Yes, it is. A geyser of protectiveness plumes inside of me. Especially when I see Myles flinch over the casual accusation. He's not made of stone. He's a protector. A good man despite what he presents to the world. How many blows can his armor withstand?

Before I perceive my own intentions, I'm across the room like a whirlwind. I pick up Myles's hand and intertwine our fingers, holding our joined hands close to my chest. "This man is very good at his job. Unfortunately, he cannot protect Jude from a jellyfish. *That* is why he's limping—"

"I wasn't seriously accusing him—" Dante starts, holding up a contrite hand.

"Well you did." I squeeze in closer to Myles's side. "You *did*. And he didn't deserve it. Yes, he comes across like a massive jerk, but he's got a soft center, you know?" I wait for Dante to nod. "He'd take a bullet between the eyes before he raised a hand to me. Those were his precise words earlier. And he feels the exact same way about Jude."

"Not the *exact* same way, Taylor," Myles mutters, shrugging at Jude. "Nothing personal."

"Too bad." Jude snaps the caps off two bottles of beer, uses them to gesture at the three of us. "I've seen that porn, too."

"Jesus," Dante sighs, but the corner of his lips are tugging. "You haven't changed at all."

Jude's expression doesn't change. "That makes one of us."

The movie star's smile drops. He and Jude go back to staring at each other and they don't stop, even when Jude limps across the floor and hands his friend a beer. They're like two alley cats waiting to see who will blink first.

"We should leave them to talk," I say, looking up at Myles—and I'm surprised to find him already frowning down at me. Not angrily. More curious or surprised.

"Massive jerk, huh?"

"That's the part you're zeroing in on?"

"No," he says quietly, cupping the side of my face. Watching in fascination as his thumb skims my cheekbone. "It's not."

"Oh?"

Grunt. "I'm waiting for the police to get back to me on Evergreen Corp. Could be an hour or so." He shakes his head. "There are a lot of other leads I need to follow, but I just keep thinking about how you never got your ice cream."

I don't know if it's possible to fall in love with a man in four days. But if it is, I think I've just soundly accomplished that feat with Myles Sumner. And there's no more pretending I'm not heading for a very steep fall.

CHAPTER 18

Myles

I don't take her back to downtown Falmouth for ice cream. There's no chance of that. After doubling back three times to make sure we're not being followed, I drive us to Wood's Hole in Taylor's Elantra. Where hopefully no one is trying to kill her.

When we walk into the ice cream shop, I barely resist the impulse to shout, "Everything. Give her one of everything." I want to buy her a scoop of each flavor. Hell, I want to buy her the whole fucking shop and hang a sign on the front with her name on it. This does not bode well for my imminent departure. Not at all. By some insane twist of fate, I've gone from wrestling convicts to the ground, dodging gunfire and nursing injuries in motel rooms to holding this woman's hand on an ice cream date. How in God's name did I get here?

More importantly, how do I go back to thinking of me and Taylor as temporary?

Can't seem to do it, no matter how much logic I shed on the situation.

Which is crazy when there are so many factors working against us. I live on the road. She's in a stable routine in Connecticut. She wants a husband and kids.

And I definitely don't want that.

Definitely not.

But while she's leaning forward and smiling down at the heaping piles of ice cream on the other side of the glass, maybe...*maybe* I just let myself imagine it. Us walking into this place with a kid on my shoulders, their grimy fingers in my hair. Taylor with another bun in the oven.

Pregnant, because I got her that way.

It takes me a moment to move on from the images *that* brings to mind.

Okay. Way longer than a moment.

Would we make love as usual and just leave it to chance? Or would she...would we fuck with the express intent of getting her pregnant? Christ. That would be...

Don't think about how satisfying it would be. Don't think about looking her in the eye when I come and knowing it serves a purpose beyond physical pleasure. Don't think of her wrapping her thighs tighter, tilting her hips and praising me for my healthy swimmers.

Unless they aren't healthy.

Then we'll have to see a doctor. Do the whole fertility thing—

Dear God, how did I get to a fertility doctor?

Back to the ice cream shop. There's a kid on my shoulders. Probably in a Red Sox jersey. Since Taylor is pregnant, she'll probably have cravings and order something other than her usual butterscotch. She'd have extra napkins in her purse to wipe our kid's face. I'd promise to rub her swollen feet when we get home.

Home.

What would that look like?

"Myles." Taylor's voice breaks into my thoughts. She's looking at me funny. "Did you hear me? I asked if you wanted to stick with cookie dough or try the vastly superior butterscotch."

"Cookie dough," I manage around the prickle in my throat. I have to let go of her hand to reach for my wallet, but I keep an eye on it as I pay for the ice cream, so I can collect it again as soon as possible. I like holding her hand a lot. I'm not sure if I like her defending my honor to her brother's friend, so much as it makes my chest feel...like sifting sand. It has been a long time since someone spoke up for me like that. My brother was probably the last person to say something nice about me. Out loud.

And for the first time in three years, I suddenly want to call Kevin.

I want to call him, tell him about Taylor and ask him what the hell I'm supposed to do about her. He had his own ups and downs with his husband, right? He'd probably be able to give me some insight. Really, I'd just like to speak to him...period. My parents, too. My old colleagues. I've been on the road, numb for three years and the thaw is wearing off.

On some level, I recognize what this means. The woman standing beside me is very good for me. She's gotten under my skin, challenged me, turned me on like nobody's business. Now her apparent belief in me is forcing me to examine myself, my life and actions.

I'm just not sure I want to do that.

I'm not sure I'm ready to face the past and do the work to overcome it.

The teenage girl behind the register hands me some change and I drop it into the tip cup. Ice cream cone in one hand, Taylor's hand in the other, we leave the shop.

"You're very quiet," she remarks, her tongue dragging around the butter yellow scoop, slowly, making my fingers tighten around hers. "Are you thinking about the case?"

"Yes," I say, too quickly.

God forbid she finds out I'm scheduling imaginary fertility doctors. Which is absolutely *not* going to happen in reality. My imagination is just a lot more vivid than I realized.

"Yeah...I'm thinking about Evergreen Corp. Who could be behind it." I scan our surroundings, parked cars, doorways, the faces of passersby, making sure there is no threat to Taylor. Since we left the house, ominous-looking clouds have moved in overhead, so there are very few people on the street. Store owners are dragging in sandwich boards from the sidewalk, diners are moving inside. Rain is coming.

Taylor seems to have that realization at the same time I do and we start to walk faster to where we parked her car, five blocks away in one of the municipal lots. We've only made it about a block when there's a roll of thunder overhead and rain starts to fall. Light at first, but slowly graduating into a downpour.

"Oh boy. No wonder we were the only two people in the shop," Taylor says, letting go of my hand in favor of shielding her cone from the falling condensation. "Should we make a run for the car?"

"With a *head injury?* No."

"You know what else is bad for a head injury? Being shouted at."

Down the side street, I see the entrance to a Catholic church. Settling my hand on the small of her back, I guide her in that direction. "I'm sorry."

She does a double take and almost slips on the rain-slicked sidewalk. "Oh, honey! You apologized!"

Honey?

A thousand pinwheels start spinning in my stomach at the same time.

"Don't get used to it," I mutter, trying very hard to stick to the mission of getting Taylor out of the bad weather, before she gets sick and has an almost-concussion. Not very easy to accomplish when she's grinning at me and rapidly turning into what looks like the winner of a wet T-shirt contest. "We'll wait out the downpour in here."

She sizes up the heavy wooden door. "You think it's open?"

"They're always open."

"Oh." I usher her into a dark vestibule. There is a dim glow coming from the church nave but a quick sweep of the place determines no one is inside. When I return to the vestibule, Taylor is leaned up against the stone wall adjacent to the door, licking her ice cream in the shadows. The heavy, outside rain echoes in the small space, no signs of lightening up. It's like we've walked into a different world. Just the two of us.

You need to stop getting carried away before it's too late.

"Let me try a bite of that," she says, distracting me from that troubling thought. Flirty. Is she being flirty or am I imagining it? "And you can try a bite of mine."

For a moment, I interpret that suggestion as sexual. At least until I remember the ice cream cone in my hands. Approaching her, I hold the cookie dough to her mouth, my balls tugging when she licks it, then sinks her teeth in, leaving a lady-sized bite behind. "Mmm." She winces. "It's good, but too rich for more than one bite."

"Lightweight."

She laughs, low and musical. "Your turn," she murmurs, lifting her ice cream to my mouth. "How do you know Catholic churches are always open? Were you raised Catholic?"

I nod, taking such a big bite of her butterscotch ice cream that she gasps. "Yeah, that was mostly down to my mother. She dragged us every Sunday. Made us wear shirts with collars and summarize the homily afterward. If she suspected we weren't listening during mass, we didn't get to play baseball with our friends afterward."

"Your mom sounds like a badass."

"She is." *She'd adore you. Everyone would.* "You didn't go to church growing up?"

"Once in a while on Christmas, since my parents traveled a lot. They couldn't really get their...*footing* in the community where we lived. They were always kind of the odd ones out. People either decided they were bad parents for putting their lives at risk constantly or they were simply intimidated by the two art crusaders down the block."

"Did that mean you and Jude had a hard time getting your footing, too?"

"Me, maybe. But not Jude. He makes friends wherever he goes. People are naturally magnetized to his ability to try anything once."

"Sure. But you're the one who gave him that confidence."

Her ice cream pauses halfway to her mouth. "What?"

"Jude. Your parents were busy, right? You raised him. And now..." I bite into my cone, sort of baffled by her confusion. She doesn't already know what I'm telling her? "You're still his biggest supporter. I'll admit he's cool. I like him. But you basically act like he shits rainbows, Taylor. His confidence and bravery comes from you."

"Oh my goodness." To my horror, her eyes flood with tears. "What a beautiful thing to say."

"It's...I'm just speaking the truth." Her dam breaks on a sob. "Jesus Christ."

She sniffles up at me. "Should you be cursing like that in church?"

"No. Please don't tell my mother."

Now she's laughing. This is like watching a fucking tennis match, except the players are using my heart instead of a neon green ball. When we've been staring at each other so long, I'm about to ask exactly how many kids she plans to have, I mentally shake myself. "Are you done with your ice cream?"

"Oh." She seems to have zoned out, too. "Yes."

I take the rapidly melting cone out of her hand and toss it into the nearby garbage can on the other side of the vestibule, along with mine. When I return to her, I'm already starting to breathe hard, because if anything, the rain has gotten more intense and we're in this little dark room, removed from the world, and my hands are itching to be on her smooth, bare skin. I might have been able to last five minutes without getting physical, but her apples scent is mixing with the rain and her natural sweetness, turning my mouth dry. I'm gravitating back toward her like a higher power—ironically—is in control and she's watching me approach with half-open eyes, her back arching ever so slightly off the wall. And so I just keep walking until my forearms are planted on the wall above her head, my mouth a few inches above hers.

"I meant what I said before, you do have a soft center," she whispers.

Those pinwheels inside me start going crazy again, spinning frantically. "No, I don't."

Her palms ride up my chest. "Yes, you do." That touch moves down, down, over my stomach and lower where she unsnaps my jeans. *Fuck.* This is happening. "When we met, I needed someone to give me rough. Maybe you need the opposite." Her hand delves into my jeans where she strokes my cock with a feather-light touch. Just grazes of her fingertips. And yet I'm already grinding my molars together to keep from spilling. "Maybe you need someone to give you slow and sweet. So you know you're capable of it. So you know you deserve it."

I'm shaking my head. No.

I don't know why, but I can't let *that* happen.

Somehow I know slow and sweet with this woman would be even more catastrophic than hard and mean. And yet I'm removing my gun, setting it on the closest ledge.

"Taylor." Why is my voice ragged? "Let's *fuck.*"

"Uh-uh."

"No?"

She leaves my erection resting in the V of my jeans and slowly, God, too slowly, she winds up the sides of her dress in her fists, puling the material up to her waist and leaving it there. Naked thighs. Hips. Her pussy *that* much closer...and covered in red lace panties.

She's wearing the hookup panties.

In a church.

"You know I was only ever going to wear them for you, right?" she whispers.

I drop my face against the stone wall to the right of her head and moan. Louder when she starts jacking me off again, her hand moving a torturously methodical rhythm and my hips start to match it, grinding, rolling.

Stroke. Pause. Stroke. Pause. So light. Yet my rasping breath sounds like it's coming from surround sound speakers in this stone echo chamber of a vestibule.

What is she doing to me?

"You make me feel safe and protected," she whispers against my chin, then higher to my lips. "But at the same time, you make me feel like I can protect myself. Isn't that kind of amazing?" She lays kisses along my jawline. "Aren't you kind of amazing?"

She feels it.

The way my cock swells over her praise. Right there in her hand.

God knows I feel it, too.

I've acknowledged it before. The fact that I need this woman's admiration. Her trust. And it's so generous of her to give me those things despite my nature. The way I act. She saw through it all. She's seeing me clearer than anyone ever has, right now, reciting a spell that is turning me to putty in her hands. I'm holding on to the wall for dear life, letting her wreck me one slide of her fist at a time. There's a niggling urge to growl at her, tell her I don't need compliments or praise. But I ignore it, teeth buried in my bottom lip, waiting to hear what she'll say next.

Fine, twist my arm. I'll start.

"*You're* the amazing one," I blurt. I'm not winning any awards for that one, but she likes it. The corners of her incredible mouth tilt up at the corners and she pumps me harder, making me hiss. "I miss you at night. When you're sleeping."

Her chest heaves faster. "You do?"

"*Yes.*"

These admissions are a bad idea. They're going to come back to bite me in the ass. But it feels too fucking good to tell this woman the thoughts in my head. I could lay all the shit in my head at her feet and she would make it better. That truth is built of concrete. My feelings for her are even more solid. Titanium. No getting around that anymore.

Taylor rises up on her toes and brushes her lips over mine. Everything inside of me races around in anticipation. It has never, ever been like this. Not even one percent. I swear to God, by the time she finally kisses me fully on the mouth, I would die having to wait another second. She doesn't make me, though. She opens her sweet, butter-scotch-flavored mouth and invites my tongue inside with a teasing lick of her own. And I go, hungrily, turning my head right and coming at her from an angle, groaning into the slick ride of tongues. The kiss is a slow, thorough entrap-ment like everything else she's doing—and I let her. I let her fucking own me. I sign my soul over, signature on the dotted line.

"Sweetheart," I break away to pant against her forehead.

What am I asking for?

She knows. She *knows.*

Her right leg lifts and curls around my hip. Not easy with our height difference. Her left leg is still balanced on her big toe. So my arms automatically drop from the wall to support her. Left arm barred beneath her tush. Right hand holding her tits through the wet T-shirt, knuckling her pebbled nipples. "Move my panties out of the way," she whispers unevenly, diving up into another kiss. Now there's a worthy job for my right hand. Sliding my fingers from her breasts to the juncture of her thighs, I all but tear the red silk from her body in my haste to reveal that place, *that place* that feels more like home than anywhere I've ever lived.

And while she drugs me with long, sensual writhes of

lips and tongue, she rubs the head of my cock against her entrance, letting me feel how wet she is. How horny.

"Fuck, baby, that's so smooth."

She nods into our kiss. "You should feel the inside of it," she says, razing my bottom lip with her teeth. "Want to?"

Good God. Taylor is dirty talking me.

Looking up at me from beneath her eyelashes while asking me if I want to fuck.

No. No, make love.

Isn't that what's happening? It must be. Because this is like nothing I've experienced before. I'm tied to her by a million invisible strings. Connected to her every breath, every tick of her hips and shudder of her body.

"Yes," I manage, hoarsely, pulling her panties more to the side, thrusting my cock into her fist, begging her to put me in. Right there. *Right there.* I could do it myself. I could throw her up against this fucking wall and have her screams of encouragement echoing off the rafters in seconds. But I can't pretend this doesn't feel good. Perfect. This slow torture. It forces me to think, to savor, to be present instead of disappearing into my head—and she deserves that from me. "Please," I growl, mouths flush. "Condom in my pocket."

Looking me right in the eye, she finds the foil pack, tears it open and wraps me up. So slowly I'm half delirious by the time it's on and she's dragging the tip of my cock through her soaked folds one final time, then pressing me to her hole. Fuck me, I start to shudder. With responsibility, with excitement. Or maybe just because what's happening is powerful and my body is acting accordingly. Corresponding to the tectonic shift taking place in my chest. I drop my face into her sweet neck and groan long and loud, while she adds more of my inches, her fist around the base of my shaft, working me in, her hips circling slowly, her wet sounds mingling with the falling rain.

We're struggling to breathe and I haven't even thrust yet. And Jesus, I want to, I *need* to. My balls are swollen and throbbing. But she's got me trapped in this spell. This woman, this perfect woman, is putting me inside of her, kissing my lips softly, drawing back every few seconds to communicate something to me with her eyes. I'm trying to decode the message when she finally voices it out loud and ruins me.

"You're in deep everywhere." Her voice is reedy, gasping. She reaches down for my right hand, which is still needlessly clutching and yanking her panties sideways, placing my flattened palm between her breasts. "Not just between my legs."

I don't know what happens. I just sort of stumble into her, crowding her against the stone wall, inhaling and exhaling into her neck. She's telling me I get to her. I've gotten to her. That's terrifying as much as it's a miracle. "*Taylor.*"

My hand moves on its own, trying to yank up her other leg, get it slung around my hips. With her two thighs wrapped tight around me, there will be no more going slow. We're going to fuck like we're possessed. But no, no, she won't let me. She pries my fingers off her knee and shakes her head, working me in and out of her slick pussy with teasing, excruciatingly hot rolls of her hips, instead. Slow. Slow. My inches slide out, then she works them back in to the fucking hilt, clamps her walls around me and grinds. All while looking me in the eye.

And I fucking give in.

I make love with her.

I slide my fingers into her damp hair and shudder

through every up and down ride of her slippery pussy. Up my johnson and back down, down. *Fuck*. It's so good. I'm keeping her elevated and balanced with my left forearm, but she's still poised on the tiptoes of her left foot, grinding on me, right leg hugging my waist. I could come just watching her go. Witnessing her absolutely screwing me for life, my soul firmly in her possession.

As much as she's trying to be in control here, her eyes are beginning to glaze over, her breath faltering. "I'm..." Her hands fist in the front of my T-shirt and the pace of her ride kicks up a notch, nearly turning my knees to ash. "I'm sorry, it's just that you're the perfect size. Just...slightly too big. Enough to hurt a little but not badly."

Consider me fucked.

No. No, I was fucked already.

This is something else. She's tapping into my basest wants and it's everything I can do to keep from peaking. Just slamming that ass up against the stone wall, one good, deep pump and blast off. "You're the right size for me, too, Taylor. A little too snug, but not enough to make me feel guilty about pounding it."

She cries out, head falling back.

My hands drop to her butt and I yank her higher, roughly, my teeth bared against her mouth while she fucks me, rounding her hips with increasingly frantic movements. "Even if we walk away, we'll still belong to each other." Vulnerable green eyes lift to mine and my heart seizes painfully. "Won't we?"

"Yes. *Yes.*"

"You're important to me."

"Taylor," I rasp.

Her mouth is all over my neck. "You're big and sweet and proud—" I stamp my mouth down over hers to stop the flow of words. Not because I don't want to hear them. Not because some deep down part of me needs them, craves them, but because I'm about to be gutted where I stand. She's either killing me or bringing me back to life. I don't know.

"Enough, baby," I breathe into our kiss.

"Let me finish."

"No." With my chest caving in and my body begging for release, I back her hard into the wall, lift that other leg and fuck her in the brutal way she loves. In the way that will distract her from her mission of dismantling me, bone by bone, brick by brick, word by word. "I've got that pretty cunt trapped now, don't I?"

The sound that leaves her is half moan, half sob, green eyes blind, her back jolting up and down against the wall, nails leaving bloody marks on my neck, my back. "Oh my God, Myles. Yes, yes, yes."

I drag my tongue up the sensitive slope of her neck. "I know what you like."

"What about what I love?" she murmurs haltingly against my mouth, her eyes squeezed shut. "What about who I could love so easily?"

Brave. She's braver than me. I stop thrusting. I crush myself against her, inhaling, dizzy from the excessive pace of my heart.

"You," she says against my ear. "I could love you so easily."

With those unbelievable words ringing in my skull, my body bucks without permission. Once. *Hard.* She whimpers and I come inside of her, my body depleting itself so swiftly, I struggle not to fall to my knees. Jaw slack, eyes unseeing, I reach between us and find her clit automatically, rubbing her out with the pad of my thumb, using the slickness of my come to circle that nub faster and faster until she's shaking between me and the wall, her thighs trembling and clenching around my hips, her voice a chant in my ear.

"Myles, Myles, *Myles.*"

Her warmth rushes around the place where our bodies join and I heave a breath of relief. "Sorry. Sorry. I don't know what happened. I—"

She shushes me, draws me into a kiss. Her legs drop from around my waist and I stoop down to prevent our mouths from separating. Or maybe to delay the moment I look her in the eye and confess the words on the tip of my tongue. *I could love you so easily, too. I already do. God help me, Taylor. I'm not sure how it happened and I don't know what's the right thing to do.*

If she's brave enough to make her admission, I can damn well make mine.

She expects honesty from me and I want to give it to her. She believes in me.

I don't know where the hell we go from here, but I can't let her get away.

"Taylor—"

Voices grow louder outside the door of the church. Taylor sucks in a breath and our hands collide in our haste to fix her panties and dress. I pull off the condom and zip my pants one handed, crossing to the trash can and disposing of it. When I return to Taylor, she's giggling and trying to collect her fallen purse at the same time. Before I know what's happening, I'm laughing, too, collecting my gun and feeling lighter than I've felt in my entire goddamn life. She makes me a better man. A better human. She makes me so much better.

I'm opening my mouth to tell her that when the church doors swing open and two nuns walk in, stopping short when they see us. Behind them, I see the rain has stopped and sidewalks are once again full with the summer crowd. How long have we been in here?

"Sisters," I say, reaching for Taylor's hand, gratified when she takes it in a way that suggests she was already reaching out. "We were just waiting out the rain."

One of them raises a white eyebrow. "It stopped some time ago."

"Did it?" Taylor has decided to feign innocence, a hand pressed to the middle of her chest. Over-the-top perplexed. "We couldn't hear through all that thick wood."

"Oh boy," I mutter, dragging a hand down my face.

I turn to find her turning crimson. "I-I mean...what I meant was the door is—"

"You're digging yourself deeper," I drawl, nodding at the nuns and pulling Taylor through the double doors. When we hit the sidewalk, I scan the street for threats. Windows, parked cars, people walking by. Nothing out of the ordinary. She's safe. So I finally let out the rush of amusement I've been holding in, laughing for the second time in as many minutes. "You just made a dick joke to a couple of nuns."

"I didn't mean to." She winces, obviously replaying the encounter. "Oh *God*."

"That's who they're talking to right now. God." I sigh, patting her on the back. "Asking him to guide you off the dark path of sin."

Laughing, she shoves at my shoulder. "Stop."

This won't be a story we tell the grandkids.

This one is just for us.

The thought is complete before I know what's happening and my pulse goes haywire. I was seconds from being honest with her back in the church, before we were interrupted. Now that we're in the daylight, it's definitely more daunting because I don't have a plan. Shouldn't I figure out how a relationship between us would work before I start spilling my feelings like some kind of impulsive idiot? I wasn't ready for a serious relationship in my twenties. God knows that. But I can't for the life of me imagine a world where I don't want to spend every second of my free time with this woman. I can't imagine having an argument with her and walking away without solving it. I wouldn't. It would torture me.

I'm...different now. I'd be different for her. I have no choice when I feel like this.

As we turn the corner onto the avenue, walking in the direction of her car, Taylor smiles up at me into the sunshine and I forget how to breathe. Fuck it. I'll come up with a plan later. "Listen, I was thinking..."

Not the most romantic opening, but okay. I've set the bar pretty low thus far in the romance department. It's only uphill from here, right?

"About what?"

My phone rings. Dammit. I fish it out of my pocket with the intention of silencing it, but Barnstable police are calling me. "This could be news on Evergreen Corp."

She stops on a dime, urging the phone higher. "Answer it."

"Yeah." I still want to throw the device into the sewer, but I grudgingly hit talk. "Sumner."

"Sumner." A low voice reaches me, barely audible. "It's Wright."

Wright, I mouth at Taylor. "Why are you whispering?" I ask the detective.

"I don't have long. Listen, Evergreen Corp. You're not going to believe this. It's registered to the mayor. Rhonda Robinson." There's a shuffle in the background and Wright says something about picking up a pizza on the way home for dinner, as if he's talking to his wife, instead of me. A beat passes and then he's whispering again. "The chief of police is a close friend of the mayor. I assumed we were going to bring Robinson in for questioning, but the brass is behind closed doors now. I've just got a feeling..."

"That they're going to bury it."

"Yeah." A door closes on the other side of the call. "You didn't hear this from me."

"Hear what?" Wright's relieved breath filters down the line. "Thanks for letting me know."

I end the call and guide Taylor down the road at a brisk pace, keeping my body between her and the road. My sixth sense is buzzing. I'm on high alert. One of the lessons I learned growing up the son of a detective and eventually becoming one myself is this. When there are politics and corruption involved in a case, there are inevitable casualties. And I'll be damned if my Taylor is going to be one of them.

She has no plans to be left out of the loop, however. As soon as we reach the car and I've buckled her into the passenger seat, circled around the front bumper and climbed into the driver's side, she starts peppering me with questions. Answering them comes naturally, I'm surprised to find. No barriers left with this woman. They're all down.

"What's going on? What did he say?"

"Evergreen Corp. is registered to the mayor. Rhonda Robinson."

"*What?*" She huffs a stunned breath at the dashboard. "I did not see that coming. She owns vacation rentals and yet she's leading the charge against them? What sense does that make?" There's a long pause while the rest falls into place. Clues knitting together for her the way they did for me on the way to the car. "Oscar was threatening to expose her as a rental owner. It would have derailed her whole campaign. Those warning notes were for the mayor."

"Yup." I back out of the space and gun the vehicle out onto the main road. "I'm bringing you home, Taylor. You need to stay put until I get back. *Please*."

"Where are you going?"

"Lisa Stanley's house."

After a second, Taylor sucks in a breath. "Because Lisa is inheriting the properties. She's got all of her brother's paperwork coming today and...that knowledge makes her a threat to Rhonda. We need to warn her, get her somewhere safe."

"Right."

"Don't waste time bringing me home. Take me with you."

An image of her lying on the floor of the library, bleeding from the head, creates a blinding pressure in my skull. "Taylor, don't ask me to do that."

She opens her mouth to argue, but a buzzing cell interrupts her. "Oh my God, it's Lisa," she says, holding up her phone. Answering it on speakerphone. "Hello?"

For a long stretch, there is nothing but garbled voices.

Scratching.

And then the distinct sound of a door smashing off the wall.

"Get out!" Lisa screams. The line goes dead.

Taylor and I trade a look of pure dread.

With icy sweat forming a layer on my skin, I floor the gas.

CHAPTER 19

Taylor

I call the Barnstable police on our way to Lisa Stanley's house and specifically ask for Wright, who is noticeably stunned when I explain that the mayor has broken into Lisa's house and is most likely a murderer. Thankfully, he doesn't waste time reporting Lisa's phone call to his superior and our belief that Oscar's sister is in imminent danger. Possibly worse. By the time we skid to a stop in front of her house, there are sirens in the distance, but if they are coming from the station, they are probably more than five minutes away.

"We can't wait. I'm going in," Myles says, removing the gun from his jacket and checking the clip. "You're going to drive to the end of the block, away from the house. Do you hear me?"

"I hear you."

"You hear me *and* you'll do what I'm asking."

I nod. I nod vigorously, but the walls of my throat are closing together at the thought of Myles going into a house with a murderer. He's so big and indestructible, I've never really had cause to worry about him before. But I am now. And I'm not one hundred percent sure I'll be able to pull the car away and leave him to possibly get killed.

"Taylor."

Can I lie? No, I can't lie. It *would* be the most expedient way to reassure him so he can stop worrying about me and do his job, but I hate lying. So I won't.

"I'm going to drive to the end of the block." I lean across the console and kiss his mouth, adrenaline bringing my voice to a higher pitch than usual. "Away from the house."

"Good." He kisses me, too—twice—looking like he wants to say more. Instead, he shoves out of the car with a curse, rapping his knuckles on the roof once. "Climb into the driver's seat. *Go* Taylor."

"Okay." My eyes are watering, hands shaking, but by the time Myles disappears around the side of the house, gun drawn, I manage to put the car in drive and pull away from the curb, Lisa's house growing smaller and smaller in the rearview. There's a pulse pounding in my ears and my stomach is folding in on itself. Oh my God. Oh my God. I don't want to nose my way into any more murder investigations. I have officially gotten my fill. Is Myles all right? Yes. Yes, he knows what he's doing. For all we know, the mayor is long gone, anyway. Or we misinterpreted the threat. Even if Rhonda Robinson is inside that house with the real murder weapon, ready to use it, I'm pretty sure a bullet would just bounce right off of Myles. Right?

Wrong. He's a human man. Flesh and bone.

The odds of him and Lisa surviving are a lot stronger if they have help and the sirens still sound like they could be a good two or three miles away. I can help. I can do *something*. What did my parents always say about being scared? That it's healthy? Yes. They used to say that anything worth doing inspires fear. Consider me inspired.

"I'm going to drive to the end of the block, away from the house," I murmur shakily. As soon as I reach the stop sign, I whip a U-turn and floor it back in the direction of the house. "I didn't say I would stay there."

What would my parents say if they could see me right now? I spent the last hour making love in a church vestibule and now I'm gunning it down a residential block in the direction of a potential crime in progress, hoping to assist my bounty hunter lover. This might be shocking even by their standards. Oddly enough, though...I'm not really concerned at all with my parents' opinion about what I'm doing. If they would think me brave or be pleasantly surprised to know I inherited some guts, after all. In that moment, I'm only concerned with how *I* feel about my actions. What my conscience is saying and what my intuition is telling me.

I've been brave all along.

I just had to stop accepting *others'* definition of it to know how much.

Parking the car in the exact same spot as before and leaving the car idling, I take stock of what I can see. All the blinds are drawn on the house. Various vehicles are parked all over the block, but I have no way of knowing if one of them belongs to the mayor. There is no sign of Myles. My scalp prickles with cold at the last part. Where is he? Is he inside yet?

Myles *and* Lisa are in potential danger. There has to be something I can do. I chew the inside of my cheek for a moment before rolling down the driver's side window. That's when I hear the shouting coming from inside the house. Women's voices. Two of them. One belongs to Lisa. The other...I think it belongs to Rhonda Robinson, although she is not using the professional voice I've heard at press conferences.

It's panicked and high pitched. And imploring.

"Please. *Please.* Listen to me. I did not kill your brother!"

"Like I said, I believe you! Just get out! The police are coming."

"Don't you understand? I can't be interrogated by the police. There are eyes everywhere in this place. Nosy retirees and busybody mamas who would love nothing more than to knock me from my perch, and oh *believe* me, this would do it. Oh, this would definitely do it. The mayor being investigated for murder? Do you think my career would *survive* that?" Several seconds tick by, a murmuring of voices. "I have no way of knowing you'll keep my name out of this. Why would you?"

There is just a hint of movement on the left side of the house. It's Myles with his back to the wall, peering into the side window, gun pointed at the ground between his feet. My wild rush of relief to see him still unharmed is quickly marred by his dark expression when he notices me sitting in the parked car. Teeth gritted, he jerks his chin down the road. "Go, Taylor," he mouths. "Now."

There's a loud crash inside the house.

Myles jerks backward, then slowly peers inside, but I can tell he's also watching me out of the corner of his eye. I'm distracting him. I can see that now. As much as I want to help, the best thing I can do in this moment is get my butt back to the end of the block and flag down the police. Putting my car into drive, I start to edge away from the curb.

The front door of the house flies open. Rhonda

Robinson comes running down the steps, a knife in her hand. A *knife?* Considering the way Oscar Stanley was murdered, I expected a gun, but I don't have time to consider this now. She's running toward a black sedan, which is parked at an angle and partially blocking the driveway of Lisa's neighbor. Clearly she parked in a hurry and she was definitely rushing again now. Trying to make a run for it before the cops arrive?

Myles steps out from the shadow of the house, gun trained on Rhonda.

"Stop where you are, Rhonda. Get down on the ground."

The mayor jerks around with an expression of shocked dread. She starts to go down on one knee and Myles approaches slowly.

"Hands behind your head. Do it."

Another, louder siren is added to the cacophony of sound and it seems to spook Rhonda. She springs back up and sprints for her vehicle, knife in one hand, keys in the other.

My eyes search the rearview, praying for red and white lights. *Where are the police?*

It feels like we've been waiting on them for an hour, when in reality, it has probably only been three or four minutes. Too long, though. Rhonda is going to get away— and she is clearly the murderer. Her name is on the property records, along with Oscar Stanley. She was profiting off vacation rentals while lying to voters about eradicating rental homes from Cape Cod. Her motive was to keep Oscar silent. Those threatening notes, written by Oscar, were intended for the mayor. She was on the verge of being outed. Her motive is rock solid.

Meaning she's the one who threw a buoy through my window.

The one who bashed me in the head with a book.

She killed a man. Someone's brother. If that happened to Jude, wouldn't I want someone to intervene so she could be brought to justice?

Am I just going to let her drive away or am I going to do something?

She could be on her way to do something drastic. Or hurt another person.

When she hops into her sedan and the engine roars to life, I make a decision. Out of the corner of my eye, I sense Myles running in my direction. He must guess what I'm planning because he belts out my name.

I'll apologize for scaring him later.

I lay my foot down on the gas, whip my car across the street and skid sideways in front of the mayor's vehicle, blocking her from leaving. Frantically, she glances back over her shoulder, but the neighbor's car is preventing her from reversing. The sirens are very close now. A quarter mile maybe. So many of them. Myles pounds a fist on the roof of Rhonda's car, ordering her to step out of the vehicle with her hands up, but she's not listening. She's looking right at me, screaming at me to move. Thank God she only has a knife or I'm certain she would have already fired a bullet through my windshield in her desperation. I've never seen anguish like this, up close and personal, and in those minutes that pass while the sirens approach, sympathy wells inside of me, despite everything she's done.

All at once, the fight goes out of the mayor and she deflates, her head falling back against the seat. Tears roll down her cheeks and she puts her hands up, palms facing out. Police cars squeal to a stop around us, Myles is shouting directions to them. An explanation of what's going on, leading with the fact that I'm not a threat. But I can barely hear any of it over the rapping of my heart. It pounds in my ear drums and my fingertips. I breathe in and out to try and get it back under control, but I'm still vibrating head to toe when Myles yanks open the driver's side door and pulls me out, crushing me against his chest.

"Are you out of your mind, Taylor?" He squeezes me, dragging me away from the scene of the mayor being handcuffed, blocking me with his back. Up ahead, Lisa stumbles out of the house and drops down onto the steps, hands over her mouth. She doesn't appear to be injured, just in shock. "My God," Myles growls into my hair. "What were you *thinking?*"

My response is partially muffled by his shoulder. "Stop shouting at me."

"I'll shout all I want. You *lied* to me. I asked you to stay down the block."

"No, you asked me to *drive* to the end of the block. And I did."

I definitely didn't pick the right moment for semantics.

With a laugh totally devoid of humor, he pulls away slowly—and I can tell right away this isn't his usual bad temper. I shook him up. Badly. He's white as a ghost, sweat soaking the front of his shirt. "She could have had another weapon in the car, Taylor. Or on her person. We would have apprehended her eventually. Lisa was safe. You didn't have to put yourself at *risk*."

I can't argue with what he's telling me. He's right. What causes me to fight might be my spiked adrenaline or the humiliation of being yelled at for trying to help—no, I *did* help. Whatever the reason, I can't bring myself to back down. Maybe I'm fighting for more than just being right. It feels like I'm fighting for us. What we could be together. "I didn't want to sit on the sidelines and watch everyone else do the hard thing. I've been doing that my whole life."

"This is about your parents again." He pinches the bridge of his nose. "Jesus."

Now it's *my* temper that's building. And it hurts. It hurts to have him bring up my parents and their influence on my choices when I've just learned to overcome the impact. When I confided those things to him with so much trust. "No, actually it's not about them anymore. It's about me. It's about participating in my own life instead of hiding—"

"Sometimes, Taylor..." He plants his hands on his hips, his upper lip curling. Hesitating. "Maybe it's better to hide."

"That's what you're doing," I whisper. "Hiding. Running away from what happened in Boston with the kidnapping."

"So what if I am?" He's shutting himself off. Lights are going out. Exits are being sealed. It's like watching a brick and mortar wall being built in fast motion capture. "I like it that way. The way it was before I accepted this job. I *like* having no connection to a case. Not getting in so deep that every failure is personal. Not having to worry that someone I care about could get taken or traumatized. Or having her fucking head blown off. *Willingly*."

"Don't group me in with what happened in Boston."

He grinds a fist into the opposite palm, knuckles white, grooves deepening around his mouth. "I will group you in, Taylor. I can't help it. You're pain waiting to happen and I'm not going to be a sitting duck. I can't fucking do it."

"Myles—"

"What do you think a relationship between us would look like, anyway?" His expression is hard now. Closed off. Intuition tells me he's about to put the final nail in the coffin and there is nothing I can do to stop him. I put myself in danger and he's not equipped to deal with that kind of trauma. That lack of control. I brought his worst fear to him on a silver platter and he's lashing out. There's nothing I can do about it. "Maybe you'll come on the road with me, half pint, and we can hunt down bad guys together. Make a cool handshake and bring your students along on stakeout field trips."

My throat starts to burn, along with the backs of my eyes. "I know you just want to push me away. I know that's what you're doing."

"You should have waited at the end of the block," he blurts, swiping sweat from his forehead. Pacing away and coming back. Opening his mouth and closing it. Silence.

So much silence.

"Maybe I made a mistake blocking the mayor in with my car when I didn't know if the threat was serious. Okay? Maybe it was a mistake. But even if I'd gone and waited at the end of the block like a good little soldier, there would have been a next time. A time for you to feel vulnerable—if we tried to make this work. In the future, I'd have gotten a flat tire on the side of a dark road without you. Or maybe I'd finally get the courage to go skydiving with Jude—"

The look of absolute horror he gives me would be funny if this conversation wasn't so excruciating.

"And you'd remember I'm a liability. A threat to the emotionless life you're so determined to lead. And you'd push me away. Best to do it now before things get too complicated, right? Get it over with?"

I take a step closer to him and his jaw bunches, fingers flexing at his sides. Almost like he's scared I'll touch him and he'll crumble. Maybe he would. Maybe he'd apologize for his harsh words and we'd kiss and go home together, but our root issues would still exist.

"There is nothing emotionless about guilt," I continue,

doing my best to keep my voice even. "About the way you're punishing yourself. Terrible things happen sometimes, but you can't avoid the high of happiness or joy, because you're too afraid of falling from a great height. Maybe I learned some of that lesson myself since we met. I just..." This is getting too hard. Standing so close to him and not walking into his arms, having that warmth permeate me when I need it the most. "You never made me any promises, Myles. Even if you wanted to. So I hereby absolve you of any guilt where I'm concerned. Okay? That being said..." Chin up, I look him right in the eye. "It's your loss, bounty hunter."

"Taylor," he rasps.

Turning on a heel, I walk away. I leave him behind me, literally and figuratively, because I don't have another choice. I won't get more attached when he's made it clear that he's an island in the middle of the ocean. Unreachable. A loner that commits to no one. My dream is to have the opposite. A warm, committed relationship where it's a given that we are in every adventure, every tragedy, together. No questions asked. Myles wants the road—and he never made any bones about it—so my only option is to give my statement to the police, go home and embark on day one of mending my broken heart.

CHAPTER 20

Myles

I have no idea how long I've been sitting on the edge of my bed in this motel room, staring into space. My bag is packed on the ground. Did I ever even unpack it?

No. When do I ever?

I should be a hundred miles from Cape Cod right now. My email is full of job opportunities. A missing parolee down in North Carolina. A hit and run driver in Michigan caught on CCTV with a ten-thousand-dollar reward on his head. Quick jobs. Easy ones that I could move on from and never think about again. If I could move from this spot. If I could just stand up, walk out the door and leave this sea foam green nightmare of a room behind. Get on my bike and go.

It's obvious why I can't light out of this place. She is the reason. And Christ, it's fucking painful to think about her.

Your loss, bounty hunter. Truer words were never spoken in this lifetime. Until she tossed her hair and strutted away from me on the sidewalk, I never stopped to acknowledge that I have PTSD. There is no way in hell a man lets a woman like that leave his side unless he's blocked up by serious mental trauma. I have post-traumatic stress. The Christopher Bunton case screwed with my head and...

And she's right. I'm punishing myself over it. Three years later, my past is leading me to do things like shout at this incredible woman when I should be kissing her, rejoicing in her safety, praising her for being brave. I did none of those things. I lashed out like a wounded bear. Knew it, too. Kept going because of the crushing residual fear. She drove her car straight at a murderer. Could have crashed, could have been shot or stabbed. Or caught in a crossfire with the police. My blood turns to ice thinking about it.

Hell yeah I'm still pissed at what she did. Sorry.

I'll probably be mad about it until the day I die.

But I'm feeling a lot worse about her not being in my lap right now.

A lot worse.

Sort of like I might die.

I try to swallow and can't, a choked noise tripping out, instead.

Taylor sure did give her statement and high-tail it out of there without glancing in my direction a single other time. She is well and truly done with me. And I just keep seeing flashes of her. Everywhere. They play out on the wall in front of me. Taylor licking her ice cream cone. Running beside me in the rain. Covered in moonlight on the beach. Dappled in a mixture of sunlight and shadows in the cave.

"Oh fuck." I manage to stand up and cross the room, feet numb, the heel of my hand rubbing at the center of my chest where an apparent eruption is happening. This woman, this woman who is in my head and under my skin, and might as well face it, buying up real estate in my heart, is done with me. I behaved like an asshole. Not just today, but most of the time I've known her. I'm not even sure why she tolerated me as long as she did.

She's going to find someone she doesn't have to simply tolerate.

She's going to find a man she likes. Who treats her like a princess.

Who gives her children.

"Shit." I drop back down on the bed, folding forward to wedge my head in between my legs. Breathing in and out through my nose. "Shit, shit, shit."

Taylor is going to have babies with someone else.

Oh my God.

When did my skin turn into fire?

Before I register my own movements, I have my phone in my hands. I start to call Taylor. I *need* to hear her voice, but I'm pretty sure I'll drop dead from the pain of her sending me to voicemail. And what would I say, anyway? Earlier today, I was ready to leap without looking. A relationship with Taylor would be nothing like my first marriage, because I'm too...*present* with her. The way I feel about her? It doesn't come close to anything I've experienced before. Or even knew was possible. But I don't have any stability to offer her. Would I be holding her back from the happiness she might find elsewhere? Jesus, I can't do that.

I need more. She deserves more. Where do I even start?

I scroll to my brother's number and hit send, holding the device to my ear in an unsteady grip. "Are you calling me on purpose or is this an unfortunate butt dial?"

It has been so long since I heard Kevin's voice, that it takes me a moment to respond. The sound of it is like walking into a wind tunnel of memories. "I'm calling you on purpose."

"Oh yeah? Well, fuck you."

"Fuck you, too." The noise in the background tells me he's in a crowd. A man's voice booms over a loudspeaker, someone shouts for a beer. "Where are you?"

"Me? Where am *I?*" The crowd makes a collectively disappointed sigh. "You don't get to ask me that when your ass has been God knows where for three years."

"You have your whole life to be a prick, Kev. Don't waste it all on one phone call."

The breath he lets out sounds like steam escaping. A moment passes. "Are you in trouble or something?"

My haggard appearance reflects back at me from the mirror above the dresser. "In a manner of speaking, yeah."

"Spit it out, Myles. I'm not a mind reader."

"You know what?" I pull the phone away from my ear, ready to end the call. "Forget it."

"No!" He clears his throat. "No...hold up. I'm listening. You called me in the middle of the Sox game. What did you expect?"

Nostalgia settles over me. The smell of hot dogs and beer. Blocking the summer sun with my hand so I can see the field. Kevin smacking me in the shoulder after a big play. I miss those afternoons with my brother. I don't think I realized how much until I watched Taylor with Jude. "You're at the game?"

He sniffs. "Of course I am. You think I gave up our season tickets just because you're not around to chip in anymore?"

"Damn." I let out a low whistle. "I guess I owe you some cash."

"Come home and we'll call it even."

The crowd cheers, the announcer's excited voice narrating a player's journey to the batter's box. Going back to Boston has been out of the question for three years, but right now...it feels possible. Everything seems possible after watching Taylor burn rubber and skid sideways in front of the mayor's car like a stunt driver. After having that incredible woman run to me, let me hold her, *nothing* in this world seems impossible.

I'm not going to disintegrate walking into my brother's or parents' home. They want me there, despite this failure I'm carrying around my neck like an albatross. Seeing Taylor with Jude made me think of my own family throughout the week. What I'm missing. How *they* would act on a snorkeling trip. Probably ridiculing the size of my feet. Or my parents and I would gang up on Kevin, claiming to have seen a shark. The typical asshole behavior I grew up with and shaped me and it's not perfect, but it's ours.

I'm not perfect...but I'm still theirs.

I could have been *hers.* She told me she could easily love me. That must mean I'm not beyond saving, right?

Maybe it's time to believe my family when they say they still want me around.

That I'm...worth having around.

"I'm in Massachusetts. Cape Cod, actually. I could...swing by."

My brother says nothing for long moments. "Really."

"Yeah. For a visit or whatever. I could do that."

"Last time we spoke, you told me you'd come back to Boston when hell froze over. What changed?"

"I, uh...I don't know." My chest winds up like a clock. "I met this woman."

"Oh. Shit." There's a smile in his voice. "I didn't see that coming."

"You and me both."

"You're the guy who always said women are a hassle, right?"

"That was me," I sigh, massaging my eye sockets.

"Just making sure." He chuckles. "What's the problem? Bring her with you for this visit."

"Seeing as how we just broke up, that's going to be hard. I mean..." I stand up and start to pace from one end of the motel room to the other. "We weren't even technically dating. She was a suspect on a case I'm working on as a favor. It's a long story. Bottom line is, she got sick of my shit and...you know. It's for the best."

"Yeah. Sounds like it's for the best. You're on the verge of tears."

"The fuck I am."

I might actually be pretty close to crying.

"Whatever your version of tears is, you're verging there."

Rolling my eyes, I cross back to the other side of the room. "This is what I get for calling you for advice, I guess."

"Advice? On *women*? Did you forget I'm married to a fellow ball scratcher?"

"No." I plow a hand through my hair. "How is he, anyway?"

"Fine." The way his voice shifts, I know his husband is sitting next to him. "Still sneaking protein powder into everything I eat and wearing running shorts literally everywhere we go." He pauses. "What's your girl like?"

An image of her rises in my mind, the way she looked on day one. In a bikini top and shorts, no shoes, sun kissed and sweet and secretly wanting rough sex. Basically a miracle on two shapely legs, dropped into my lap from heaven. "She's a second grade private school teacher from Connecticut. She's...well." The lump in my throat expands. "Beautiful is an understatement. She's a planner. A caretaker. Always making sure everyone eats and has enough coffee. Smart as hell. Brave. She also cries a lot, but in a way that, I don't know...it's just fucking cute, all right? She's stubborn and mischievous." I turn and bang my head against the wall, which shakes loose the part I didn't mean to say out loud. "She blows my mind in bed."

"Christ, you're a lot more open and honest than you used to be."

The tips of my ears burn. "Sorry."

"Don't be. I can't wait to use that information against you at a later date." Kevin laughs. "So where are you now? And where is she?"

I turn in a circle, looking around. Nothing is familiar because I spent all of my time working or with her. "I'm in my motel room in Cape Cod. She's back at her rental house."

"Drive your ass over there and apologize for whatever you did."

"How do you know I'm in the wrong?" He says nothing. "Fine. It was me. All me. But I can't just go over there and apologize. Apologizing doesn't make us compatible. Did you miss the part about her being a teacher in Connecticut? My next job is in North Carolina. Then who the hell knows where. Taylor wants to get married. Be a parent. Settle down and be happy."

"Sounds terrible. Who wants to be happy? Gross."

I curse under my breath. "You're not taking this seriously."

"Yes, I am, asshole. What sounds better to you? Going back out on the road like some damaged desperado? Or moving in with your teacher and waking up naked with her?"

Oh. Oh sweet Jesus.

I never got a chance to wake up with her head on the pillow beside mine. She'd be so warm and snuggly. And horny for morning sex. She'd be so hot on top, those hips rocking up and back, our bellies slipping together. Sweaty. Afterward, I'd kiss her everywhere. Just kiss her all the way down to her toes while she laughed—and I am so completely ruined.

I'm decimated.

"Damaged desperado really rolled off the tongue," I manage to push through my crowded throat. "Is that what you've been calling me since I left?"

"No. It's what Mom has been calling you."

"Ouch."

When did I sit on the floor? I have no idea how I got here.

"Listen, Myles. You need to go grab your patch of happiness with two hands. They don't come around very often. Some people don't get this chance at all. You're squandering it, man. Do you think she's better off without you?"

"Yeah, probably—"

"Forget I asked that." His finger taps against the receiver, like he's thinking. "Imagine she made the same mistake as you. On the Bunton case. Do you think she'd deserve to be happy at some point in the future? Or would you want her depriving herself of everything good to try and make up for a human error?"

"Of course I wouldn't want that," I rasp, loathing the idea of her unhappy.

"I'm sure she doesn't want that fate for you, either."

"Yeah." I tip my head back and notice a crack in the ceiling. It runs straight through the crown molding. Making me think of the peepholes in Oscar Stanley's house.

There's a loud gurgle in my stomach. I sit up straighter, my skin turning clammy.

The mayor couldn't have fit in that crawl space, either.

Didn't we decide that based on there being two holes, eye distance apart and angled downward, that someone must have actively been peeping at some point? Oscar couldn't have fit in the crawl space, neither could Rhonda Robinson. It would make sense that the mayor would want to keep tabs on Oscar, since he was threatening to expose her duplicity, but...

But she wouldn't have done it herself.

And this morning during the rally, when Taylor was hit in the head with the book, no way could Robinson have slipped away unnoticed in that crowd. But I know who could have.

Small, non-descript. Loyal.

"The assistant. The fucking assistant."

"What?"

The contents of my stomach lurch upward. "I have to go. I..."

Taylor is out there. Vulnerable.

I left her without protection.

I don't remember hanging up the phone on my brother. I'm already dialing Taylor. Holding the phone to my ear while ripping my keys out of my pocket, running at full speed into the parking lot. No answer. Of course not. The sound of her musical voice on the outgoing voicemail recording almost buckles my knees. Christ, oh Christ. I could lose her. Permanently. No. No, I can't breathe. "Taylor, the peepholes," I ramble, voice threadbare. "It had to be Rhonda's assistant." I'm barely able to think straight with her in potential danger. We might have arrested *a* guilty party. There are two of them, though. One is out there—and he's violent. "Get somewhere safe. *Now*, sweetheart. Please. You and Jude. And wait for me. I'm coming."

CHAPTER 21

Taylor

*W*eird how I'll cry over an Allstate commercial or two senior citizens holding hands, but right now, when my heart hurts worse with every pound, I can't eke out a tear.

I'm sitting on the beach in a sweatshirt and bare feet, arms wrapped around my raised knees. We came down here after letting the men in to replace the broken window in the back bedroom and simply never left. Now there is a magnificent sunset painting the sky with pinks and grays and I want to enjoy the beauty, but I'm too numb. It helps to have Jude sitting beside me, not talking, just occasionally rubbing a circle on my back or showing me a pretty shell. I want to ask him what happened with Dante, who was gone by the time I returned home, but if I open my mouth, I think I'll just start shouting about pigheaded men and never stop.

"It hurts now. Feels like it'll never stop," Jude says

quietly. "But it'll get easier to ignore. One day you'll be able to convince yourself it never happened."

It sounds like he's speaking from experience, but I don't have the heart to point that out. So I just nod.

Stupid bounty hunter with his secret soft center and tortured past. I fell for it. Leave it to the teacher to fall for the textbook temptation to fix a man. To incorrectly believe, somewhere deep down in my heart, that he wouldn't be able to walk away. That was nothing but a bad assumption. I'm just a Bond Girl in a long line of Bond Girls. He'll look back on me in fifteen years, squint his eyes and say, *oh yeah, the one who liked grandma ice cream.*

And I'll probably have a family and be settled down.

"Settled down," I murmur. "But I'm not going to *settle.*"

Jude raises an eyebrow at me. "Huh?"

"Well." I wet my lips, grateful to be talking and thinking about something other than Myles. "You know I've been dating men who have a serious eye toward marriage. But I don't think I'm going to do that anymore. I think maybe...I just want to live and see what happens." Saying that out loud loosens a little bit of the pressure in my chest. "I don't have to be practical and play it safe, just because I've always been told that's who I am. I'm who *I* decide to be, you know? I can play it safe in some aspects of my life, but in others, maybe I just want to help catch a murderer or have a fling with a bounty hunter. I'm more than one thing. I decide my own course. Nobody else."

Jude is nodding along with me. "You're damn right."

I pick up a handful of sand and throw it. "Shoot. I didn't mean to bring him up. I don't want to talk about him."

"We don't have to."

"But since we're on the subject, I hope his long hair gets stuck in a toaster."

"Savage."

"I mean, not in a way that he gets electrocuted," I rush to clarify. "Just in a way that is inconvenient and embarrassing."

"I'll see what can be arranged."

"Maybe I should look at this whole torrid affair as a positive thing. He shook me up. Make me realize what I need to be...to feel. To feel. And now I'm determined to expect more out of my future real, *functioning* relationships."

"Gratitude is a healthy way to approach anything."

I wrinkle my nose. "Gratitude is a little bit of an over-statement. Maybe once the hostility fades." We share a laugh and I reach over to squeeze his hand. "Are you all right?"

He blows a long breath out at the ocean. "No. But I will be."

We sit in silence for several minutes, watching the sky turn from pink to orange to cerulean and finally, midnight blue. Stars wink to life on the canvas of the sky, the brush blowing behind us on the hill. Laughter reaches us from backyards up and down the beach, fire pits glowing and barbeques smoking.

I'm unsettled—and I know it's because of Myles. The way things ended. The way everything feels so woefully unfinished. I miss his big, grouchy ass. But there's more. There's a little niggling sensation buried in the nape of my neck that won't quit. I tell myself the itch comes with the territory of being hit over the head with an encyclopedia, having the best sex of my life and catching a murderer all in one day...but the worry just keeps churning. Eventually it moves to my stomach. I'm getting ready to voice my—prob-ably—unfounded concerns to my brother when a wind rolls off the turbulent Atlantic and lifts the hair off my neck, making me shiver.

"Hey, I'll go grab us some blankets and beers from the house. Sound good?"

"Sounds great." I fall back onto my elbows, watching him plod through the sand toward the stairs. "Hey, can you bring my phone down? I left it charging in the kitchen."

"Yup."

After a few minutes, I let myself melt back completely onto the sand, not caring if it gets in my hair or into my clothing. It's cooled down from the day's sunshine and from here, I can look up at the gigantic sky above. Me and my problems are miniscule compared to it—

There's a metallic click behind me.

It's a gun being cocked.

My muscles tense up, my mouth going dry, but I don't move. I'm frozen.

"You're pretty relaxed for someone who goes around ruining lives."

I know that voice, but it's not overly familiar. Belonging to a young man.

Where have I heard it before?

Footsteps approach, then I'm kicked in the ribs. Not hard, but forceful enough to make me cry out. Hand pressing to the throbbing spot, I sit up and scramble backward awkwardly on my elbows, heels shoving at the sifting sand.

The man comes into view.

The mayor's assistant. Kyle?

No. *Kurt.*

Kurt is pointing a gun at me—and of course this is the moment everything clicks into place. Very convenient.

The assistant just barely tops five feet. Everything has

happened so fast since this afternoon, I haven't stopped to review all of the evidence and reconcile it with the mayor's guilt. But of course Kurt was involved. He's always at her side, ready to serve. He would have spied on Oscar for her, easily fitting into that area behind the bedroom wall.

"Piecing it all together? Took you long enough. Maybe you and your boyfriend aren't as smart as you think you are."

Myles.

He's going to flip out.

For some reason, that's really comforting.

Or it will be, if I don't die.

He's also going to be so hard on himself when he realizes this oversight. Who could have seen it coming, though? Rhonda didn't implicate Kurt at the scene. She only denied her own guilt.

Wake up. Think.

Hostages usually survive by keeping their captor talking. Personalizing themselves. I'm not technically a hostage—yet?—but the same logic should still apply, right? Although, if I keep Kurt talking and Jude comes back, my brother will be in danger, too.

No, I can't have that.

My pulse is almost deafening in my temples, but I force a deep breath.

"Did she know?"

"Who?"

"Rhonda. The mayor. Did she know you were spying on Oscar?"

"No," he spits, as if I'm an idiot for asking. "Do you think I *wanted* to watch a live feed of that sad sack while he binged *Bake Off* all day? I didn't. Although it was better than keeping tabs on him from the closet." He shivers. "Oscar Stanley. What an idiot. Did he really think Rhonda was *actually* going to pass any laws to restrict him from renting? She was telling people what they wanted to hear to secure reelection. That's what we do. We stay in office at all costs. And it's my job to make sure the mayor doesn't have to worry about the details. That's what makes me the *best*. After one more term as mayor of this middle-class hell hole, she was going to run for state senate and I would have been right there, indispensable. No one overlooking me, like I'm nothing but an inconsequential flea."

"You're not inconsequential."

"Don't pander to me." He jabs the air with the muzzle of the gun. "The cops would have pursued that meathead father who kicked Oscar's ass. He probably would have been found innocent. But by then, everyone would have forgotten about the murder of a man no one knew. The Barnstable police wouldn't have been motivated to dig and ruin a good thing with Rhonda. But you had to poke. And prod. And you didn't take my warnings, did you?"

Slowly, I inch sideways, hoping he'll turn in the same clockwise motion so his back will be to the stairwell. "You clocked me with the book. You threw the buoy."

His finger moves on the trigger. "Should have just shot you and gotten it over with."

"You're going to get caught."

"Oh, I know I'm going to be caught. The cops are already bringing me in for questioning. Rhonda is putting it all together, I'm sure. And will she appreciate what I did for her? To keep her double life out of the press? No. I'm sure she'll act horrified on the evening news. But if she found out what I did and I never got caught? She wouldn't have said shit. Because that's politics."

Out of the corner of my eye, I see Jude coming down the stairs.

No. *No.*

It's clear there isn't going to be any reasoning with Kurt. He's got nothing to lose.

I suck in as much air as I can and scream for everything I'm worth. "Jude! Run!"

Myles

*I*t's my nightmare come to life.

I didn't resolve a piece of evidence and now the woman I've fallen for could pay the price.

My bike is moving so fast down Coriander Lane, the tires are barely meeting the asphalt. Sweat pours down the side of my face, a pit yawning open in my stomach. None of the lights are on in the house when I park outside. Please tell me they went out to dinner or somewhere the assistant hasn't located them yet. Kurt. Kurt Forsythe. I had his last name confirmed by the Barnstable police, who I called on the way here. I only recall the conversation in snippets. Could barely hear the chief's voice over the roaring in my ears. After what Wright confided to us about the police potentially looking the other way with the mayor, part of me wanted to come alone, but I had to weigh the risks—and the risk I absolutely cannot take is with Taylor's life.

House door locked.

A quick glance in through the front window shows no signs of life—

There's a movement to my right, in the distance. Someone on the stairs leading down to the beach. "Please be Taylor. Please be them."

I lunge off the porch and jog in the direction of the figure. Hard to make out who it is now that the sun is down. But when I'm about fifty yards away, I recognize the hair, the build. Jude. And immediately, I know something is wrong. Very wrong. His hands are up and he's shaking his head. That's when I hear Taylor's hoarse scream and my legs almost liquify.

"Jude! Go! Please!"

"What the fuck is going on? Who is that?" Jude's tone is laced with fear. "Put the gun down!"

Gun. Taylor. There's a gun on Taylor.

My skin is nothing but a sheet of ice, heart lurching and racing.

No. No, please God, no. Not her.

Focus. You have to focus.

Number one. If there is a gun down on the beach, Jude is in harm's way, too.

"Jude," I growl, not recognizing my own voice.

His head whips around and his horror-filled expression threatens to derail whatever composure I have—and it's not much.

"Myles." He turns awkwardly and trips over the step behind him. "There's a guy down there pointing a gun at Taylor."

My icy skin thaws rapidly and now I'm hot. Piping hot. Chest burning. No. *No, no, no.* A memory of Taylor inviting me for tacos catches me off guard and a rough sound escapes. She'd want me to get her brother somewhere safe. "Jude. Come here. You need to come here now and let me handle this. The police are on the way."

He's incredulous. "I'm not leaving her down there!"

"*We* are not leaving her down there. Of course we're not. But if she thinks you're in danger, she might do something erratic and get herself hurt."

Jude curses and swipes at his eyes. "He's going to shoot her."

Hold on. Hold on to your control. "Is he on the shorter side? Glasses?"

"Yeah. Yes."

"Okay. You're going to trade places with me, all right? I'm going to speak to him."

The static in my head is so loud, when I finally hear the sirens approaching, I have no idea how long they've been wailing. But they're close. Very close.

"Jude! *Go!*" Taylor hollers from the beach again, her scream mingling with the crashing waves. "Please!"

It's hard. It's hard to think in logical terms when she's in danger. When she sounds so scared that my heart wants to tear through my chest. My instinct when it comes to Taylor and her safety is animalistic. I want to hop the stair railing and hurtle down the hill at full speed and plow down everything standing between me and her. But impulsive behavior gets people killed. I need to be calm right now and *think*.

What do I know?

One, Kurt obviously doesn't care if he gets caught. There are countless houses positioned along the beach, all of them facing the water and the sun has barely gone down. People are awake. Roasting hot dogs. Likely watching this whole scene unfold and probably calling the police. Not to mention, Jude has seen him holding a gun on Taylor. Kurt is potentially unbalanced. He's not going to act reasonably.

Two, Kurt's motive is revenge. We arrested his boss. Cost him his job. One or both of them is going to be charged with the murder of Oscar Stanley—depending on Rhonda's knowledge of Kurt's actions. But I was present when the police questioned Rhonda Robinson—and unless she's the world's greatest actress, she doesn't know what Kurt did to prevent Evergreen Corp. from being exposed. Out of loyalty.

Loyalty to the mayor.

Dedication.

I can use that.

My hands are shaking as I punch out a quick text to Wright, shoving my phone quickly into my back pocket once again. "Back up slowly, Jude," I say, trying to sound reassuring, even though my heart is in my mouth. "We're going to get Taylor back safely. You know I'm going to do everything I can to make that happen."

Jude hesitates for another few seconds, then finally crawls up the remaining stairs, sitting on the grass landing with his head in his hands. Red and white lights flash at the bottom of the hill. Finally. Sirens turned off, as instructed, they race up the street and pull to a stop at haphazard angles. Wright climbs out of his vehicle first and jogs over to me, handing over the bullhorn and a phone, a call live on the screen, seconds ticking upward.

With those tools in hand, I move toward the staircase, praying like hell my appearance doesn't set Kurt off. Or induce him to pull the trigger. If he's going after Taylor, it's because of her role in the investigation. I was involved, too, more heavily than she was. He's seen us together. He picked the only one of us he could bully, but I wouldn't put it past him to use violence against Taylor to pay me back for my role in the case. He doesn't have an earthly clue how much it would ruin me, though. My fucking heart would stop beating.

I could let the police chief run point on this, but I can't put her safety in someone else's hands. I won't do it. Especially when there is a chance they were planning on covering for the mayor and therefore might be operating in a morally gray area.

I take another several steps and they come into view. Kurt. Taylor. The gun. My stomach lurches violently at the sight of my Taylor with her hands up, trembling. I can tell she's trembling from here. She looks so fragile from this distance and I'm going to kill this motherfucker. I'm going to kill him. Scalding hot rage starts to bleed into my thoughts, blur them together, but I fight to remain calm. Composed. Thinking clearly. Taylor is at stake.

Our life together is at stake.

Did I really think I could just walk *away* from her?

I would sell my soul to the devil to be holding her right now. To hold her forever.

"Kurt," I call, as evenly as possible. "This is Myles Sumner. Do you know me?"

He takes a step closer to Taylor, as if he means to grab her, use her as a shield, and she lurches backward, out of his reach. Good girl. She can see what I see. That despite being a murderer, he's not confident holding a gun. He can barely hold it up at this stage. He's using his opposite hand to brace his elbow.

"Of course I know you," he shouts up the stairs. "I know everything that happens here. It's my job. I'm good at my job."

This is what I was hoping for. Pride in his work. Dedication to the job and loyalty to Rhonda Robinson. "Is Taylor all right?"

"She won't be for much longer. I was just waiting for you. I wanted you to see this."

My throat closes in.

This is how he's going to come for me. A fight between us would be a mismatch, but he can knock me out in a death blow by pulling that trigger. "You don't want to hurt Taylor." I'm all but gasping for air when I say that, so I take a moment to regain control. "You're not a killer, Kurt. Just a man who goes above and beyond for his job."

"I'm not buying your attempts at psychology."

"That's fine, man. But the mayor needs to speak with you."

"What?" He lowers the gun in surprise, but raises it back up just as quickly. "She's not here. She's in custody."

But he's splitting his attention now between me and Taylor. Good.

Just have to keep chipping away until it's all on me and she can escape.

I bring the phone to my ear. "Mayor Robinson?" I say into the receiver.

"Yes," she responds, briskly, but with an underlying weariness. "I didn't know about Kurt. I didn't know—"

"You were briefed by Wright?" I cut in.

She sighs. "I was, yes."

"Good." I swallow hard, inhaling and exhaling through a wave of dizziness. "Please. I need you to talk him down. He's holding a gun on my girlfriend. If something happens to her..."

"I understand. I don't want anyone else to get hurt over this. Put me on."

The sudden confidence in her tone doesn't make me feel better. Nothing is going to make me feel better until Taylor is out of the line of fire. Praying to a maker who I haven't spoken to in a very long time, I hold the phone up to the bullhorn.

Rhonda's voice carries down to the beach, accompanied by an opening squeal of feedback. "Kurt?"

The assistant's head whips around. "Mayor?"

She can't hear his response. Not yet, anyway. But she continues as if he's listening. "I knew the day I hired you that it was one of the best decisions I ever made. And you have never let me down. Not once. There is no one on my staff that I trust more. No one that believes in my vision for this county and has the tools to help me execute it."

"I had to do it!" he calls back, thinking Rhonda can hear him. "Stanley would have killed our chance at being reelected."

I drop the phone away from the bullhorn, bringing the speaker to my mouth. "Kurt, the mayor has some things she would like to say to you in private. For your ears alone. Are you okay with me bringing down the phone?"

I hold my breath. *Come on.*

He's torn. His attention shifts from the staircase to Taylor, back to me. "Leave your weapons up there. All of them. Or I'll fucking shoot her, I swear to God."

No.

Not going to let that happen, sweetheart. Have faith in me.

"Okay." I set down the bullhorn and the phone, taking my gun out of my waistband and putting it on the ground. I lift both of my pant legs to show him I have nothing. "I'm unarmed, all right? I'm coming down."

This guy might be book smart or politically savvy, but he's an idiot to let me come within ten feet of him. I just have to hope he doesn't realize that as I get closer. Holding up the phone like a peace offering, I travel down the steps slowly, heart ricocheting in my ribcage. Kurt is not stable. The closer I get, the more obvious that becomes. He's muttering to himself. Every once in a while, he punctuates the air between him and Taylor with the muzzle of the gun, as if to remind her who is in charge. The tide could turn at any second.

Please just let me make it over there.

"Are you ready to speak to the mayor, Kurt?"

"Toss me the phone."

I'm down on the beach now. It's high tide, so I'm only about twenty yards from where they stand and I'm continuing to inch forward slowly, over the crunching seaweed and pebbles. "You're pretty close to the water, man. I don't know if that's a good idea." *Breathe. Breathe. She's right there. Don't think about how terrified she looks or you'll lose it.* "How about this? You let Taylor head back up the stairs and point the gun at me, instead. That way I can come over there and hand you the phone safely."

"No. No way. I don't know."

"The mayor told me you would never hurt an innocent woman. She's right, Kurt. I know she's right. And she has a lot more to tell you. Let's just let Taylor go home."

"Myles," she whimpers, shaking her head.

"It's okay," I rasp. I can't look at her. I can't look at her, even to reassure her. There's still a gun pointed at her and I'm not good. The longer it's trained on her, the more rapidly my sanity deteriorates. "Kurt?"

When he points the gun at me, I'm nearly felled with relief. "Go, Taylor."

She hesitates.

"Go. *Please*."

With a sob, she starts to run. Thank God. *Thank God.* I don't move a single step until I hear her footsteps fade on the wooden planks of the stairs. Until I hear Jude's exclamation and the flurry of police movement. Safe. She's safe.

I hold out the phone in my right hand, the palm of my left hand visible.

One step, two, my boots sinking into the sand.

"We found the same gun on the beach," I say, nodding at his Glock, which he is struggling to keep aloft. "Did you plant it to delay the investigation or throw us off your trail?"

He's staring at the phone. "Both."

"Well played."

"Don't humor me," he hisses through his teeth. "Give me the phone."

I nod evenly, edging forward another step. Two. "Here you go. It's all yours."

He's so eager to speak with his boss and absorb more of her false praise for what he's done that he's distracted for a split second. But that's all I need. I toss the phone up in the air and his attention goes with it. My left hand clamps around the wrist of the hand holding the gun, angling it toward the ocean. It goes off. A bullet fired into the black water where it will hit no one. Especially not Taylor.

The reminder that this man meant to kill her causes me to subdue him with a harder punch than intended, the crunch of cartilage not nearly enough. Nothing will ever be enough. But that's all it takes for him to go down in a heap on the sand, the phone landing beside his outstretched hand. I remove the clip from his gun and toss it down, too, my adrenaline crashing with a vengeance. From all sides. I see Taylor flying down the stairs in my direction, but I'm shaking my head, not quite ready to declare the beach danger free for her.

She keeps coming, though, leaping, our chests colliding, her arms wrapping around my neck. I'm still so numb with the fear of potentially losing her that I can't even pick up my arms to hug her back. For long moments, all I can do is breathe in the scent of apples, rubbing my face in her hair, until finally my limbs start to work again and I crush her tight to my body, overcome by the fact that she's alive. She's alive and she's not hurt.

"Taylor."

"I know. I know."

"*Taylor.*"

She kisses my cheek, my jaw. "I know."

I'm trying to process out loud the fact that I almost lost her, but she seems to understand without words. She seems to know it would have killed me. Good. Good, we'll work out the rest. Everything else is details as long as she's alive. I'm surrounded by police officers now who want statements. They are trying to rouse Kurt on the sand and he's stirring. There's no way in hell I'm trusting anyone but myself to cuff him and bring him to jail. This man was going to kill the incredible woman I'm holding in my arms. This woman who trusted me to keep her safe. *My* woman. I'm seeing this through. "Give them your statement," I say, kissing her temple. "I won't be able to relax until he's locked up and he probably needs medical attention first."

Her lips twitch. "Thanks to you."

I tuck some windblown strands of hair behind her ear. "He had a gun pointed at you. He's lucky he doesn't need a coroner."

She smiles at me, but something is off.

Why does she seem...sad?

Her arms drop from their position around my neck, her hands sliding into the rear pockets of her shorts. "Thank you. For what you did. Trading places with me and...all of it."

"You don't have to thank me."

After a second, she nods. "I know. You were doing your job."

What the hell? "You're more than a job."

She nods, as if she was expecting me to say that. But I don't really think she understands. I need to spell this out for her. "Taylor, I'm—"

"Sumner!" Wright shouts. "The chief has some questions—"

"In a minute!" I bark over my shoulder, before facing Taylor again. "Hey. Listen to what I'm telling you. Even when I thought we had this case solved, I couldn't leave. I want to do this. Us. I need to be with you. Do you hear me? I'm done running. I want to run to you."

"Wow," Wright says to my left. "That's poetic, man." He sniffs. "Ah shit. I need to call my ex-wife."

"Walk away," I grit out.

"Sorry. Sorry."

When we're alone again, Taylor still looks sort of resigned and Christ, I'm starting to panic. "You feel this way right now, Myles, because we just went through something scary together." She squeezes my arm. "But tomorrow or the next day you'll remember all the reasons you told me this wouldn't work and you'll be right—"

"No. I was a fucking moron, Taylor. I said that shit out of anger and fear."

Isn't this supposed to be the happy ending? Guy saves girl, guy kisses girl and they ride off into the sunset? The girl isn't supposed to say *nah, thanks, I'm good*.

This isn't happening.

"I was supposed to come here. I was supposed to meet you. The road was leading me *here*. To you. All right?" Here we go. The final wall has collapsed. I'm exposed. "You made me remember I love Boston. Because you reminded me of what home feels like. You made me call my brother. Because you made me remember what love feels like. You did that. I'm not walking away from you. We're going to fight until we meet in the middle, Taylor. End of story. You're not cutting me off. I'm taking you home to meet my family. I'm doing the whole fucking thing, all right?" I clasp the sides of her face in my hands. "Please let me do the whole thing?"

Everyone is listening.

There is a crowd of officers and detectives hanging on my every word. I'm pretty sure even Kurt is invested and the mayor is still listening on the other end of the line. Ask me if I care. Ask me if I care when I'm performing my own open-heart surgery and this women who I can't live without still looks dubious. "You've moved on, in your head. I can see that." It guts me to acknowledge that out loud. "You've written me off. Okay. Tell me you feel something for me and I'll write myself back in. I'll bust my ass doing it."

"Of course I feel something for you," she whispers.

Our audience lets out a collective sigh of relief.

Nothing compared to mine. It's like I just made it from the ocean floor to the surface.

"Thank God," I say on a rocky exhale, leaning down to kiss her. But her eyes are still cloudy. She needs more than words. I've spent our entire acquaintance telling her I commit to nothing and no one. Actions are the only thing that will convince her.

Done.

I'm in it for keeps—and she's not going to doubt me for long.

CHAPTER 22

Taylor

"What is he doing?" I ask, staring outside the front of our rental house.

We're packed, ready to leave, suitcases by the front door.

We were preparing to load the luggage into the trunk of my car when I spotted Myles across the street, sitting on his bike. Or more like...waiting? Helmet in lap, arms crossed over the powerful breadth of his chest. A duffel bag is secured to the rear of his seat.

What is he *doing?*

Is he waiting to say goodbye?

There is no way I'm holding him to the promises he made last night. Those were words soaked in adrenaline and residual fear. Promises he made because he feels protective of me and I was in danger. Now that the sun has come up, I'm sure he's back to his bounty hunter mindset.

Quick, no-strings jobs are what he wants. If he doesn't get attached, he can't get hurt.

"Maybe you should go out and talk to him?" Jude suggests.

I could. I should.

I'm just not sure I'm prepared to hear goodbye. Because despite my best intentions, the things he said to me last night in that passionate tone of voice...they might have given me a teeny tiny bit of hope. Dangerous, stupid hope. *Ignore it.*

"Let's go. We want to beat the traffic."

I pick up my suitcase, hesitate in front of the door and push it open. When Jude passes me, I close the door behind him, lock it and leave the key for Lisa under the large ceramic starfish on the porch. On my way to the car, I frown at the biker across the street. "Good morning," I call, handing my suitcase to Jude so he can lift it into the trunk. "We're getting a jump on the traffic. Back to *Connecticut*."

He nods at me. *Nods.* But says nothing.

Then he puts on his helmet and the bike roars to life.

Huh. So he's not even going to say goodbye? Maybe we're taking the easier route of parting ways without any of the messy apologies or lies that we'll call each other. Fine. I'll follow his lead. Never mind that my heart is withering like a grape left too long on the vine.

I crank the volume on the AM traffic station and back out of the driveway, my eyebrows drawing together when Myles follows our next three turns. Just a coincidence. We're both heading toward the interstate, obviously.

When we reach the interstate, Myles takes the same ramp. Same direction.

He barely leaves enough room between us for other cars to merge.

I switch lanes, he switches lanes.

"Is he *following* me?"

A laugh bursts out of my brother. "It took you way too long to figure that out."

"All the way back to Hartford? Uh-uh. No way."

"All the way to your front door, Taylor. You *know* that's what's happening." Jude turns in his seat to observe Myles through the rear window, grinning ear to ear. "Admit this is romantic."

"No," I say, breathily. "It's not."

"He sacrificed himself for you on the beach last night and now he's literally tailing you home." Jude drops his voice and switches to an Australian accent, as if he's narrating the Discovery Channel. "This appears to be some kind of unique bounty hunter ritual, Taylor. Be mean to the potential mate as long as possible, then wife her when she least expects it."

Oh God. My lower lip trembles a little bit. That smidgen of hope he lit inside of me last night is growing...and that's dangerous. This whole idea is dangerous and stupid. "That is not what is happening here. He's just making sure I don't trip on the way home and land in the lap of a serial killer or something."

"You're not getting knifed. You're getting wifed."

I wring my hands on the steering wheel. "He changed his mind too fast. If he came and stayed with me, he would regret it eventually."

"You know him better than I do, but he doesn't strike me as fickle."

"No. He's not." I chew my lip, my eyes continually straying to his giant, helmeted figure. "But he still has all these unresolved issues with his family."

"Everyone on this highway has unresolved issues with

their family," he responds without a second's hesitation. "Didn't you say he called his brother?"

"Yes. Because I reminded him...because..."

"You reminded him what love feels like."

"That was the adrenaline talking."

Jude clearly wants to argue with me, but we spend the next few minutes in silence—save the rumble of the motor-cycle engine behind us. "Look, I'm with you, T," my brother says, finally. "Whatever you want to do, I'll back you up. If you want to pull over and tell him to get lost, that's what we'll do."

I swallow hard. "That's what I want to do. It's for his own good. He has a sense of misplaced responsibility for me and I'm going to set him free."

"Okay, cool. Let's do it." He squints at the approaching highway sign. "Pull over somewhere I can get coffee."

After driving another three exits, I spot some golden arches and take the off-ramp. Waiting to see if Myles will follow, my throat turns dry and my pulse moves at a breakneck pace. There is no mistaking the relief that washes over me when he guides his bike off the highway after us.

Okay. I can do this. I can be strong, rip off the Band-Aid and do what's best for myself, as well as Myles. I'm definitely not going to get even *more* attached to this man, just so he can blaze off into the sunset in a month or two, tired of my crying jags and thrifty habits. That would absolutely kill me. I've only known him for five days and the prospect of never seeing him again was nearly unbearable. What would it be like after weeks? Months?

No. I'm not going to find out.

When I pull into the McDonald's parking lot, Jude turns to me. "Do you want me here when you give the speech?"

"No. I can do it alone." I take a deep breath. "Get me an iced coffee, please. I'm going to need it."

"That's probably an understatement."

I don't get a chance to ask my brother what he means by that ominous statement, because Myles rumbles into the spot beside me, switches off his engine...

And then he takes off his helmet, tossing back his mane of sweaty hair, biceps flexing as he hangs it over the handlebar. He grabs the hem of his shirt and lifts it, swiping sweat from his brow and briefly exposing his thick, muscle-packed stomach. Those sharp ridges shift with his movements, covered in a light sheen of perspiration. *Oh my.*

When my view of Myles is obscured, I realize my breath is fogging the window.

Shaking myself, I exit the car on suddenly gelatinous legs. I clasp my hands together at my waist and straighten my spine, as if I'm getting ready to address the parents on back-to-school night. "Myles, this is simply not necessary—"

A big hand settles on my hip, cutting me off. Scorching me through my dress.

"Come here," he says in a low voice, drawing me forward. "I like what you're wearing."

"Oh." My right hip meets his inner thigh and a hot shiver wracks me, blazing a path through my belly and straight down to my toes. "I...um. Thanks, but—"

"These aren't vacation clothes, are they? They're regular life clothes."

"Correct."

He leans in to peer at my neckline, so close I can taste the salt of his sweat on my tongue. My nipples tighten in response. Quickly. Painfully. And so, when he says, "Are those little pearls sewn into the collar?" in that guttural tone of voice, I almost climb up on that very large, very sinewy thigh and scandalize the McDonald's parking lot.

"I...yes. I suppose they are."

"Mmm." He fists the material of my dress and tugs gently until my breasts are a mere inch away from his chest. "Should I expect you in prim and proper dresses like this year-round?"

I don't understand the question.

I'm too busy counting the grains of his stubble. Even his ears are attractive. Why have I never taken the time to notice his *ears* before? Heat rolls off his big shoulders in my direction, making it necessary to curl my fingers into my palms before I do something unwise like trace the swell of his pectorals or brush back his long hair.

"What you're thinking is in no way showing on your face, Taylor," he says gruffly.

"Good," I respond briskly. Until those words actually penetrate. "I mean...what?"

He uses his grip on my dress to tug me close, laying his mouth against my ear. "You're beautiful, sweetheart. You're so fucking beautiful."

"Okay." I'm shaking, hot moisture held at bay by the backs of my eyelids. "But you can't just keep following me, Myles."

"Taylor?" He captures my mouth in a long, hard kiss. "I'm going to keep following you."

"Oh." I stare at his perfect, one-of-a-kind mouth, wondering how I can get a little more action out of it. Without committing to anything, of course. This whole situation is ludicrous. "Well, I guess we can discuss this in Connecticut and you can leave from there."

"We can discuss whatever you want. But I'm not leaving."

How can I still want to climb onto his lap when he's being so obstinate? "Have you been this stubborn the whole time?"

"Yes. Just not about the right things."

"What does that mean?" I murmur, heart fluttering. *Stop fluttering. Please.*

"It means, I should have been less damn stubborn when pushing away the best thing that ever happened to me." His voice resonates with sincerity and regret. "And more stubborn about locking her down."

"I'm n-not property to be locked down."

"*I* am. I'm your property." His lips skim my jawline. "Inside and out."

"Huhhh," I whimper, embarrassingly, gravitating closer despite my best intentions, biting my lip to trap another second humiliating sound when my breasts flatten against his hard chest. "I appreciate all of this. You...saying things. Nice things." Oh my God. Speak coherently. You're a teacher. "I'm just worried you're jumping into this relationship too fast and that you'll regret being so hasty down the road."

I'm arrested by his sudden grin. "You called it a relationship."

"Don't focus on that part."

"I'm laser focused on it, Taylor." His grin fades into a serious expression. "We experienced more in five days than most people experience in a year together. We got to know each other's strengths and weaknesses and fears and dreams. Fast. And I'm drawn to every single piece of you. Everything that makes you Taylor. By the grace of God, you're drawn to me, too, or you wouldn't be halfway into my lap right now in a McDonald's parking lot. Wave at the nice family, sweetheart."

With a wince, I turn to find a Happy Meal toting family

of five hustling to their station wagon through the parking lot. The mother is covering her youngest child's eyes and shaking her head at me. "There's a time and a place, folks," she calls.

"Sorry!" I put several inches of space in between me and Myles, smoothing the new wrinkles from my dress while he chuckles. "As I was saying..." *Was* I saying something?

Myles's mouth is still twitching, so much affection in his eyes that I feel another lip tremble coming on. "I'm coming over, Taylor. To your place." He rakes a set of fingers through his hair. "Maybe right now a relationship sounds crazy to you. Maybe you need to see me there to believe it's happening. *We're* happening."

"You think if I see you in my kitchen...I'll be more inclined to believe this could work."

"It's a start."

"Maybe you're just trying to get me into bed."

He laughs without humor. "I need you in bed so bad, I could barely zip up this morning."

"Wow." Jude comes to a stop beside me, shaking my ice coffee until I reach for it. "Really feels like I've been an intimate part of this process. About ready to bow out, though."

Face flaming, I fumble with my free hand for the driver's side door handle. "I guess I'll see you in Connecticut, then."

"Damn right you will," Myles says, putting his helmet back on.

Jude waves his coffee. "Please drop me off first."

---

*I*t's already working.

Just watching Myles park in one of the guest spots in my complex makes everything between us feel real.

He's here. He's not a figment of my imagination. Of course, just like anywhere else Myles goes, he dwarfs everything around him. People in the lot. Even the cars seem tiny in comparison. But he doesn't seem to be noticing anything but me. He crosses the lot in my direction, duffel bag thrown over one ox-like shoulder, determination hardening every line of his body—and I can already feel myself caving. We aren't even *inside* yet.

"So..." I start to lift my suitcase out of the trunk, but he does it for me. With one finger. Is that supposed to impress me? Because it does. "Thank you. So..." I wave my car keys in the direction of the guest lot. "That's where you would park."

"Would."

"Uh-huh." I walk ahead of him, unlock the gate and take one flight of stairs up to my apartment. And I only drop my keys twice because of the ferocious way he's looking at my butt. I also drop them to delay the moment this colossal bounty hunter enters my boho chic living space with his size thirteen steel-toed boots and remembers we're nothing alike. And leaves. Back to his nomadic, commitment-free life.

"You need some help unlocking the door, Taylor?"

"No, I've got it."

"Your hands are shaking."

"I'm cold."

He's kind not to point out that it's July and eighty degrees. Finally, I get the door open and he follows me inside, stepping in so I can close the door behind him. There is enough sunlight that I don't need to turn on any lamps, so I fuss with the thermostat, instead, getting the air flowing. "Taylor."

"Yes?"

"Look at me." I do what he asks, watching him set down my suitcase, followed by his duffel bag. Slowly. "This is me inside your door."

My stupid heart crawls up into my throat. All I can do is nod.

He toes off his boots. Crosses the room to me and takes my hand, leading me into the kitchen. "This is me at your refrigerator." He raps his knuckles on the appliance and smirks at me. "I'll be here a lot." My laughter is winded. He leans down, studies my face closely, then kisses the sound off my mouth very thoroughly. "I'll cook for you."

"When you're here?"

"What do you mean?" he asks patiently, facing me.

Almost like he *wants* me to ask questions.

"I mean...you'd be on the road a lot," I say, wetting my lips. "Doing jobs. Didn't you say they take weeks sometimes? Therefore, you would cook on the infrequent occasions that you *are* here."

He hums in his throat. "I see your point. Guess bounty hunting is out."

I must have misheard him. "Sorry, what?"

"I guess I'm done bounty hunting," he says, brushing back my hair. "I'm not spending weeks at a time away from you, Taylor. No fucking way. I want to be here. With you."

"But..."

"But what? You think I'm jumping into this without any thought or preparation?" He props a forearm above my head on the fridge, his free hand playing with the ends of my hair. "Remember the private investigation firm I was planning to open with my brother? We spent the night working on the details. He's going to run the Boston end. I'm going to find some office space and work from here. We'll cast a wider net this way. He's already signed on a few retired detectives who need some action."

Every inch of my body is buzzing. Goosebumps are springing up everywhere. I'm barely capable of breathing. "You...so you're actually..."

"Moving here." He tilts his head. "I thought that was clear."

"You left out a lot of particulars," I manage.

"I figured we'd get around to them." Both of his hands fall to my hips, squeezing them roughly while he makes a sound in his throat. "Show me the rest of your place."

"Um. Where?"

His lips twitch. "How about the bathroom?"

"Okay." I slide out from between Myles and the fridge, moving on trembling legs down the hallway to the bathroom, flipping on the light. I gesture for him to step inside and he does—but he pulls me with him. Positions me at the sink, facing the medicine cabinet mirror.

"This is me in your bathroom," he says into my hair, his fingertips trailing up and down my bare arms. "Can you see us brushing our teeth together here in the mornings?"

I tilt my head consideringly. As if I don't want to scream yes.

As if I'm not a millisecond from launching myself into his arms and never letting go.

When I don't answer right away, he leans back a little and strips off his shirt. "How about now? This is more accurate since I sleep naked."

Brain meltdown. "You do?"

"You will, too, Taylor." He dips down behind me and comes up flush, his lap to my butt, that hard part of him parting my cheeks through the material of my dress. We both moan, two sets of hands clutching at the edge of the sink. "If we're going to share a bed—and by if, I mean when —you'll be too worn out to wear anything but whisker burns and the top sheet." He elevates me onto my toes, his warm breath puffing onto my neck. "How are you doing visualizing me here now, sweetheart? Starting to seem real yet?"

"Starting to. Yes."

I'm watching his face in the mirror and witness the blaze of relief. The way his breath shudders out as if he's been holding it since the parking lot. "Thank God. That's some-thing." He turns me around to face him. "I know this is moving fast, Taylor. I'm going to get an apartment close by, so I don't scare the hell out of you. I'm coming on too strong? You throw me out for the night. But I'll be here as much as you want me here. And then one day, we'll merge your fringed throw pillows with my functional man shit and we'll be in one place. Our place. When you're ready."

There is no way I'm letting him rent an apartment, but I don't get a chance to tell him that. Because his mouth is on mine and he's walking me out of the bathroom, down the remainder of the hallway and into my bedroom, matching me step for step. Before we can crash down onto the bed with Myles on top, he breaks the kiss and lifts his head, looking around the room. Taking a deep inhale. Of the room, then my neck. "Apples."

I lean in and rub my nose on his throat. "Sweat."

His deep chuckle makes me shiver. "Better work on that."

"No." I let him peel my dress off over my head. "I like it."

He unhooks the front clasp of my bra, pushing it open on a groan and kneading my breasts in his hands, head falling forward as if he's been desperate to touch them. "You should like it. You're the reason I'm sweating all the time."

"Who, me?"

"Yeah you," he says, gruffly. Pausing in the act of thumbing my nipples. "This is me in your bedroom, Taylor. Can you see me here?"

"Yes," I whisper, shaken down to the ground by what I feel for this man. How is it possible that he wasn't in my life a week ago? Now that I'm letting myself believe this is real, a wealth of emotion rushes in and chokes my next breath. "I can see you here."

His eyes close briefly, chest dipping and rising dramatically. "Good."

In a flash, my back is pressed to the mattress and his hard, heavy body is coming down on mine, our mouths moving feverishly together while he works my panties down to mid-thigh, pushes them down past my knees, where I hook my toe into the waistband and drag them off completely. Our hands clash in an effort to unzip his jeans, my core throbbing for him. Needing him. Weeping over having been without him so long. "Wet, baby?" he asks in between mind scrambling kisses, his hardness finally, finally springing out into my waiting palm.

Transferring to his, mid-stroke.

"Yes," I gasp—and he enters me in a mighty shove, shouting my name into my neck while my cry of his name resonates in the hazy bedroom, the headboard cracking hard off the wall. "*Myles.*"

I'm aching for him to thrust. To dominate me. To give me a break from this tension that only he has ever inspired. But he tilts my chin up and looks me in the eye, instead, love naked on his features. Right there for me to witness. No holding back. "This is me in your body, Taylor." His hips rear back and rock forward, deep, deeper than before. "You feel me here?" he asks, raggedly, pressing my knees up toward the pillows.

"*Yes*," I gasp.

And because he's been vulnerable, because he's given up so much ground to make me believe, I pull his forehead down to mine and take the biggest leap of all—the emotional one—meeting him halfway. "This is you in my heart," I say, voice uneven. Kissing him softly. Once, twice. "Do you feel yourself there?"

"Yeah," he chokes out, eyes suspiciously damp. "Keep me there. All right?"

"There's no getting you out. I don't want to."

Visibly overcome, he drives my body up and down the bed, in that hard, pumping rhythm that we make together, limbs tangling, offering our moans to the ceiling. "You're inside me for good, too, Taylor," he says into my neck, just before pleasure tightens its grip on me. "From the first second I saw you to the last second I'm given. Stay with me. Watch me prove it."

EPILOGUE

Myles

Two years later

*B*reathe in. Breathe out.
   Expand the diaphragm.

I've spent hours of my life ogling my girlfriend while she does yoga on the floor of our apartment and it appears I've picked up a few of the relaxation techniques. So why the hell aren't any of them helping me remain calm? I'm so nervous, my stomach is stuck to my fucking ribs.

I pace the entryway, yanking at the tie around my neck. Maybe I shouldn't have worn the tie. I never wear these damn things. She's going to know something is up. Mid-yank, I stop in front of the picture collage on the wall. Every time I walk through the front door of our place—the spacious first-floor apartment of a Boston townhouse—I stop to look at it. At everything we've done together over the last two years.

In the upper right-hand corner is a picture Jude snapped that first week in Cape Cod, both of us unaware we're being caught staring at each other, lovesick, while eating breakfast burritos. A little farther down we're at a Celtics game with my family and Taylor is heckling the referee after literally one beer. One. It's my favorite picture. Or maybe my favorite is the one where we're packing her trunk in Connecticut and getting ready to move to Boston. Taylor was trying to smash a champagne bottle against her bumper, but it wouldn't break and I captured her open-mouthed amusement.

Oh my *God*, I love my girlfriend.

I'm whipped and I know it. Every second of it is pure heaven.

It scares me to picture life without Taylor. Maybe that's why I always stop at the collage. To remind myself our relationship has all been real. That when the private investigation firm needed me in Boston full time, she agreed to apply for teaching jobs here and move with me. Not counting today—and her being held at gunpoint—asking Taylor to relocate to Boston was the most nervous I've ever been in my life. What if she said no? What if I hadn't done enough to prove I'm going to be her man until the end of my life?

I can still remember that afternoon. Showing her the apartment I wanted to buy for us on my laptop, leading with the fact that Jude would have his own room, for whenever he could manage a visit. I showed her the brochures for several private elementary schools, hoping one of them would appeal to her. I would have stayed in Connecticut, no questions asked, if she'd said no to moving, but thankfully that didn't happen. She'd fallen in love with my family, as much as they'd fallen in love with her, and wanted to be closer. *I think Jude needs some space, anyway*, she'd said. *I'm up for an adventure, as long as you're with me.*

Like I'd ever be anywhere else?

Happiness doesn't even begin to cover what this woman makes me feel. I'm grateful. I'm in fucking awe, to be honest. Finally I can see a future that isn't shaded by the past. And I'm never spending a day without her. Which leads me to the box in my pocket. The engagement ring inside of it. When we moved in together two years ago, I was in a rush. I wanted to give Taylor everything she'd ever dreamed of—immediately. A ring. Kids. Ironically, Taylor ended up being the one to slow us down. *I've met someone I want time with first. Let's take our time.*

She said that while I was Googling "what is a princess cut" on my phone.

Thank God I didn't pull the trigger, because she's way more of a cushion cut type. And the fact that I know engagement ring styles by heart might shed some light on how truly crazy I am for this woman. Is she going to say yes?

She's going to say yes, right?

My knees almost buckle at the sound of a key being slid into the lock. I bang a fist on the living room wall to quiet down everyone waiting on the other side. Silence falls abruptly, except for the tap of Taylor's heels when she enters the apartment.

Oh Jesus. Look at her. Beautiful beyond words.

Why did she have to wear the light pink dress today?

I can never think straight when she wears that thing.

"You're home?" Beaming a smile in my direction, she tosses her coat onto the wall hook. "I thought you had meetings all day. Is that why you're wearing a suit?"

She starts to cross the entryway, but stops short, gesturing to her dress, which I'm just now seeing has green splotches on the front.

"Art class got a little spirited. I can't hug you or I'll get paint on your suit."

"I don't mind." I blurt—whipped. I can hear my brother's eye roll from here.

"No! You'll have to get it dry cleaned. Besides..." She gives me a long, leisurely once over and sends way too much of my blood south. "You should leave it on for a while. Remember that time you pretended to interrogate me? The suit could really make it believable—"

"Taylor," I rush to interrupt her, pretty sure I hear a choked snort from the other side of the living room wall. "Why don't you go change and I'll—"

"Ooh, I have a better idea." To my simultaneous delight and horror, she reaches back and unzips the pink dress, letting it drop and pool on the ground around her ankles. "Problem solved." She steps out of the dress in a seductive move, running her fingertips up and over her tits. *Jesus Christ.* My tongue turns useless in my mouth. "Now I can hug you all I want..."

Yeah, there is simply no way I can stop my arms from opening when she's walking toward me. It's a deeply rooted impulse that will never go way. *Here comes Taylor. Open your arms. Get her as close as possible and keep her there.*

Still, there is that seriously pressing matter of seven people waiting in the living room to witness my marriage proposal. Dammit, I wanted to do this on a walk in our favorite park, but my brother convinced me that she'd like friends and family present. That she would want pictures. Now she's in a bra and panties and I'm halfway to stiff. Last time I listen to Kevin.

"Listen, sweetheart. There's something going on here."

"I know." Laughing, she rubs her belly against my cock. "I feel it."

"Okay, there are *two* things going on here."

She's winding my tie around her fist, tugging me down for a kiss and I give it to her, because I don't have the strength to turn it down. Not when her mouth is so soft and she's being horny and playful and perfect. Would it be inappropriate to bring her upstairs for forty-five minutes or so prior to this proposal or—?

Yeah, don't even think about it.

Harnessing every speck of my willpower, I break the kiss. As she watches me in confusion, I remove my jacket and wrap it around her—

Just in time for my brother to walk out of the living room, tossing a shrimp into his mouth. "Come on. Let's get the show on the road."

Taylor screams and hides against my chest.

My brother notices the dress on the floor and bursts out laughing. "The honeymoon comes *after* the proposal, you two."

"What is going on?" Taylor gasps, all but climbing me for coverage. I block her as best as I can, but I can't do anything about the mirrors on the wall. Or the fact that her legs are so gorgeous and attention grabbing, they should be illegal. "Why...I thought we were alone..."

My mother and father amble out, crowding into the entryway. Along with Jude. And Kevin's husband. It takes Mr. and Mrs. Bassey a moment to join the party, but of course they do, drawing the same conclusion of everyone else. That we were about to knock boots with seven people waiting in the living room. And I'm not so sure we weren't. Damn that pink dress.

"Does this mean she said yes?" Taylor's father asks, peering at us through his glasses.

"It certainly doesn't look like a no," responds Mrs. Bassey, as if they're discussing one of the art installations they love so much.

My father pats me on the back. "Congratulations, son."

This isn't happening. I've had nightmares about this proposal going awry, but never in my wildest dreams, did I imagine it could devolve into a shit show of these proportions.

"I haven't asked her yet," I grit out over my shoulder. "Could everyone just be quiet and let me try and salvage this?"

Before the situation can get any worse, before she says no to marrying me and I have to go throw myself into traffic, I lean back a little and wrap Taylor more securely in the jacket, making sure she's covered from neck to mid-thigh. And then I take out the ring box and get down on one knee, my pulse seeming to echo throughout the entire room.

Eyes full of unshed tears, she looks down at me and gives me a watery laugh.

She's going to say yes.

With that one sound of joy, she knows and I know that everything is going to be fine.

We get each other forever.

But she's still going to hear what I've got to say, just in case I haven't professed my love often enough over the past two years. Spoiler alert: I have. And I'll never stop.

"Taylor Bassey. You became the most important person in my life overnight. I didn't have a pulse when I found you and now it never slows down. Because you exist. Because somehow you're mine. You not only reminded me of who I used to be, but you made me believe I could be even better a second time around. But I'm only better with you beside me. I want you for my wife." My voice cracks and I have to pause to clear my throat. "Will you please be my wife?"

"Yes," she says, without a second's hesitation. As if she knows I couldn't bear waiting. "Of course I'll be your wife. I love you."

"Christ, I love you, too, Taylor." Happiness and relief and love are overflowing inside of me, only growing more intense when I stand and she's right there in my arms, where she's supposed to be.

But of course, the jacket has fallen off. And we have a new photo to add to the collage.

We continue to add to it for the next six decades. Until it takes up the entire wall and spills into the living room. A tapestry of joy.

HE END

Don't miss the sizzling, feel-good winter romance from *New York Times* bestselling author Tessa Bailey

'The perfect reverse grumpy-sunshine holiday romance – Aiden and Stella brightened my holiday season!'

Amazon review

Do you love contemporary romance?

Want the chance to hear news about your favourite authors (and the chance to win free books)?

Kristen Ashley
Ashley Herring Blake
Meg Cabot
Olivia Dade
Rosie Danan
J. Daniels
Farah Heron
Talia Hibbert
Sarah Hogle
Helena Hunting
Abby Jimenez
Elle Kennedy
Christina Lauren
Alisha Rai
Sally Thorne
Lacie Waldon
Denise Williams
Meryl Wilsner
Samantha Young

Then visit the Piatkus website
www.yourswithlove.co.uk

And follow us on Facebook and Instagram
www.facebook.com/yourswithlovex | @yourswithlovex

PIATKUS